X March 2006
X Feb 12 - 2016

"Hell on Earth and Eden, all rolled into one."

So far, it wasn't Mack Bolan's notion of a holiday.

It felt like coming home.

Bolan had grown up in a jungle, spilled blood there and earned the nickname that would follow him through his life, even beyond his early grave. That jungle was located on the far side of the world, but all of them were more or less the same. The predators and prey varied by continent, but it was still survival of the fittest in a world where no quarter was asked or granted.

The one rule carved in stone was kill or be killed. The Executioner knew that rule by heart. Forest primeval. He knew that it would eat him alive, given half a chance.

And somewhere in the midst of it was Nathan Weiss.

Don Pendleton's Mack Bolan®

Survival Reflex

A GOLD EAGLE BOOK FROM

WORLDWIDE®

TORONTO • NEW YORK • LONDON
AMSTERDAM • PARIS • SYDNEY • HAMBURG
STOCKHOLM • ATHENS • TOKYO • MILAN
MADRID • WARSAW • BUDAPEST • AUCKLAND

First edition March 2006

ISBN 0-373-61510-8

Special thanks and acknowledgment to
Mike Newton for his contribution to this work.

SURVIVAL REFLEX

Printed in U.S.A.

That man travels the longest journey who
undertakes it in search of a sincere friend.
                              —Ali ibn-abi-Talib
                                 (Seventh century)

Between friends there is no need for justice
                              —Aristotle

We all need justice sometimes, and the best test of
friendship is a trial by fire.
                              —Mack Bolan

To all suffering victims in Iraq

CHAPTER ONE

Mato Grosso State, Brazil

The battle never really ends. It's true that guns stop firing, smoke clears from the field and politicians mutter through negotiations in the name of statesmanship—but what about those who fight and bleed?

Who tends the ragged wounds and clips the severed arteries? Who stitches or removes the ravaged organs? Who sets shattered bones and searches for new skin to cover burns?

I do, the surgeon answered silently. For all the good it does.

One truth Nathan Weiss had learned in years of military practice dogged his thoughts through every waking hour and in nightmares: no wound ever truly healed.

Bones mended. Torn flesh produced scar tissue. Spilled blood could be replaced. Some organs were expendable.

But what about the soul?

How did a man really recover after he'd been shot, stabbed, tortured, set on fire or blasted with explosives? Even if he learned to walk again without a cane or limp, if he could show a more or less unblemished visage to the world, what was going on inside?

What did he wish, hope, dream, regret?

How did he claim the life he had before?

Weiss couldn't answer that one, and he'd long since given up on trying. Elbow-deep in blood again, he concentrated on the open body that demanded his attention at the moment. It was male, peppered with shrapnel wounds that seemed almost innocuous from the outside, but which wreaked havoc with the vital parts inside.

"Do something, please," he said, "about these goddamned flies."

His two assistants blinked at each other, each raising a bloody hand to point accusingly. They didn't speak, but the expressive eyes above their surgical masks said everything the surgeon needed to hear.

"I'm sorry, never mind," he told them. "Please, just keep them from the wounds."

Heads bobbed in unison. They could do that, at least.

Flies were a part of working in the field, along with ants and roaches, the occasional pit viper, leaky tents and wheezing generators that could fail at any time and plunge the operating tent into lethal darkness with the job unfinished.

Just another day at the office.

The young man before him had suffered wounds to both kidneys, but one of them could probably be saved. The spleen was gone, which meant that the young man—assuming he survived the night—would have some difficulty fighting off infections in the years to come. His perforated stomach had been sutured and its spillage cleared away. Two feet of shredded small intestine had been excised, the remainder spliced. A deep wound to the prostate might or might not leave him impotent.

But none of that would kill the young man.

In the operation's second bloody hour now, Weiss had moved on to things that took a bit more time. Two surgeons might've finished up the job by now, but he was on his own, as usual. There were no shortcuts, no Get Out of the OR Free cards in this life-or-death game.

He was the only surgeon in the area—or, anyway, the only one who'd work on battle wounds without a hotline heads-up to the same men who'd inflicted them.

And so he did it all, with two assistants who were learning as they went, eye-rolling when the blood flowed freely, grimacing as charnel odors filtered through their masks.

"Forehead, someone, please," he requested. "I've got my hands full."

One of his helpers found a sponge and moved around the table, careful not to block the surgeon's field of vision as he dabbed sweat from the tan expanse of forehead.

"Thanks," Weiss said. "Let's clean this up and close."

TEAM PANTHER WAS on schedule, closing on the target with determination borne of knowledge that there might not be another chance. They had already missed the target twice during the past six months. A third failure was bound to have unpleasant repercussions.

Following his point man down a muddy jungle trail, Team Panther's leader thought, Strike three. You're out.

A third miss wouldn't cost his life, but it would be embarrassing. He'd lose prestige and likely be passed over on the next attempt. He might be shuffled to some post in the middle of nowhere, with nothing to do but slap mosquitoes and type his resignation on a rusty portable.

An air strike might've done the trick more swiftly and effectively, but killing from the sky was not always reliable. The air force had no "smart" bombs in their inventory, and they could've strafed the jungle all day long without scoring a verified hit on the target.

So much for high technology.

When wet work was required, it still came down to men who weren't afraid of dirtying their hands.

Behind their leader and the point man, moving through the rain forest in single file, two dozen soldiers focused single-mindedly upon their goal. It helped distract them from the swarms of biting insects, mud that tried to pull their boots off, lukewarm rain that fell just long enough to soak them to the skin then waited for their camouflage fatigues to nearly dry before it started up again.

The nagging irritations made them anxious for a fight.

Eager to kill.

They were the best at what they did, these men. Team Panther had a reputation to defend, which had been sullied by their failed attempts to burn the target in October and December. Now they had another chance, and every member of the team had sworn a blood oath to succeed this time.

The leader checked his compact GPS unit. Assuming that their information was correct, they had another half mile left to go, dense jungle all the way.

WEISS'S FIFTH PATIENT had once been fairly handsome, if his eyes and brow were any indication, but the bullets that had ripped into his cheek and jaw had spoiled his face forever. It was something of a miracle they hadn't killed him on the spot, in fact, but there was grim determination in those eyes, before the morphine blessed him with oblivion.

Why do you bother? asked the small voice in his head. Why heal them, so that they can maim and kill?

Because somebody had to do it.

And Weiss wasn't altogether sure that they were wrong.

Shouting outside the operating tent distracted him, but he recovered so quickly his aides never noticed. Split-second hesitation on the scalpel stroke, but when he made the cut it was deep, clean and sure.

A runner burst into the tent and stopped short on the threshold, gaping at the deconstructed form in front of him.

Shifting to half-baked Portuguese, Weiss told the newcomer, "You're risking this man's life by coming in here. Turn around and leave."

The interloper stood his ground, though he was trembling as he said, "They're coming, Doctor."

"Who is *they?* More casualties?"

"The enemy."

That made the surgeon pause. He glanced up at his two assistants, found them staring back at him, and swiveled toward the messenger. "How long?"

"Perhaps a quarter of an hour."

"That's too soon. I still have work to do."

He knew the words were nonsense, even as he spoke. The

surgeon's enemies wouldn't withdraw until he finished with his patients. They had come to stop him, after all. If they could finish off the job they'd started with the wounded, it would just be icing on the cake.

"What should we do?" the messenger inquired.

"Get ready to evacuate. And buy some time."

"We'll try," he said, and fled the tent. Weiss wondered whether he had sent the messenger to meet his death.

Too late to think about that now.

He had a short while left to finish with the patient on his operating table. Enough time, anyway, to close the last incision, though he couldn't manage any of the fine work needed to reduce scarring.

All wasted effort if the patient couldn't be evacuated safely in the time that still remained to him. There'd be no mercy from the enemy when they arrived. They'd come in killing and be quick about it this time, trying to make sure no one escaped.

Weiss glanced back toward the corner of his makeshift operating room that served as sleeping quarters when he wasn't carving flesh. Jungle fatigues lay folded there, and resting on the bundle of his hiking clothes, an Uru submachine gun.

Kill or cure.

This day, perhaps, he'd do a bit of both.

TEAM PANTHER'S leader listened to the terse report from his point man. The target lay five hundred yards ahead, though still invisible from where they stood, surrounded on all sides by looming trees and dangling vines like ropes in a gymnasium.

"How many did you see?" the leader asked.

His scout considered it, a moment dragging as he did the mental census. "Six or seven men with weapons, sir," the point man said at last. "They carry others in and out of tents."

"And did you count the tents?"

"One big, three small, sir. Also, they have an open space covered by tarp on poles, with men laid out on stretchers. And a generator near the big tent."

"Is that everything? No vehicles?"

The point man stared at him as if he'd lost his mind. "There is no road, sir."

"None on this side that we know about. Answer the question."

Sulking, the soldier said, "No, sir. No vehicles."

Team Panther's leader did the calculations swiftly. Six or seven armed and able-bodied men against his twenty-five. The wounded would present no difficulty. They were enemies, presumed guilty of crimes against the state, condemned by their own treasonous behavior. He would leave them where he found them, after making sure they didn't live to fight another day.

And he would have the one who'd managed to elude him for so long, making a mockery of each attempt to capture him.

This time, the leader told himself, I will succeed.

He'd be a hero back at headquarters, or at the very least erase the black marks placed beside his name the last two times he'd led teams through the jungle, searching for the man his enemies referred to simply as *O Médico*.

The Doctor.

One who gave them hope when they should have none,

who restored the broken bones and ravaged flesh of terrorists, enabling them to spread more carnage and imperil everything Team Panther's men were dedicated to defend.

This day it would end.

They would eliminate *O Médico* once and for all. If he surrendered, they would take him back for trial and the inevitable prison cell. If he resisted…well, Team Panther would be forced to remedy the state's misguided abolition of capital punishment.

Either way, the doctor was finished. He'd already seen his last patient.

He simply didn't know it yet.

Team Panther's leader fired a rifle shot into the air above the smoking tent and shouted to his hidden troops, "Attack! Attack!"

THE SPOOK SAT at his desk, chain-smoking while he studied maps and photographs, sitreps and transcripts of interrogations. He was looking for a bright spot, but it stubbornly eluded him.

The telephone beside his elbow was an enemy, a traitor. For the past six months it had refused to transmit anything except bad news from sources in the field and criticism from his boss. Each time it rang, these days—as it was ringing now—the spook experienced the urge to rip its cord out of the wall and drop the damned thing in his wastebasket.

Instead he lifted the receiver to his ear.

"Downey."

"It's me."

He recognized the caller's voice. It was a gift that served

him well, despite accents. The caller was a valued asset, though he hadn't been performing well of late. In fact, he'd left a fair amount to be desired.

"I need good news," the spook advised. And from the silence on the far end of the line, he knew there would be none forthcoming. "All right, then. How bad?"

"We missed again."

"When you say missed…"

"My people found the place, all right. Just where you promised it would be. A scout saw people in the camp, guerrillas, some of them on stretchers."

"So?"

"We still aren't sure what happened. By the time he came back with the main force and they had the camp surrounded, there was no one there."

The spook reached for another cancer stick. "You tipped them off somehow," he said accusingly.

"We're looking into it."

"Fat lot of good that does." He smoked and fumed.

"It's worse," the caller said.

"Worse than another empty bag? All right, tell me."

"The team took casualties. One man dead, another six or seven injured."

"How the hell? You said there was nobody there."

"Some kind of booby trap, or maybe just an accident. We're—"

"Looking into it, I know. This isn't what we talked about at all. You understand that, right? This doesn't just reflect on you."

"Of course, you'll blame me all the same," the caller answered back, showing some attitude.

"I call 'em like I see 'em," the spook said. "You said yourself, the intel I provided led your hunters to the target. They saw people in the camp, for Christ's sake! Now you see 'em, now you don't. What kind of crazy shit is that? You want to say it's my fault that your people can't throw down on targets standing right in front of them?"

"I will find out what happened."

"Beautiful. And what about the mark?"

"We'll have to try again."

"Just like that, is it? Let my fingers do the walking through the goddamned business pages, maybe. See what they've got listed under traitor comma dirty fucking."

"You have contacts," the caller replied. "*We* have contacts."

"And they've told us where to look for him three times. How many strikes are you entitled to, I wonder?"

"Strikes?" The caller was confused now.

"Never mind. Forget about it. I'll put on my thinking cap *again* and see if I can find another angle. In the meantime, it's your job to make sure that the latest screwup does *not* go public under any circumstances. Are we clear?"

"I hear you."

"Right. But are you listening?"

"I'll handle it."

"I hope so, for your own sake."

And for mine, the spook thought as he dropped the telephone receiver back into its cradle. Once again he felt the urge to rip, discard, destroy.

Instead he lit a fresh smoke from the one he'd had clenched between his teeth and waited for the nicotine to work its magic on his jangling nerves.

Spilled milk, he thought. No use crying about it.

What he needed now, and goddamned soon, was some spilled blood to solve his problem. One more chance, if he was very lucky, and he didn't dare waste it.

But what was left?

He needed specialists.

And with that thought in mind, he reached for the hated telephone.

CHAPTER TWO

San Diego, California

Mack Bolan took his time on Harbor Drive, westbound, checking his rearview mirror frequently. He hadn't been in San Diego for a while, no reason anybody should be looking for him here, but vigilance was the price of survival. The first time Bolan let his guard drop, taking personal security for granted, it was safe to bet that negligence would turn and bite him where it hurt.

No tails so far.

His progress in the rented Chevrolet was leisurely enough that other motorists were glad to pass him, but he wasn't driving slow enough to risk a ticket for obstructing traffic. Just the right speed, Bolan thought, for someone seeking a specific address in an unfamiliar neighborhood.

The address in question belonged to a block of professional offices, one of those buildings designed to resemble a twenty-first-century bunker. It was bronze and brown, metal and stone, with windows that reflected sunlight in a painful glare across the nearby lanes of traffic. In short, it was an eyesore, but the ritzy kind that advertised the affluence of those who had their offices within.

He wheeled into the parking lot and checked the rearview mirror once more, just to play it safe. Nobody followed him, none of the other drivers slowed to track his progress as they passed.

Now all he had to think about was what might be inside the ugly building, waiting for him.

Theoretically, it was a friend he hadn't seen in better than a year. The contact had been clean, secure on Bolan's end, no glitches to excite suspicion. Still, he was alive this day because he always took that extra step, preparing for the worst while hoping for the best.

The parking lot was only half full at this hour, approaching lunchtime, and he found a space within a short sprint of the revolving glass door. No one was loitering outside, but tinted windows wouldn't let him scan the lobby from his vehicle.

Twelve minutes left.

He didn't have the hinky feeling that an ambush often prompted, small hairs bristling on his nape, but Bolan didn't live by premonitions. Instinct, training and experience all went together in the mix, occasionally seasoned by audacity.

Do it or split, he thought.

He didn't need to check the pistol slung beneath his left armpit in fast-draw leather—fifteen cartridges in the Beretta's magazine and one more in the chamber—so he simply had to squeeze the double-action trigger. Two spare magazines in pouches underneath his right arm gave him forty-six

chances to kill any assailants who might try to jump him at
the meet.

Relaxed? No way.

Frightened? Not even close.

He locked the car and left it, crossed the sidewalk, stepped
into the maw of the revolving door. This was the first chance
for an enemy to take him. Shooters waiting in the lobby could
unload on him while he was sandwiched between panes of
glass, most likely take him down before he could retaliate. It
didn't happen, though, and in another moment he was standing in the lobby, bathed in frosty air-conditioning.

There was an information desk to Bolan's left, manned by a
senior citizen. Off to his right, a wall directory served those who
didn't want the human touch. Bolan ignored them both, sweeping the empty lobby as he moved directly to the dual elevators.

Bolan didn't need to check the floor or office numbers.
They had been supplied, and he'd memorized them, end of
story. Now he simply had to hope there would be no nasty
surprises waiting for him on the seventh floor.

The smooth and solitary ride lasted no more than ninety
seconds, but it gave him ample time to think about the call
that had surprised him, coming out of nowhere with a plea
for help. The caller was a man whose martial prowess nearly
rivaled Bolan's, one who rarely bluffed and never folded if
he had a prayer of staying in the game.

They hadn't talked details, an indication that the caller
was concerned about security, despite precautions taken when
he made the link-up. The arrangement of their meeting was
another warning sign, behind closed doors, using the office
of a lawyer Bolan didn't know from Adam.

Hinky? Not so far.

Cautious? Believe it.

Bolan's circle of devoted friends was small and dwindling over time. It was the nature of his life and his profession that attachments came with price tags. Sudden death or worse lay waiting for the careless. He had more friends in the ground than standing on it, and the trend would always run that way.

It was a law of nature in the hellgrounds where he lived.

Bolan had no suspicion that the caller might betray his trust. It was unthinkable. That didn't mean, however, that some rude third party couldn't find a way to horn in on the meet. Technology was only one short step behind imagination, these days, and he couldn't discount pure bad luck.

There was a chance, however minuscule, that Bolan's contact might be followed to the meet, or that a leak inside the lawyer's office might produce a most unwelcome welcoming committee. Bolan doubted it, but it was possible, and that meant he would have to be on full alert throughout the interaction.

SOP, in other words.

Another normal day in Bolan's life.

He felt the elevator slowing into its approach and stepped back from the door, to the left side. A straight-on spray of bullets when the door slid open wouldn't take him, though he'd have to watch for ricochets.

Jacket unbuttoned for swift access to his pistol, Bolan stood and waited with his hand almost inside the jacket, feeling like a caricature of Napoleon. The elevator settled and its door hissed open to reveal an empty corridor.

A small sign on the facing wall directed Bolan to his right.

He moved along the hall with long strides, radiating confidence and capability. He had no audience, but they were qualities the tall man couldn't hide. He might not stand out in a crowd on any given street corner, but when push came to shove he was the leader of the pack.

Make that lone wolf, most of the time.

But not today.

His destination was a door like every other on the floor, with a bronze plate that gave a number and the lawyer's name. The knob turned in his hand and Bolan stepped into a small but suitably luxurious reception room.

Four empty chairs faced an unattended desk. No sign of a receptionist or anybody else.

He didn't need to check his watch. A stylish wall clock told him he was right on time.

Bolan was running down a short list of his options when a door behind the vacant desk swung open to reveal a smiling face.

"I'm glad you found the place okay," Rosario "The Politician" Blancanales said.

BLANCANALES HAD EARNED the "Politician" nickname in another life, a tribute to his skill at soothing fear and agitation among Asian villagers whose lives and homes were threatened daily by the ever-shifting tides of war. He had been part of Bolan's Special Forces A-team, one of several thrown together in the hellfire moment who had forged lifelong alliances.

One of the few who somehow managed to survive.

"I guess the staff is out to lunch," Bolan remarked as they shook hands.

"We have an hour to ourselves. Friend of a friend, you know?"

He didn't bother running down the details of a family in peril, spared against all odds, with gratitude that reached beyond the limits of a long lunch on a busy afternoon. Pol knew that Bolan didn't need the details, didn't really care how they had come to find themselves alone in an attorney's office on the seventh floor of a building he'd never visited before this day and wouldn't see again.

"He sweeps the place, I guess?" Bolan asked, thinking of security.

"I swept it, coming in. It's clean."

"Okay."

"You want to talk out here or use the inner sanctum?"

"This is fine."

Bolan took one of the four matching chairs. Blancanales noticed that he didn't touch the arm rests with his hands. It was a small precaution, probably unnecessary since his law-enforcement files across the country had been closed and marked "Deceased," but playing safe was second nature to the Executioner.

"I'm glad you had some time," Blancanales said, easing into it.

"No sweat," Bolan replied. "What's going on?"

"I caught a squeal the other day, through Toni."

Toni Blancanales was the Politician's sister. She was also CEO of Team Able Investigations, a private security firm Rosario Blancanales had launched years ago with another war buddy, electronics wizard Hermann "Gadgets" Schwarz, to make ends meet in peacetime. Now that Pol and Gadgets op-

erated more or less full-time for Hal Brognola and Stony
Man Farm—the same covert nerve center that fielded Bolan
for various do-or-die assignments—Toni ran the show and
rarely needed her big brother's help.

"Why that route?" Bolan inquired.

"Long distance. A long time out of touch."

"A mutual acquaintance?" Bolan asked him, frowning.

"You remember Bones."

Blancanales didn't phrase it as a question. There was nothing wrong with Bolan's memory, and he saw instant recognition in the warrior's eyes.

The nickname came from "sawbones," as in "doctor"—or
from *Star Trek,* same damned thing. In their Special Forces
days together there'd been many medics, too many M.A.S.H.
units, but only one Bones.

"Nate Weiss," Bolan said.

Blancanales nodded. Make it Captain Nathan Weiss, M.D.
A wizard with a scalpel, long on empathy for patients, short
on tolerance when military red tape hampered his attempts
to care for sick and wounded soldiers. Thinking back, Blancanales could remember Weiss cutting and stitching under
fire, while Bolan's team faced down the enemy, one of their
own guys on the table leaking life.

The frown was still on Bolan's face. "I haven't thought
about him in…"

"About a hundred years?"

"Seems like it. How'd he track you down?"

"It wasn't him, exactly."

"Oh?"

"An intermediary. Bones gave her my last name and remembered that I came from San Diego. No real hope of getting through, I guess, but Toni's in the book. She caught a break."

"And 'she' is…?"

"Marta Enriquez. She knew some jungle stories that could only come from Bones. It feels legit."

"So what's the squeal?"

"Long story short, the way she laid it down, he's in Brazil, running some kind of floating hospital for anyone who needs him in the bush. Somewhere along the way, he started stepping on official toes."

"How's that?"

It was Blancanales's turn to frown. "She claimed it has to do with Indians. The Amazon is one huge place, as you well know. We hear a lot about the forest being cut and burned for shopping malls, whatever, but the fact is, they've got tribes down there no white man's ever seen. Some others sit on land the government and certain multinationals are anxious to 'improve' and put a few more millions in their pockets. When the honchos in Brasilia want a stubborn tribe to move, it can get Wild West messy. I've seen some of that, up close and personal."

"But you have doubts about her story," Bolan interjected, going to the heart of it.

"Let's say I have some reservations, pun intended."

"Why?"

"You know the history. They've had civilian government for only twenty years or so. Before that, it was hard-core juntas all the way. Some wouldn't mind a switch back to the bad old days. You've got guerrillas in the backcountry, fighting for one thing or another, and banditos everywhere you turn. I wasn't kidding when I mentioned the Wild West. Jivaro headhunters, covert Indian wars—Bones could be into damn near anything."

"And someone's hunting him?" Another cut, right to the heart.

"Sounds like it, yeah."

"Whatever it is, he can't turn to the law."

"The way it was explained to me," Blancanales said, "that's not an option."

"So, either the government is hunting him or it doesn't mind someone else doing the dirty work."

"I'd say that sums it up."

"It's not like Bones to ask for help."

"Unless he really needs it, no."

"I'm guessing, since you called, that Able Team can't take it on," Bolan said.

Blancanales shook his head. "Not soon enough. I'm stealing time as it is from a job in Baja."

"Have you talked to Hal?"

"He isn't thrilled about it, but he says it's up to us. Resources as available, but no hands-on collaboration till we've got a clear fix on the problem."

Bolan's smile took Blancanales by surprise. "'We' meaning me," he said.

"If you decide to do it, right."

"And is the woman still around? This Marta?"

"Waiting for a verdict as we speak."

"Not here?"

"Nearby. The way it seems to me, she's used to hiding out."

"When can we talk?"

Blancanales felt himself start to relax inside. "How do you feel about right now?" he asked.

THEY TRAVELED separately, Bolan trailing his old friend to form a little two-car caravan that traveled half a dozen blocks on Harbor Drive, then swung inland. Blancanales led him to the spacious parking lot of a motel located near the U.S. naval station, then drove around the back with Bolan following, and parked close to the open stairs. The Executioner said nothing as he trailed his friend upstairs and left along a balcony to Room 252.

"I called ahead," the Able Team commando told him, "so we wouldn't spook her."

Blancanales knocked and waited while the tenant of that room surveyed them through the peephole's fish-eye lens. There came a fumbling at the locks, and then the door swung open to admit them. Only when they were inside, door locked again, did Bolan have a clear view of the woman he had come to meet.

Marta Enriquez was approximately thirty-five years old, a slim Latina with a curvaceous figure. A pinched look almost spoiled the face, framed by a fall of raven hair, but large, dark eyes and high cheekbones redeemed it.

Blancanales made the introductions, using Bolan's relatively new Matt Cooper pseudonym, and the woman surprised him with the strength of her handshake.

"If we could all sit down," Blancanales said, "this won't take long." He settled on one corner of the queen-size bed, leaving the room's two chairs for Bolan and their nervous hostess. "Marta, why don't you tell my friend what brings you here."

"I want to help *O Médico*," she said. "He has done so much for my people in the past three years, I must somehow repay him if I can. The danger that he faces now is too much."

"What kind of danger?" Bolan asked her.

"From the army and the death squads," she replied. "I know your press tells you Brazil is free and all are equal there, but things aren't what they seem. My people—the Tehuelche—have been driven from their homes and deep into the forest, where the hunters seek them still. They are shot on sight. Sometimes a 'gift' of food or clothing is delivered, and more of us die."

"It's classic," Blancanales interjected. "Your manifest-destiny types did the same thing right here, with poisoned grain and blankets spiked with smallpox. Talk about weapons of mass destruction."

"*O Médico*—Dr. Weiss—has helped us without charge since he arrived. He offers care to anyone in need, and for that crime, the state will kill him, or at least expel him from Brazil."

"You've witnessed these attempts?" Bolan asked.

Enriquez nodded. "Once, when we went to Diamantino for supplies, three men approached us. They insulted me, touched me and Dr. Weiss told them to stop. They turned on him then, but he left all three of them unconscious in the street.

"Later," she continued, "they sent helicopters to the village of my people, shooting from the sky. *O Médico* treated the wounded, even while bullets flew around him."

"I don't know what you're asking us to do," Bolan told her.

"If the government wants to get rid of him, they'll find a way to do the job. We can't declare war on Brazil."

"Nathan told me that he had friends of great ability in the United States. He sent me here to ask for help, but I am not a fool. I know he cannot stay and help my people any longer without giving up his life."

"What, then?"

"You must persuade him to give up, go home, before he's killed. Take him by force, if necessary. Be his friend and save his life."

"Just drop into the jungle there and kidnap him."

"Maybe he'll listen if you talk to him," she said. "Remind him that he is American and not Tehuelche."

"Couldn't you do that?" Bolan asked.

"To my people, Nathan—Dr. Weiss—is almost like a god. They need him to survive and love him for the help he offers them, but they think first about themselves. Sometimes, it seems as if they think he is immortal and cannot be harmed by common men."

Bolan had picked up on her use of Weiss's given name and wondered whether there was something more between them than a simple doctor-patient relationship. Despite the time they'd spent together under fire, some jungle R and R between engagements, Bolan didn't know the details of his old friend's private life, his taste in women, anything along those lines. He knew the man's determination, though, and the soldier didn't like the odds of him persuading Bones to leave his self-appointed mission.

"You say he's being hunted just because he helped your people?" Bolan asked.

"It's one reason," the woman answered, "but the government has ample cause to hate him. Before us, he was in Rio de Janeiro. There, he had a clinic for street children. Did you know that some policemen, after hours, drive around the streets and shoot the homeless children as if they were rabid dogs?"

"I've heard the stories," Bolan said.

"They're true, and sometimes worse than what you read in newspapers or magazines. After six months in Rio, the police got an injunction to prevent Nathan from treating children without the consent of their parents. Orphans! You see? When he continued, they put him in jail. Before he was released, they burned his clinic and declared the fire an accident."

"So he moved on?"

"To spare the children, after a police lieutenant told him every one he treated would be thrown in prison to amuse the perverts. It hurt him, but he left to find new patients."

"It's a jump from Rio to the Mato Grosso jungle," Bolan said.

"He tried some other places first. AIDS patients in São Paulo. Plantation laborers at Uberlândia. Guarani Indians in the Serra Dourada. Each time it was the same. Suspicion, threats against his life and those he tried to help."

"It's obvious he isn't listening," Bolan replied. "What makes you think that he'll hear anything I have to say?"

"Because he asked for you, his friends."

"Unless you're holding back, he didn't ask us to come down and snatch him out of there."

"Perhaps he'll listen. But if not, when it is done, at least he will be safe."

"What's to prevent him turning right around and going back?" Bolan asked. "We can't lock him up and throw away the key."

"Perhaps, when he has time to think in peace, he'll realize that nothing can be gained by what he's doing in my country."

"What about your people?" Blancanales inquired.

Stone-faced, she said, "We're finished, don't you see? Nathan can't save us. No one can. He'll only waste his life, when he could be of such great help to others, somewhere else."

"Would you be coming with him?" Bolan asked.

"I don't know," she replied. "Perhaps, if Nathan wants me."

"When are you going back?"

"Tomorrow. One way or another, I must give him your decision."

"I'll tell him myself." Turning to Blancanales, he said, "We need a minute to ourselves."

THE MOTEL BALCONY was adequate, no one in the adjoining rooms to eavesdrop as they leaned against the rail in hazy Southern California sunshine.

"Now I've heard her," Bolan said, "give me your take on this."

"I think Bones may be losing it. Looking for a cause, some way to make his life count for something. Hell, for all I know it could be your basic midlife crisis."

"Maybe. But who's picking up the tab? Free clinics may be free to patients, but they eat up money just the same, and plenty of it."

"I can answer part of that," Blancanales said. "I ran a check on Bones through Stony Man. He had some money from his family, back East. Not Rockefeller money, but they did all right. He's the last of the line, never married, no siblings. Had a good adviser, made some smart investments. Most of it was liquidated when he left the States. Call it a cool half million, give or take."

"That's seed money," Bolan replied. "A big seed, sure, but he's been working with the lady's tribe for three years now, no charge, and all the other deals she talked about before he focused in on them. The Rio clinic and what-have-you. Would half a million last that long, paying for medicine, equipment and facilities, travel?"

"I doubt it."

"So, I'll ask again. Who's picking up the tab?"

Blancanales shook his head. "Don't know."

"One thing we do know," Bolan said. "If Bones has his mind set on helping these people, he won't be talked out of it."

"No."

"And I don't fancy trying to carry him out of Brazil on my back, bound and gagged."

"Why are you going, then?"

"First thing, to have a look and see what's really happening." He nodded toward the door numbered 252. "I think we've got a case of hero-worship here, or maybe love. I don't believe she's told us everything she knows about what Bones is doing in the big, bad woods."

"You figure it's political?"

"She talks about a man who's looking for a cause. Maybe

he wants to be a martyr. I won't know until I see it for my-self."

"Wish I could back you up," Blancanales said.

"I'm just observing," Bolan told him.

"Rii-iight. And I'm the next Olympic figure-skating champion."

"I'll need a flight. One way for now," Bolan said. "Find out where she's touching down and send me somewhere else. I'll catch a shuttle to the airstrip nearest Bones. Don't tell her when I'm flying."

Blancanales frowned. "You figure she's a sell-out?"

"Why take chances? If she's straight, there's still at least a fifty-fifty chance she'll be picked up when she gets home. If someone sweats her, I don't want her spilling my itinera-ry."

"Right," Blancanales said. And then again, "You're right."

"I'll need a contact on the other end for various supplies, including hardware. Play it safe and don't use anyone con-nected to the Company or NSA."

"I know an independent dealer in Belém."

"That's fine, if I can get a charter flight from there to Mato Grosso with no questions asked."

"I'll check it out today," the Able Team commando prom-ised. "If it doesn't work, your best bet for a touchdown where you want to go will be Cuiabá. I'll find somebody there."

"Before you cut her loose," Bolan said, "get the best fix that you can on where Bones has his chop shop. If he's mo-bile, try for base coordinates, at least. I'll GPS it and go solo in the bush."

"That's risky, man."

"Hiring a guide is worse. I won't know who he's really working for until it hits the fan."

"You're right again. Has anybody ever told you that's an irritating habit?"

Bolan smiled. "My childhood aspiration was to be a know-it-all."

"And how's that working for you?"

"I'm still working on it."

Blancanales went somber, then. "I'm having second thoughts about this whole damn thing," he said.

"It's Bones," Bolan reminded him.

"I know that, but you've got me thinking now. Suppose someone's already bagged him, squeezed him. Now they're putting out feelers to see who'll try a rescue mission. Pick off Santa's little helpers one by one."

"It doesn't have that feel about it," Bolan said. "Somebody wants to take out Bones for helping Indians, whatever, why would they go fishing in the States?"

"Because they can?"

"It's thin," Bolan said, "but I'll keep an eye peeled, just in case."

"It may be too late, once you're down there."

"Maybe not. Let's see what happens."

"The more I think about it," Blancanales said, "the more I wish I hadn't called you."

"Spilled milk, guy. Just make those calls and let me have the word before you head back down to Baja."

"It'll be a couple hours, give or take."

"You've got my number."

"That's affirmative. Where will you be?"

"Around."

"Okay. I'll be in touch."

Blancanales lingered on the balcony as Bolan went downstairs. No one was lurking near the rented Chevy, no one peering from the nearby rooms. Behind the wheel, the soldier took time to stop and think about the mission he'd accepted and what it would mean to follow through.

A friend in trouble, right.

But he could only help the willing.

And if Nathan Weiss had asked for help, that made him willing, on the surface. But what kind of help was Weiss expecting?

Extrication or combat support?

Bolan had no illusions concerning his ability to make a one-man stand against the whole Brazilian army, even if a friend's life might be riding on the line. Weiss might be looking for a martyr's end, but that would never be a part of Bolan's plan.

Die fighting if he had to, absolutely.

But to throw his life away?

Forget about it.

He would have a look, as promised, and take it from there. The next step would be up to Bones.

And Bolan hoped the bones he left behind him in the jungle wouldn't be his own.

CHAPTER THREE

Belém, Brazil

The first leg of Bolan's long journey was a two-hour flight from San Diego to Mexico City, with ninety minutes in the airport terminal, waiting to make his connection. He stayed alert from force of habit, even though no one he could think of had any reason to be hunting him in Mexico.

His enemies in that troubled country were all either dead or in prison, as far as he knew, but it never hurt to be careful. He bought an English-language guidebook for Brazil and started reading it at the departure gate, killing time.

The authors considered Brazil a Latin miracle of sorts, emerging from military rule to reclaim civilian democracy in the mid-1980s, battling back from a decade of economic crises to stand head and shoulders above its neighbors, national triumph symbolized by five straight victories in World Cup soccer finals. There was only passing mention of the country's long-time military junta and its brutal violence, countered by rebel insurrection in the cities and the hinterlands.

No mention at all of homeless children hunted through the streets by death squads or the covert policy of "relocating" native tribes at any cost.

Bolan wasn't surprised by the guidebook's omissions. Tourist economies thrived on illusion, whether it was Carnivale in Rio, Atlantic City's neon boardwalk or the Las Vegas Strip. No advertising agent pointed out his client's warts or called attention to the smell of rot that wafted from behind most glittering facades.

In Bolan's personal experience, there was no government on Earth without a dark core of corruption at its heart. No tourist paradise without a nest of vipers in the garden or a school of sharks cruising offshore. No end of problems for a die-hard altruist to tackle in the autumn of his life.

But why in hell had Nathan Weiss chosen Brazil?

He was a doctor, and more specifically, a trauma surgeon. Weiss would find trauma to spare in Brazil, but the same could readily be said for New York City, San Francisco, London or Madrid. Unless Shangri-la had been discovered since the last time Bolan watched CNN, there was no shortage of victims anywhere on Earth.

So, why Brazil?

It wasn't for the love of jungle climates. Bolan knew that much from time he'd spent with Weiss in another green hell, on the far side of the world. Bones didn't often complain, but mosquitoes and tropical germs were among his pet peeves in those days.

Why seek them out, then, when he could've written his own ticket at any stateside hospital and most of those in Europe?

Pol Blancanales had been clueless on that score, nothing in Weiss's file from Stony Man to clarify the mystery. Bolan was still puzzling over the problem when they called his flight, and during the four-hour transit to Belém. He skipped the in-flight movie, browsed his guidebook, ate the packaged pseudo-food they set in front of him, but still the question nagged him.

Why Brazil?

Whatever the reason, Bones had gotten in too deep, and now he needed help. He'd reached out for The Politician because Blancanales was traceable. If Weiss thought of Bolan at all, these days, he would presumably accept the media reports describing Bolan's fiery death in New York City. Surgery had altered Bolan's face more than once, made him unrecognizable if he had passed Weiss on the street.

And would *he* recognize the doctor, after all that time? Would he want to see what Bones had become?

And what was that, exactly?

Being hunted by the government proved nothing, either way. One man's criminal or terrorist was another man's heroic freedom fighter. Bolan himself had once graced every Top Ten list of fugitives in North America and western Europe, and he'd been guilty as sin in the eyes of the law, convicted by his own admission on multiple counts of murder, arson, kidnapping and sundry other felonies.

Being a fugitive meant different things, in different times and places. Ditto criminal indictment and conviction. On the basis of the sketchy data in hand, Bolan couldn't tell if Nathan Weiss was being hunted for crimes against humanity or for helping the underdogs survive.

All he had, at the moment, were his memories of Bones and an ingrained sense of duty to a friend who'd never let him down. As to where that led him, and to what result, the next few days would tell the tale.

Bolan had a twelve-hour wait for his charter flight to Cuiabá, in Mato Grosso State, departing at six o'clock the next morning. There'd been no way to speed it up, but Blancanales had supplied him with the name of certain hardware dealers in Belém and the assurance that a private flight within Brazil involved no baggage checks. As soon as he was settled into his hotel, Bolan would take his rented car and embark on brief shopping tour to prepare for his time in the bush.

Still hoping for the best, and bracing for the worst.

BLAINE DOWNEY COULD'VE braced his target at the airport, but he thought it lacked a certain style. There was a piss-off factor, too. If he got in the stranger's face and spooked him into turning around and leaving Brazil on the next available flight, it would minimize the meddler's inconvenience. On balance, Downey preferred to let him rent a car, check into his hotel, and *then* realize it had all been a huge waste of time.

One thing, though. Looking at the man who matched the photo faxed from San Diego, Downey didn't think he was the kind who frightened easily.

Of course, he could be wrong.

It wouldn't be the first time, as his supervisor frequently reminded him.

The photos hadn't told him much. A team in San Diego had observed the woman, snapped as many pictures as they could of anyone she'd spoken to in the city. There'd been

waitresses, two cab drivers, a motel maid—and two men who
had called upon her in her room. One showed up twice, the
second time with company. Nice head shots for the pair of
them, and Downey wondered now if someone should've used
a rifle instead of a Nikon's zoom lens.

The two-timer had been identified, after some effort, as a
private investigator and security specialist named Rosario
Blancanales. He was a Special Forces veteran whose service
history included black ops in the Badlands. These days, as far
as Langley could determine, he was more or less retired, letting his sister run the business he'd built from the ground up
after his discharge. The handful of customers identified so far,
including Uncle Sam, pronounced themselves entirely satisfied with the performance of Team Able Investigations.

So, the woman wanted help—and who could blame her?

Why she'd look for it in Southern California, and specifically with Blancanales, was a riddle Downey longed to solve,
but it eluded him. Right now, he had a problem closer to
home.

Number two. The new arrival.

The guy took a good photo, but his mug shot wasn't stored
in any high-tech archive the Agency had thus far been able to
tap. The car he'd used in San Diego led them to the rental
agency, where Downey's counterparts had obtained a second-
generation photocopy of the guy's Virginia driver's license.
The license, in turn, gave them Matthew Cooper's birth date,
social security number and last-known address.

Which, in turn, led them nowhere.

The birth date might be accurate, for all Downey knew, but
he couldn't confirm it from any known source. The target's

address was a mail drop in Richmond, and his social security number—while technically active—revealed no activity of any kind since it was generated two years earlier.

Which made him…what? A criminal? A spook?

If he was in the cloak-and-dagger trade, who paid his salary? Not Langley, Downey was assured by his superiors. The Agency had worked against itself from time to time, the old right-versus-left-hand syndrome, but he'd been promised that no such snafu was in progress this day.

And that, unfortunately, didn't reassure him in the least.

Who stood to profit if his operation in Brazil went belly up? Downey couldn't have guessed with anything approaching certainty, so he declined to play the game. Sometimes he had to treat the symptoms, put out brush fires as they sprang to life, and let someone else track the roots of the problem.

Downey couldn't be everywhere at once, and right now his target was standing in line at a car-rental desk on the airport concourse. He might've been a businessman whose flight to Belém was pure coincidence, unrelated to his meeting with the woman the previous day.

But Downey didn't think so.

Not a chance in hell.

That's why he watched and waited, trailed the guy until he found his car, then swiftly doubled back to meet his driver waiting at the curb, parked at the red curb with a traffic cop fuming and glaring at the diplomatic license plate.

That's why he trailed the mark to a hotel downtown and went inside to meet the stranger, one-on-one. A little face time, just to break the ice and see what Matt Cooper was made of.

It was easier that way, than bringing in a crew and taking him apart.

UNPACKING WAS a waste of time, so Bolan didn't bother. He changed shirts, pocketed a knife he carried in his check-through luggage and decided not to bother shaving. Halfway to the door, he heard the unexpected rapping and went on to use the peephole, checking out his uninvited visitor.

The man stood three or four inches below six feet, looking burly or just overweight in his suit. The lens made it difficult to judge, but at least his hands were empty and he was alone.

Bolan opened the door and stood waiting, silent.

"Mr. Cooper?"

Bolan didn't answer, didn't step aside. "Who are you?" he demanded.

"Downey," the stranger said, thrusting out a hand, which was ignored. "Blaine Downey, from the U.S. Embassy."

Bolan knew what that meant. He simply didn't know, yet, if the man was CIA, NSA or attached to some other intelligence service that made up the Washington-Pentagon alphabet soup.

The bad news was, they had him marked.

But how deep did it go?

"What do you want?" he asked.

"A minute of your time, that's all. May I come in?"

Bolan considered making him explain his business in the hallway, but security took precedence. His cover might be blown, but that was still a long way from announcing his mission to every guest on the hotel's fifth floor.

"Five minutes," Bolan said, "is all I have to spare."

"Suits me," Downey said, brushing past him in a beeline

for the small room's single chair. He sat, leaving Bolan to pick a corner of the bed or stand.

He stood.

"My hope, in a nutshell," said Downey, "is to save you from a world of hurt."

"How's that?"

"You're in Brazil on business that is bound to turn out badly," Downey said.

"Which is?"

"Marta Enriquez. She's a subject of some interest to the U.S. government, as well as to authorities here in Brazil. You met her yesterday, in San Diego. Now you're here. I don't believe in that kind of coincidence."

"Nobody asked you," Bolan said.

"That's right. Nobody did. Sometimes, unfortunately, there are situations where you have to deal with consequences, even if you'd rather not. Catching my drift?"

"Not even close," the Executioner replied.

"I'll spell it out, then. Whatever Marta Enriquez and Mr. Rosario Blancanales may have told you in Dago, whatever they asked you to do, whatever they offered in return—you don't want to go there."

Denial seemed pointless. Confession, while possibly good for the soul, was unthinkable.

Time to stall.

"Because…?"

"Because I say so, Mr. Cooper. And because I represent the U.S. government."

"We're not in the United States."

"You weren't born yesterday," Downey replied. "In fact,

according to your social security records, you're almost two years old. Happy birthday, Mr. Cooper."

Bolan had decades of practice at keeping surprise off his face. Instead, he smiled and asked, "You're IRS?"

"Heaven forbid! I couldn't care less what you do with your hard-earned money, friend. Declare it, don't declare it. All the same to me. But if you travel any further down this particular road, you'll be stepping on some very tender toes."

"You've got sore feet? Try Dr. Scholl's."

Downey put on a deprecating smile. "I'm just the messenger. You get one warning, friend."

"What happens next?"

"I don't believe you want to know."

"No hints?"

"Let's say you won't enjoy it."

"I should turn around and go back home, you're saying."

"To the Richmond mail drop, or wherever home may be."

Showing his hand like that, Downey had to think he had it covered. Bolan, on the other hand, wasn't convinced.

Not yet.

"I'll think about it."

Downey rose, rubbing his hands together like a miser in a high school play. "That's all we ask," he said, mock-cheerful. "Somber thought about the risks of pissing off your Uncle in D.C. and various locals who may have even shorter fuses."

"Hey, I thought Brazil was friendly."

"That depends," Downey replied, "on you."

"I get your drift."

"Smart man. I thought you would." There was a brief pause on the threshold, Downey turning with another phony smile and parting shot. "Enjoy your flight."

I must be slipping, Bolan thought. He'd missed the watchers back in San Diego, and again at the airport. It was an inauspicious start, but Bolan didn't feel like backing down.

Not yet.

He thought of calling Hal Brognola in Washington and then decided not to risk it. If they had his room, they likely had the telephone, as well.

He'd have to fix that, taking one step at a time.

Slight change of plan.

He had a tail to shake before he could begin his shopping spree.

THE TAIL WAS obvious.

Either they wanted it that way or Downey had a bunch of amateurs on staff, and Bolan didn't think that was the problem.

They were dogging him to send a message and to make sure Bolan—or Matt Cooper—didn't rendezvous with anyone he may have come to meet. They would observe him every moment he was in Brazil, and thus prevent transaction of whatever covert business he'd agreed to in the States.

But how much did they know?

If they had Marta Enriquez covered, why not wait until Bolan made contact, then drop the net over all of them at once?

Because they don't know where she was, thought Bolan.

And they wouldn't get a fix from him.

Not here. Not now.

The black American sedan trailing his rented car was obvious. He drove around downtown Belém for fifteen minutes, circling blocks and twice ignoring stoplights, to make sure the glaring tail was no coincidence. When he was satisfied on that score, Bolan turned his mind to losing them and treating Downey to a message of his own.

Step one was getting out of the hotel. They didn't try to stop him when he walked out empty-handed, confident that even if he lost them somehow in the city, he would have to come back for his bag.

But they were wrong.

Bolan had packed light for the trip, knowing that most of his civilian trappings would be useless in the bush. Stuffing his pockets with the necessary items—wallet, money, passport, cell phone and GPS unit—he walked out of the place without a backward glance.

The black sedan was waiting for him, and it had been on him ever since.

After the downtown circuit, Bolan reckoned that he wouldn't shake his watches by racing through alleys or running red lights. He'd satisfied himself that there was only one team watching him, which made it easier.

Not easy in the classic sense, of course, but better than a running battle in the streets.

Especially since he was still unarmed.

He set off in the general direction of the hardware dealer, then sidetracked himself when he was halfway there, seeking a place where he could ditch the watchers and their disappearance wouldn't be reported for a while.

All cities had bad neighborhoods, omitted from the tourist guidebooks and sightseeing tours, where locals walked in fear and the police patrolled in two- or three-man teams. Bolan found one such neighborhood, parked on its outskirts where his car probably wouldn't be stripped down for parts within the hour, and made his way from there on foot.

One myth about the world's great urban slums was that they teemed with cutthroats waiting to snatch any man or woman off the streets in broad daylight. The thugs existed, of course, but they were typically nocturnal predators, and long experience had taught them how to pick and choose their prey.

Some people were natural victims, defeated by life and timid to a fault. They seemed to lurch from one disaster to the next, recognized by bullies on sight. Others were strong and confident, broadcasting an alert that told potential hunters any confrontation might prove hazardous.

Belém's slum dwellers noticed Bolan as he made his way across their turf, but no one tried to intercept him. Even if he hadn't been a clear-cut Alpha male, the fact that he was trailing heat had registered before he covered half a block.

Both trackers from the black American sedan came after him on foot. It was their first mistake, and Bolan meant to save them the embarrassment of making any more. He led them three blocks deeper into hostile territory, then picked out an alley that was well-shadowed despite the midday hour. Turning in, he ducked behind the nearest garbage bin and stood back to wait.

The stalkers followed him, then passed him by. One of

them started to say something, but his partner shushed him.

"Quiet now, and watch your step," he said.

"Too late," Bolan advised.

THEY TURNED as one, to find him standing in the middle of the alley, blocking off their access to the street.

"What's this?" the seeming leader asked him.

"You tell me," Bolan replied.

"I don't know you from Adam, pal."

"Which makes me wonder why you're tailing me," Bolan said, standing fast.

The leader's ruddy cheeks flushed darker still. Apparently his brief didn't include a face-to-face with Bolan, even though they clearly meant to spook him out of town.

"You must have us mixed up with someone else," he said.

"Convince me."

"How would I do that?"

"You could show me some ID," Bolan suggested. "Maybe tell me why you've been tailgating me since I left the hotel."

The second spook had worked up nerve enough to speak. He said, "Hey, now!" before his partner cut him off.

"You've got some nerve," the leader said. "I'll give you that."

"Your boss left that part out when he was briefing you, I guess," Bolan replied.

"My boss?"

"Downey."

The two men blinked as one. "I don't know anybody by that name," the leader said, too late.

"So, he won't miss you, then."

"Miss who?" The second spook had trouble keeping pace.

"We're going now," the leader said. "Have a nice day."

"I don't think so."

They telegraphed the rush with sidelong glances, back and forth. Not certain what to do, now that their crude surveillance had backfired, the pair surrendered to machismo. Bolan saw it coming and was ready when it got there.

Number one, the mouthpiece, led his partner by six feet or so, looking to tackle Bolan, taking him down and maybe thumping him for a while before he tired of it and left.

It didn't quite work out that way.

The Executioner dropped to a fighting crouch at the last second, while his adversary's thick arms closed on empty air. He fired a rabbit punch into the spook's short ribs and heard him grunt with pain as he was doubling over. No time to evaluate the damage as he drove a rising knee into the stranger's nose and flattened it across his florid face.

The leader dropped to hands and knees, while Bolan turned to face his sidekick. Number two was growling as he sprang toward Bolan, one arm cocked to throw a mighty haymaker. If it had landed, Bolan would've been in trouble, but he ducked the punch instead, seized the extended arm and used his enemy's momentum as a weapon, flinging him to earth.

The spook went down, then came up cursing, red-faced, instantly forgetting most of what his martial-arts instructor would've taught him during basic training. What he tried and failed to execute was a high kick toward Bolan's face.

Bad move.

It was a simple thing to block the kick and grab his ankle, twist it sharply, and kick through the knee of his remaining leg where it supported him. This time, when he went down, the spook was squealing in pain.

Bolan turned back to number one and found him struggling to his feet, blood streaming from his broken nose to stain his white dress shirt.

"Bathtid," he growled. "Ahm gawn kitchur ath."

Bolan feinted a swing, then caught him with a roundhouse kick behind one ear. The guy went down, poleaxed, and hit the ground this time without a whimper.

Leaving one.

His backup had rolled to the garbage bin, clutching one rusty side as he struggled to drag himself upright. It was painful to watch, and he was wasting precious time.

Bolan chose his spot, the base of the skull, and aimed his elbow shot for maximum effect without the killer follow-through. It dropped his man, inert, and he was pure dead-weight as Bolan hoisted him into the bin. Moments later, when the two spooks lay together on a bed of reeking garbage, Bolan dropped the bin's lid and left them to their troubled dreams.

Sleep tight.

Don't let the slum rats bite.

No one appeared to notice Bolan as he walked back to his car. He found it at the curb, untouched, and saw the black American sedan parked on the far side of the street. It might still be there when the two spooks woke and crawled out of the garbage bin.

Then again, it might not be.

Too bad.

Still watching out for tails, he joined the flow of traffic and set off to see a man about some combat gear.

THE DEALER'S SHOP was half a mile from where Bolan had left his two incompetent shadows. Out front, bilingual signs offered repair of watches, small appliances and such. Inside, a man of middle age was hunched over a cluttered workbench, peering at the guts of an electric motor through a jeweler's loupe. He glanced up as a cow bell clanked to signal Bolan's entry and set down his screwdriver.

"Boa tarde, Senhor."

"Fala inglês?" Bolan asked, thus exhausting his Portuguese vocabulary.

"English, yes, I speak. How may I help you?"

Bolan spoke the phrase Blancanales had provided, watching as the merchant's face registered first surprise, then caution.

"Ah. You wish to see my special stock?"

"That's right," Bolan confirmed."

"One moment, please."

The shopkeeper rose from his stool and limped past Bolan to the door, which he locked while reversing a small cardboard sign.

"Is siesta time now," he explained with a smile. "You will please follow me."

Bolan trailed him through a curtained doorway to a tiny, cluttered storeroom, where another door opened on steep wooden stairs. The proprietor descended first, taking the stairs without complaint despite his limp. Bolan followed into another storeroom, this one spotless and smelling of gun oil.

Bolan could've launched a small war with the dealer's inventory, but he had no plans to mount a grand offensive. He passed on the heavy machine guns, rocket and grenade launchers, and the Barrett M-82 A-1 Light Fifty sniper rifle. In their place, he chose a Steyr AUG assault rifle, a Beretta 92-F semiauto pistol and a Ka-Bar combat knife. Spare magazines and ammunition, with a side order of frag grenades, completed his heavy-metal shopping list. The rest came down to camouflage fatigues, web gear, an Alice pack and shoulder rig for the Beretta, two canteens and sturdy hiking boots. The purchases filled two stout duffel bags and took a fair bite out of Bolan's bankroll, but he didn't quibble over price.

The money, strictly speaking, wasn't even his.

Before leaving the States, he'd tapped a San Diego crack dealer for sixty thousand dollars and some pocket change. Six different banks had sold him nine grand worth of AmEx traveler's checks, and thus avoided mandatory red flags to the IRS. The rest had funded Bolan's flights, the rented car and his unused hotel room where his bag and civvies were waiting to be seized by someone from the Company.

He hoped the clothes turned out to be a lousy fit.

Before packing the gear, he loaded the Beretta and two spare magazines, adjusted the quick-draw harness to fit his torso, and covered the setup with his windbreaker. The waning day outside was cool enough, here on the coast, to prevent him from standing out by the jacket alone. After he cleared Cuiabá, farther in-country, concealment of his weapons would no longer be an issue.

Climbing the stairs behind the shop owner, Bolan slung one bag over his left shoulder and carried its mate in his left hand, leaving the right free for action if need be. He didn't anticipate trouble this early, but in most cases preparedness was more than half the battle.

Exiting the shop, he paused to scan the street in both directions, but aside from the neighborhood pusher, he saw no one who qualified as suspicious. Bolan walked back to his car and stowed both bags in the trunk, satisfied with the pistol for now. He would bag it, as well, when the time came to fly, but he still had hours to burn in Belém before his crack-of-dawn rendezvous with a charter pilot who asked no impertinent questions where payment in cash was concerned.

Bolan used an hour of that time to scout the airstrip, studying the hangar and its layout on the drive-by. He would return before dawn to check it again, watching closely for any lurkers in the shadows, but he retained an air of cautious optimism.

So far, so good.

And if experience was any guide, his chosen road could only go downhill from here.

Belém isn't Rio, but Bolan had no problem getting lost in the crowd, alternately driving and walking, never straying far enough from the rental to put his new hardware at risk from light-fingered locals. Staying awake through the night was no challenge. Call it a familiar ritual, divorced in Bolan's mind from any concept of fatigue.

He could sleep in the air, on the long flight westward to Cuiabá. And after that—who knew?

In the grand scheme of things, feeling weary was the least of a combat soldier's problems. In the days ahead, Bolan expected to be faced with worse.

All for the sake of friendship.

For the sake of duty.

And to find out what in Hell was going on with Nathan Weiss.

CHAPTER FOUR

The pilot was a twenty-something woman with short red hair and a black patch covering her left eye. The one Bolan could see was emerald-green and flicked suspiciously in the direction of his duffel bags before he loaded them aboard a Piper PA15 Vagabond at least a decade older than its owner.

Whatever she was thinking, cash resolved the lady's doubts about her passenger, and they were in the air by 6:15 a.m., soaring southwestward over rain forest that could've swallowed regiments with ample room to spare.

Where are you, Bones? he thought. What brought you here?

Bolan was glad to get out of Belém and out from under scrutiny, at least for the time being. He had no illusions about pulling off a long-term fade, if agents of the CIA made any serious attempt to locate him. They'd find him in Cuiabá, given time, but Bolan didn't plan to hang around to see the sights.

If they pursued him on his mission through the jungle, it

would be another story. They would be on his turf, then, and nothing in their past experience would've prepared them for a contest with the Executioner.

The weak part of his plan was still Marta Enriquez. Spooks had followed her to San Diego, where they'd picked up Bolan's trail without him noticing. That was a personal embarrassment, but he could live with it. The extra bad news was that if they'd spotted him, they also had to have marked Pol Blancanales, which, in turn, might lead them back to Able Team and Stony Man, if they dug deep enough.

Granted, the Company had been aware of Stony Man from the beginning, and a team of Langley rogues had once attempted to destroy the Blue Ridge Mountain farm, but general knowledge and specific details were two very different things. Bolan was on a private errand in Brazil, albeit with the knowledge of his old friend Hal Brognola, who ran Stony Man from Washington. What Bolan hadn't known, before he left the States, was that his mission placed him in direct conflict with agents of the CIA.

That was the kind of problem that could boomerang on Brognola in nothing flat, and friendship demanded that he warn Brognola at the very least.

And if the big Fed tried to call him off, then what?

He couldn't answer that until he reached Cuiabá. Enriquez was supposed to meet him there and help him with the next stage of his journey. If she didn't show, or if a swarm of spooks was trailing her, he might be forced to scrub the play.

As for the risk that he might pose to Brognola and Stony Man by pushing on, Bolan would have to weigh that against his prevailing sense of duty to an even older friend.

Cruising over the primeval forest at 130 miles per hour, Bolan reviewed what he knew so far. Blaine Downey hadn't mentioned Nathan Weiss at their brief meeting in Belém. Rather, he'd warned against collaborating with Marta Enriquez—but why?

Was the woman herself a target of investigation, distinct and separate from Weiss? It seemed unlikely, but Bolan had seen enough of politics in various banana republics to know that anything was possible.

Then again, if the Company *was* after Weiss, presumably acting in conjunction with the Brazilian government, what had Bones done to provoke their anger? Was it really just a matter of him helping persecuted aborigines, or was there something else at stake?

Bones was a healer. Even in the midst of war, he'd treated wounded soldiers of both sides impartially. His dedication was to mending flesh and lives, not scrutinizing racial pedigrees or weighing ideology. A man of peace, he'd volunteered to serve in combat, where he thought his skills were needed.

Most people found that kind of dedication laudable, until it trespassed on their politics. Healing *our* side was fine, of course, but hands off the alien-radical-subversive-demonic other side. Under no circumstances could healers help *them*.

Bones hadn't toed that line in Asia, and the odds against him heeding it now were astronomical.

But had he tipped the other way at some point, in the years since Bolan saw him last? Had he abandoned his trademark impartiality to join some cause that placed him in the outlaw ranks?

And if so, what could Bolan do about it?

Nothing, Bolan thought.

Not if the doctor's mind was set.

But he was flying on the wings of guesswork now, and that was reckless. He would wait to see if Marta met him in Cuiabá, if she had the means of putting him in touch with Nathan Weiss. And if she could, he'd find out what Bones had to say for himself.

Until then, the trick was just staying alive.

Belém

"YOU STINK, the two of you," Blaine Downey said.

"Yes, sir. We came straight back," Sutter replied. "I didn't want to phone it in."

"Straight back from where? The city dump?"

"Almost."

"Explain yourself."

"You ordered us to keep an eye on Cooper, sir, and follow him if he left the hotel."

"There's nothing wrong with my memory, Sutter."

"No, sir. Anyway, he did leave the hotel, and we trailed him. Making it obvious, just like you said. He saw us, all right, started boxing the block to make sure, then he led us downtown. Parked on the outskirts of the red-light district."

"Window shopping?" Downey asked.

"That's what we thought," Sutter replied. "We figured if he tried to score a little action, we could break it up and spoil his evening for him."

"Fair enough. How does that bring us to your tragic choice of aftershave?"

"We followed him a couple blocks from where he parked, and then he ducked into an alley."

"And?"

"We went in after him."

"Of course you did."

"First thing, I thought we'd lost him somehow. Maybe he ducked through a door we didn't see or something. Then, before you know it, he's behind us."

Downey saw where this was going, but he let the flow of words continue.

"Anyway," Sutter continued, "we had words."

"Such as?"

"He challenged us," Sutter said.

"Challenged us," Jones echoed, speaking for the first time since he'd entered Downey's office. "Right."

"Who made the first move?" Downey asked.

"Well…"

That answered it.

Downey refused to let the two incompetents provoke a raging outburst, though the pair of them deserved no better. He preferred to take his time, dissect them with a surgeon's skill, enjoying every slice.

For all the good that it would do him now.

"I see," he said. "The target *challenged* you, and one or both of you attacked him. Did I order you to rough him up, Sutter?"

"You didn't say—"

"Thank you. I'll take that as a no. The two of you exceeded your instructions and then, what? He kicked your asses, I suppose?"

Jones fidgeted with eyes downcast. Sutter was fuming, anger radiating from his body like the stench of garbage that surrounded him, but he was wise enough to keep his mouth shut.

"Right," Downey continued. "So, he kicked your asses for you. Knocked you both unconscious, I presume, since your report is hours late. And from the way you stink, I'd guess he dropped you down a manhole. Were you floating in the sewer all this time, ladies?"

Nothing.

"I can't hear you."

The crunching sound from Sutter had to be grinding teeth. His face was red enough to fit a stroke victim. Beside him, Jones reluctantly answered, "A garbage Dumpster, sir."

"How's that?"

"He put us in a Dumpster, sir, not down a manhole."

"I'm relieved," Downey said. "I don't think that I could stand another load of shit from either one of you."

"No, sir," Jones answered.

"Will you shut up!" Sutter hissed.

"I'm gravely disappointed in the pair of you," Downey announced. "You've turned a simple job into a screwup that's left the Company exposed on levels you don't even understand. You wouldn't catch me lighting any candles if the mark had bled you out instead of marinating you in garbage. Are we clear?"

Apparently, since neither of the smelly two replied.

"My choices, broadly speaking, are to can your asses on the spot or to send you back to Langley for retraining and potential reassignment. That's if I report your sorry asses for the mess you've made."

"And if you don't? Sir?" There was something close to hope in Sutter's surly voice.

"You must redeem yourselves," Downey said.

"How can we do that?"

"Begin by thinking for a change. What do you think might change my mood, right now?"

"Locate the mark!" Jones said, pleased with himself despite his reek.

"And…?"

"And…trace him to his contact?" Sutter asked.

"At which time," Downey prodded, "you would…?"

That one stumped them for a moment, until Sutter hit upon the obvious. "We take 'em out," he said. "Use locals if we can. No comebacks on the Company."

"Be careful, gentlemen, and shower thoroughly before you start, for God's sake. I'll expect good news within…shall we say, forty-eight hours?"

"Yes, sir." A two-man chorus.

"If you can't manage that, I suggest you keep going. Find a hole and burrow deep. Pray I don't find you alive."

Cuiabá, Brazil

THE RED-HAIRED PILOT beat her own best ETA by forty minutes, even after bucking killer turbulence over the Serra Formosa. Bolan tipped her thirty percent of her fee and got an inkling of a smile in return before she left him to fuel the plane for her return trip to Belém.

When Bolan turned, hefting his bags, he saw Marta Enriquez standing in the shadow of the airstrip's terminal. She raised a hand and Bolan nodded in return, while scanning left and right for any sign of watchers in the neighborhood. He'd missed them back in San Diego, and he was determined not to make the same mistake again.

This time around, his life depended on it.

Bolan crossed the tarmac and a strip of poorly tended grass to reach the terminal. He didn't go inside, because the country's rural landing strips demanded nothing in the way of customs declarations or security procedures. It was why he'd gone the charter route, instead of booking a commercial flight.

Enriquez put on a smile to greet him, saying, "I was worried that you wouldn't come."

"I'm here. You have a car?"

"This way." She eyed his bags. "May I...?"

"No, thanks."

She led him to the far side of the small building and a bare-dirt parking lot of sorts. Three vehicles stood baking in the sunshine, the woman's four-door model Bolan didn't recognize. Something domestic, he decided, patterned on some U.S. model from the 1960s.

Bolan put his bags in the back seat and let himself into the oven on wheels. The sedan's air-conditioning gave out asthmatic wheezing sounds, and Enriquez left the windows down, raising her voice as she accelerated on the highway to Cuiabá.

"Were there any difficulties on your trip?" she asked.

"I had a welcoming committee in Belém," Bolan replied.

"Oh, yes?" She sounded nervous.

"A guy from the U.S. embassy. He doesn't like the company I'm keeping lately."

"Oh?" Her eyes flicked back and forth between the road and Bolan's face.

He didn't feel like tiptoeing around it. "Did you know you had a tail in San Diego?"

"Tail?"

"That you were being shadowed. Watched."

The horrified expression on her face answered his question well before she found her voice. "I didn't know. I promise you."

"You put them onto me, and they were waiting when I touched down in Belém."

"What did they say?" she asked.

He gambled on the truth. "They called you 'a subject of interest' and told me to leave you alone, go back to the States, this and that."

"But you came anyway."

"I like to judge things for myself," Bolan replied.

"Did they say anything about Na— About Dr. Weiss?"

It wasn't the first time she'd caught herself speaking of Bones in a familiar way. Or was that intimate? Bolan couldn't swear the question was relevant to his mission, but it might have some bearing on how much he trusted the woman.

"He wasn't mentioned."

"Oh? Perhaps they just want me."

"Why's that?" he asked.

"I've been involved in antigovernment protests since they began to drive my people off the land."

"That's a domestic problem," Bolan said. He guessed the answer to his next question before he spoke, but asked it anyway. "What does it have to do with Washington?"

"Your country has involved itself in Latin American matters for two hundred years, from the Monroe Doctrine and the Panama canal to Noriega and the Contras. Some say Washington supports regimes that favor U.S. businesses."

"And what do *you* say?" Bolan prodded.

"Dr. Weiss needs help," she said. "Soon, it may be too late. If you're his friend, please help him."

"First, I have to find him."

"I will show you where he is," she said.

"That wasn't part of the agreement," he reminded her.

"How else will you locate him?" Enriquez asked.

"Technology. You give me the coordinates and I take it from there."

"I'm sorry," she responded with a calculating smile, "but I don't understand such things. I'll have to show you where he is. Are we agreed?"

Washington, D.C.

HAL BROGNOLA TOOK the call from California on his private, scrambled line. He recognized the voice at once and asked, "How's Baja?"

"Hot and dry," Rosario Blancanales said. "I've got another problem, though. You ought to know about it."

"So, let's hear it."

"Toni had two visitors at the home office earlier today. They claimed affiliation with the State Department, but she says they smelled like Company."

Brognola frowned at that. "How sure is she?"

"Ninety to ninety-five percent."

"That sure. Okay."

"They asked about Brazil," Blancanales said.

"Asked what, specifically?"

"Whether Team Able handles foreign clients, and by any chance is one of them Marta Enriquez?"

"What did Toni say?"

"She cited confidentiality. We often work for lawyers, so it's covered unless they come back with a warrant. In which case, there's nothing to find."

"But they still made the link," Brognola said.

"Exactly. I don't know how they tagged us, but I'm working on it. Anyway, it made me think about our friend."

Brognola was thinking about Bolan, too. If the CIA had tracked Marta Enriquez from Brazil to San Diego, then it stood to reason they'd be waiting for her when she got back home. They might have Bolan's face on film already, though it wouldn't take them far. More troublesome, to Brognola's mind, was the prospect of a hostile welcoming committee waiting for him in Brazil.

The private task Bolan had taken upon himself for friendship's sake was difficult enough, without yet another chef stirring the pot. And if Langley backtracked Bolan far enough, under one of his code names, would the trail lead back to Stony Man Farm?

Brognola needed to check his firewalls, but first he asked Blancanales, "Did Toni get names?"

"Smith and Thomas, if you can believe it."

He didn't, but that was par for the course. The CIA had covert millions to spend, but Langley often suffered from a near-criminal lack of imagination. Mr. Smith, for God's sake. Mr. Thomas.

"I'll do what I can on this end," Brognola said. "Thanks for the heads-up."

"About our friend…"

"No word, so far. I don't really expect to hear from him, since this is unofficial."

"Then we won't know if he hits a snag."

Brognola had considered that when Blancanales briefed him on the woman's story, asking for a dossier on Dr. Nathan Weiss. It made him nervous, then and now, but there was little he could do about it. Part of Bolan's deal with Washington and Stony Man included freedom to reject assignments, or to tackle missions of his own when he was off the clock. It hadn't often been an issue in the past.

But now...

It galled Brognola, thinking that his best field agent, one of his oldest living friends, might come to fatal grief while handling a private errand on the side. He'd braced himself a hundred times for news of Bolan's death, had privately rehearsed the secret eulogy, but this eventuality had troubled him beyond all else.

The Executioner was only human, after all.

Like all flesh, he was prey to accidents, disease and plain bad luck. The fact that he had led a more or less charmed life to this point didn't mean it would continue.

Luck could turn in a heartbeat.

Life could stop on a dime.

"I need to make some calls," Brognola said. "Take care, and call me back if anybody gets in touch."

"Will do."

Brognola cradled the receiver, scowling at the modest clutter on his desktop. Life went on in Washington, no matter who was being threatened, maimed or killed halfway around the world.

He started taking stock.

Brognola knew where Bolan was, at least approximately, and he knew one contact's name. He had a slim file on the man Bolan had gone to see, perhaps to extricate from trouble of the killing kind—and possibly in contravention of local authority. Now Langley had a fat thumb in the pie, and that potentially changed everything.

Except the fact that Bolan's mission was a private one, unsanctioned by Brognola's superiors. And if Bolan's personal pursuits placed him in conflict with the government, where did Brognola's loyalty lie?

His paychecks came from Uncle Sam, but Brognola had forged a bond with Bolan long ago, back in the days when the Executioner was a Top Ten fugitive and the big Fed had been assigned to bring him in, dead or alive. He'd bent the rules to work with Bolan then, against the Mafia—but could he do the same against the CIA, despite the closed-ranks posture of the War on Terror?

Maybe. Maybe not.

Before he made his choice, Brognola needed more hard information.

And he needed it right now.

Cuiabá, Brazil

"I UNDERSTAND," Anastasio Herreira said. In his rage, he clutched the telephone so tightly that his knuckles blanched from olive to a shade of ivory.

"Do you?" the sharp voice in his ear demanded. "Do you *really* understand our problem? I'm not sure you grasp it, Major. I don't think you're up to speed on this at all."

Stiffly, cheeks aflame, Herreira answered, "Mr. Downey, I assure you that I'm doing everything within my power to locate this rogue American. He has invaded my country, not yours, where he would be at home. He serves my enemies, not those of the United States. And frankly—"

"That's exactly what I mean," Downey said, interrupting him. "I hear you say something like that and I can tell you haven't got a clue about the big picture. When we talk about big pictures in the States, we don't mean giant paintings on the wall. Understand?"

"Senhor Downey—"

The caller forged ahead, oblivious. "When we say big picture, we're talking the long view, wide-screen, all-inclusive. A man coughs in Moscow, they catch cold in China and sneeze in Manila. You get me?"

"If you have some point to make—"

"That *is* my point, amigo. Right there, in a nutshell. You've got creeping Red cancer in your country, and it's going to eat you alive if you cut it out, root and branch. Now, if you think that only affects Brazil, and not the States—or the whole freaking world, for that matter—you're not only blind, you've got your head stuck in your ass."

Major Herreira wasn't sure how many more insults he could endure from the crude Yankee before he exploded in fury. That, of course, would jeopardize his agency's relations with the CIA, which in turn would outrage his none too tolerant superiors. Better, perhaps, to rage in private and placate the Yankee. They *were* allies, after all, engaged in a common struggle.

"What would you have me do?" Herreira asked Downey.

"I'm sending a couple of men out to help you," Downey said.

Herreira bristled at the notion. He needed Yankee "helpers" as he needed jungle rot or syphilis—and having suffered both, the major knew the irritations they produced.

"Senhor Downey—"

"Before you get all territorial, they have information that can help you wrap this up, okay? They've seen the new kid on the block, this guy recruited by your woman for whatever reason."

"She is not my—"

"Anyway, they've met him. They can spot him, where your men might think he's just another gringo tourist looking for some action."

"Photographs would do as well," Herreira said.

Downey ignored him, saying, "More importantly, my men can take him out with no reflection on your team."

Herreira wasn't easily deceived by specious arguments. The Brazilian government had no qualms about jailing foreign intruders or killing those who resisted arrest. A simpleminded blind man could've seen that Downey's primary concern was to prevent embarrassment for the United States.

The doctor had been bad enough, but if he'd started to recruit allies from the U.S., some might regard it as more than intrusion. It could mean invasion, perhaps an act of war.

"Your men must willingly submit themselves to my authority," Herreira said.

"Sure thing, Major," Downey answered with a broad smile in his voice.

Herreira knew that he was lying, that his agents would behave as they had always done in "Third World" countries for the past two hundred years. Imagining that only the U.S. was fit to form opinions, dictate terms, decide what should be done in any given situation from Latin America to Europe and Southeast Asia.

"In that case," Herreira replied, "I welcome their assistance."

"That's my boy. Expect a call within the hour."

So, Herreira thought, they were already in Cuiabá or well on their way. His agreement, once more, meant no more to Downey than a rubber stamp on plans already finalized. He'd have to watch them every moment, to be certain they didn't overstep their bounds.

Or if they did, and tragedy ensued, Herreira had to make sure that he couldn't be blamed.

And if some accident befell them in the process, it was Downey's job to deal with it, smother the breath of scandal.

Let the Yankee do his job, then. And together, they might just manage to save Herreira's career.

"I STILL THINK it's a bad idea," Bolan insisted.

"Senhor Cooper, I'm Tehuelche. What you see—" the hands that smoothed her dress had polished nails "—is only one facet of what I am."

"I understand that, but—"

"I know the jungle," she informed him. "I was born and raised there, educated in a mission school. Your high technology may locate map coordinates, but it won't tell you if the doctor has been forced to flee again or where he's gone this time."

"He's moving?"

Marta Enriquez shrugged. "We won't know that until we reach the meeting place."

"I've done some tracking of my own, from time to time," Bolan informed her.

"Were you hunting men?"

"Yeah, I was."

She frowned at that. Sometimes the newbies asked what it was like, killing and almost being killed, but Enriquez had to have seen that for herself. Instead she simply asked, "Why are you here, really?"

"Bones is—or was—a friend of mine. If he's in trouble now, I'd like to help him."

"With no politics involved?" she asked.

"The man I knew wasn't concerned with politics. He was a healer."

"Tell me why you call him 'Bones.'"

Bolan explained, briefly. When he was done, she asked, "And you would help him, even if he now heals those who might be enemies of the United States?"

"If he needs help—*wants* help—I'll do my best. I didn't come to join a cause or fight against one. If there's fighting to be done, though, you'll be in the way."

"In any case," she said, "it makes no difference. I have supplies for Dr. Weiss. If I don't go with you, then I must go alone into the forest."

Bolan saw that argument was futile in the face of such determination. He had no doubt that Marta would proceed without him, and it was entirely possible that she'd withhold Weiss's location if Bolan refused to cooperate.

At last, resigned, he said, "All right. We need an early start tomorrow."

"Is dawn early enough?" she asked him, smiling.

"Just about."

"I'll let you sleep, then." At the door of Bolan's hotel room, she paused and turned. "What if they follow us, your people?"

It was Bolan's turn to shrug. He didn't think he'd seen the last of Downey's people yet. "I shook them once," he said. "I can do it again."

But shaking might not do it in the jungle. He might have to bury them, if they were bent on doing some irrevocable harm to Nathan Weiss or to himself. It wouldn't be the first time he'd clashed with Company spooks, where lives were at stake.

"I hope you can do it," she answered. "They may be here already." And having said that, she slipped out of the room.

Alone, Bolan got busy with his fear. He would be wearing street clothes when they left the following day, in Enriquez's car, but he wanted his canteens full and his weapons ready to go. He'd change clothes when they reached their jumping-off point, where they'd have to ditch their wheels and take to water, then proceed on foot. There were no roads where they were going, yet.

What was waiting for them at the end of the trail?

A friend, perhaps—or maybe not.

Time changed minds, hearts, people. Bolan didn't think that Nathan Weiss had been transformed into a villain or mad scientist since they'd last seen each other, but it was entirely possible that Bones had found himself a cause to follow. And it might be one that ran against the grain with Bolan, one way or another.

Insurrection, revolution—the American tropics bred them like fever. Most countries south of the Rio Grande had battled their way through long series of rebellions, civil wars and military juntas over the past two centuries, and some were still embroiled in that struggle. Brazil had seemingly beaten the trend.

Bolan would see what waited for him when he reached trail's end, and not before. Meanwhile, he needed sleep, in case he couldn't find it in Green Hell.

CHAPTER FIVE

Cuiabá

"I hope the dirty SOB resists," Dirk Sutter said.

"I'm counting on it," Clement Jones replied.

They sat together in a plain brown van, with three secret police types huddled in the back. Waiting. Jones had a MAC-10 submachine gun in his lap, fat sound suppressor extending its abbreviated muzzle, but the weapon still looked almost toylike in his black-gloved hands. Sutter had picked a micro-Uzi, likewise silenced, and was feeding it a magazine of Parabellum hollowpoint rounds.

"It needs to look good, though," Sutter remarked.

"That's why we brought the three amigos," Jones reminded him.

The locals all spoke English, more or less, but Jones saw no reason to spare their feelings. He was an American, for God's sake. Anywhere he set his feet was home, thanks to the megabillions spent on foreign aid and the new atmosphere of militancy prompted by the War on Terror.

It wasn't the natives he worried about, sitting sweaty and tense in the van. He worried about Downey and the man they'd come to neutralize.

Jones still wasn't sure how Downey had zeroed the target's hotel in Cuiabá. Some kind of high-tech hocus-pocus, he supposed, or maybe an old-fashioned squeal from an informant. Either way, they had his crib on quarantine, nobody in or out, and in another five minutes or so they would be going in to smoke him out.

Or waste him, as the case might be.

Downey had given them some latitude, after the fuck-up in Belém. He wasn't letting them forget it—likely never would, the bastard—but at least he hadn't sent them out unarmed this time. They were prepared, complete with reinforcements duly authorized to make arrests.

Not that he planned on taking Mr. Hot Shit into custody. Not even close.

There'd been a time when asshole bullies used to get their kicks by stuffing Clement Jones in lockers, trash cans and the like, but Jones had turned that trend around by pumping iron for two years straight, then kicking ass and taking names. To save himself from bullies, he'd *become* a bully, and his path was set for life.

Until the moment in Belém, when all his muscle got him was a headache and the stink of garbage in his hair.

Somebody had to pay for that insult, the damage it had done to him in Downey's eyes, and one Matt Cooper was about to rue the day he ever fucked with Clement Jones.

But Jones was nervous, sweating through his lightweight suit despite the early morning chill. The three studs waiting on the van's rear bench seat seemed immune to nerves, but Jones saw Sutter fidgeting behind the steering wheel. Jones wasn't psychic, but he had a fair idea of what was going on in Sutter's head.

He didn't want to give this Cooper prick another chance to kick their asses, nothing hand-to-hand unless the guy surrendered and they got him handcuffed. Maybe tune him up a little then, to settle scores, but if he offered anything resembling physical resistance, they would put him down.

Case closed. No second chances.

"Room 228, you said?" he asked Sutter.

"You got it."

"And the woman's in 230?"

"Right next door," Sutter replied. "Connecting rooms, for all I know. Maybe they're playing house. Guy wants to change his luck."

"It's changed, all right," Jones said.

Sutter glanced over at him from the driver's seat. "Remember, now, the first move's his. We're playing by the rules."

"No sweat."

It wouldn't have to be much of a move, Jones thought. The prick could blink his eyelids, maybe clear his throat, and that was all the physical resistance it would take to spark a storm of automatic fire.

Their cleanup gear included body bags.

Jones didn't really care about the woman, one way or the other, though the trouble had begun with her. He wished someone had taken care of her in San Diego, maybe left her in the desert with the others who were robbed and killed crossing the line from Mexico. It would've been the easy way, but no one thought of it.

Dumb bastards.

Now Jones had to kill a man who'd kicked his ass and dropped him in a garbage Dumpster. Maybe kill the woman, too, though she'd done nothing to offend him yet.

"It's time."

Sutter was out and moving, even as he spoke, tucking the micro-Uzi underneath his jacket. Jones opened his door, half turning toward the goons in back, and said, "Let's rock and roll, amigos."

They breezed through the lobby without opposition, rode the elevator up two floors, and followed the wall-mounted arrows to their target. Jones and Sutter took the door to Cooper's room. Their three companions, pistols drawn, staked out the entrance to the woman's crib. On *three* they kicked both doors and rushed inside, shock troops of the apocalypse.

And found both rooms deserted.

"Shit! He isn't gonna like this," Sutter said.

Jones scanned the empty hotel room and muttered, "That makes two of us."

THEY WERE MAKING fair time, but Bolan still wished the old riverboat could've gone faster. Its diesel motor labored, fouled the air around them, and propelled them at a steady four to five knots with the current, but he'd hoped for more.

Broad daylight now, and if the Company was looking for them in Cuiabá, then its spooks would soon know they were gone. The question would be *where*, and Bolan wished they could've gained a better lead before the hunters started tracking them afresh.

An airlift would've done the trick, but Marta didn't skydive and she'd finally convinced him that trackers would waste more time questioning Cuiabá's several thousand river rats than checking out a hundred-odd bush pilots. It made sense and gave the warrior time to think.

But he still wished for speed.

The Rio Cuiabá flowed southwestward from the city that shared its name, winding through primal forest toward the Bolivian border, where it met and fed the Rio Paraguai. Bolan and his companion didn't plan to follow it that far, however. They were landing fifty miles downriver and would hike from there, through wilderness that one early explorer had described as "Hell on Earth and Eden, all rolled into one."

So far, it wasn't Bolan's notion of a holiday.

It felt like coming home.

Bolan had grown up in a jungle, spilled his first blood there and earned the nickname that would follow him through life, even beyond his early grave. That jungle was located on the far side of the world, but all of them were more or less the same. The predators and prey varied by continent, but it was still survival of the fittest in a world where no quarter was asked or granted.

The one rule carved in stone was kill or be killed.

Bolan knew that rule by heart, and he was still alive.

The captain of their boat ignored them after he'd collected cash up front, which suited Bolan perfectly. He lingered at the rail and watched the forest pass, unscrolling like the background footage in a wildlife film. Bright-colored birds hovered or swooped among the trees, while monkeys swarmed and chattered. Caimans waited on the bank for fish or careless swimmers to present themselves.

Forest primeval. Given half a chance, he knew that it would eat him up alive.

And somewhere in the midst of it was Nathan Weiss.

Bad choice, Bones, Bolan thought. And once again, Why here?

Enriquez was suddenly beside him at the railing. She'd changed into khaki hiking clothes and sturdy boots, hair pulled back from her face and cinched with an elastic band. She wore no makeup, and she didn't seem to miss it.

Both of us were going home, Bolan thought, but it didn't warm the cockles of his heart.

"It shouldn't be much longer," Enriquez told him, eyes fixed on the wall of forest opposite. "I know a place where we can stay tonight. A village. By nightfall tomorrow, with luck, you can speak to your friend."

"After all this time," Bolan said, "you're a closer friend to him than I am."

"Maybe not."

"I'm betting on it. And I'm hoping you can shed some light on why he chose this place."

"We've never talked about it," she replied. "I felt so lucky that the choice was made, for both my people and myself. I didn't want to question it."

"Okay."

"But if I had to guess," the woman went on, "I think he feels a need to heal the world. It sounds ridiculous, perhaps."

"Not necessarily."

"I think, for Dr. Weiss, it's not enough to have an office in the city or to work at an important hospital. He talks about red tape sometimes. You know of this?"

"It rings a bell," Bolan replied.

"He hates red tape and rules. Out here, I think, he finally feels free."

And Bolan was supposed to talk him out of it.

Welcome home.

Belém

"WHAT DO YOU MEAN, you lost them both?"

Downey could feel the anger stirring, rising through his body like a head of steam seeking an outlet, throbbing in his ears, a second pulse. He didn't need a mirror to imagine the pink color in his face.

"Um, well, sir," Sutter stammered over the long-distance line, "we took the team as planned and checked that address you supplied us, half-past five in the a.m. They were already gone."

"Checked out?"

"No, sir. I asked the desk clerk, after. They just walked. Nobody saw them go."

Was that pure luck, or had somebody put a bug in Cooper's ear? He would've been expecting company, after the ruckus in Belém, but not so soon. How could he know they'd pin him down that fast?

He couldn't, Downey thought.

Luck, then—or else, the kind of skill that made dumb luck superfluous.

"All right, here's what you do," he said. "Get after them.

I don't care what you have to do, just find out where they've gone and follow them. You understand."

"Yes, sir. But—"

"But nothing," Downey cut him off. "You have one job and only one. Find Cooper and the woman. If they're hiding in Cuiabá, root them out. If they've gone native and they're swinging from the goddamned trees, you grab a vine and follow them. I hope you're reading me."

"Yes, sir."

"And when you find them, liquidate the problem, Sutter. Rub it out. Until that job is finished, you and Jones will *not* return. Under no circumstances known to God or man will I accept one more report of failure. Are we clear?"

"Yes, sir!"

"Then move your ass and get it done."

Downey put down the telephone receiver, then immediately lifted it again. The urge to share his misery was irresistible. He dialed the number of security police headquarters from his memory, one of perhaps five hundred crucial numbers filed inside his head, and waited while his call was passed along to Anastasio Herreira's desk.

"Está?" Herreira greeted him.

"Está, yourself. Are we secure?"

"Of course."

"I've got bad news."

"It's the only kind you ever bring to me."

"Somebody screwed the pooch this morning, in Cuiabá," Downey said. "I'm not assigning blame, you understand. Mixed signals, who knows what it was. Long story short, we missed the woman and her friend at the hotel."

"I see." Herreira's voice was glum.

"Now, what we need to do is find out where they're going. Either head them off or trail them to their destination. Maybe wrap it up once and for all."

"You make it sound like meeting old friends in the park," Herreira said. "You think they'll leave a trail for us to follow?"

"Everybody leaves a trail. It's a fact of life. The trick is knowing what to look for, how to read the signs."

"Mato Grosso is the third-largest state in Brazil, Senhor Downey, and the most sparsely populated. Outside Cuiabá—"

"I don't need a geography lesson. I need hunters who aren't afraid to get their hands dirty."

Herreira lowered his voice as he asked, "What is it you propose?"

"We have a chance to wrap this up once and for all, within the next few days, if we're not squeamish. We've already missed our chance to stop the woman slipping past with her hireling, but the mistake may work for us if we're quick enough."

"You think they'll lead us to the doctor?"

"That's exactly what I think. Of course, we have to find them first."

"And I must say again—"

"Don't tell me what you can't do. I need a can-do attitude for this job. Think about the money Langley's pumped into your service, and the cut you've skimmed off for yourself."

"Senhor—"

"Nobody's faulting you," Downey said. "Hell, I know the way things work. All I'm suggesting is that you should earn

a little of that money, now and then. You need to work a little overtime, put extra bodies on the street."

"What am I looking for?" Herreira asked, resigned.

"Smart money says they've left Cuiabá. If we find out
how they went, we also find out where they've gone. Get
those coordinates, a drop-off point, and we can start to hunt
for real."

"All right," Herreira said. "I'll see what I can do."

"And let me know, ASAP."

"Of course."

"Good man," Downey said, smiling even as he broke the
link.

THE FIRST HOUR on foot was the worst, Enriquez thought. It
still surprised her, after all this time, that her body was forced
to reacclimatize each time she returned to the jungle from a
trip away. Even a weekend in Cuiabá, with its running water,
fans and air-conditioning could tip the balance of her metab-
olism it seemed, and had her sweating like a rank tourist
when she came back home.

Moving along the narrow, unmarked trail, she made a point
of watching Cooper on the sly, quick glances from the corner of her eye or underneath an arm when she paused to wipe
her brow. He seemed to bear up well, with both the heat and
the equipment that he carried. He was cautious, yet almost
casual about it, not like one of those big-city "sportsmen" who
clutched his weapon as if danger waited behind every tree.

Though it might, she admitted.

They hadn't left danger behind by escaping from the city
and the men who hunted them through the streets. Those

hunters would follow, or send others in their place, and still
more peril waited on the trail ahead.

Marta hoped Matt Cooper was equal to the task, and for a
moment she almost felt guilty for bringing him into the jungle.

Almost.

Dr. Weiss—her Nathan—needed help to stay alive. If that
meant taking him away, so be it. She would either find some
means of joining him, or she would stay behind and nurture
fading memories of what they'd had together.

Either way, the most important thing was his survival and
the good work he could still do elsewhere, if he lived.

He had such talent, such compassion, and it would be
wasted if he died here, clinging to a futile hope that he could
change the hearts and minds of common men.

"Within two hours," she told Cooper, "we should reach the
village."

"Is it yours?" he asked.

"The people are Tehuelche and they welcome me," she
swered, "but it's not my home. A smallpox epidemic k
most of my people years ago, while I was in the reside
mission school. I've seen where they were heaped and bu
together for the public good. My parents have no graves.

"I buried mine," he said. "The markers aren't much h

"You may think I was lucky to be off at school."

He shrugged beneath his heavy pack. "You're still ali

"The residential schools were meant to break us, wipe
old beliefs and fill our heads with something new."

"It looks like you outsmarted them," Bolan said.

Grim-faced, Enriquez shook her head. "They broke

with the rest," she answered. "Only in the past few years have I recovered what was lost."

"Still, that's a victory," Bolan replied. "They knocked you down but couldn't beat you."

"Oh, they beat me," she corrected him. "Nobody in the mission schools escaped beatings—and worse. You've heard the stories, I suppose."

"From Canada," he said. "Not so much from Brazil."

"They're much the same. It was a silent holocaust of torture, rape, indoctrination. No one who survived it was unscathed. Recovering the culture that was beaten out of us may take a lifetime, but the time is what we don't have, Mr. Cooper. Even as we speak, the government and industry are finishing the slaughter that began more than a hundred years ago."

"Is that what brought Bones to Brazil?"

"It may surprise you that we never talked about his motives. He is a very private man. I was too grateful for his help to question it."

"Okay."

"You don't believe me?"

"I just want to understand what we're all doing here," he said.

"The doctor heals. You're here to save his life."

"And you?"

She frowned again and said, "I'm not sure, yet."

They spoke little over the next hour, their silence broken only when Enriquez pointed out some animal or plant that posed a threat. On those occasions, Bolan listened, paid attention and moved on.

She smelled the village from a half mile out, wood smoke and food in preparation for the evening meal. Before she could alert Cooper, she realized that he had smelled it, too.

Clearly, he wasn't just another handsome face.

They were two hundred yards from contact when the first shot made her jump. Two more immediately followed, wringing from her throat a strangled protest.

"Please, God, no!"

Bolan released his weapon from its shoulder sling and plunged into the jungle, following the sounds. Fearing what she would find, Marta Enriquez clenched her teeth and followed him.

A QUICK COUNT made it ten or fifteen shooters dressed in mismatched clothes, no military trappings other than their weapons. Bolan had no time to scout the village, making sure. The gunmen he could see were busy when he got there, herding unarmed Indians in the direction of a long house built from logs. Its thatch roof was already smoking. Bolan saw one of the raiders shoot a woman with a baby in her arms, a single bullet drilling both.

He fired instinctively, a 3-round burst dropping the shooter in his tracks. Most of the raiders were distracted, but a couple saw the dead man drop and spun to find out where the killing shots had come from.

Bolan didn't keep them in suspense.

He shot the nearer of them in the forehead, saw his 5.56 mm tumbling projectile spread a misty crimson halo as the shooter fell, and tracked on to the next stunned target.

That one triggered off a short burst from his automatic

rifle, but the bullets didn't come within a dozen yards of scoring. Bolan's two rounds of return fire punched the gunman backward, off his feet, and left him twitching in the dirt.

The rest had noticed him by now, distracted from their genocidal chores. Bolan picked off a fourth before he started taking concentrated fire, then ducked away and circled to his left along the village's perimeter.

He didn't know where Marta was, but hoped she would be smart enough to keep her head down while the firefight lasted. There was no time to go looking for her now.

Inside the village, some of the tribesmen were taking advantage of Bolan's distraction, seizing actual or makeshift weapons and lashing out at their would-be murderers. Moving along the tree line, Bolan saw one of the shooters topple with a hatchet sprouting from his skull, before two of his friends killed the hatchet man.

Bolan unleashed a short burst from the hip, running, and cut one of the shooter's legs from under him. Three Indians immediately fell upon the wounded man, punching and kicking while they grappled for his gun, but others shot them down.

Bare hands against hot lead was bound to be a losing fight.

Bolan veered closer to the tree line, ducking, firing, watching targets fall. As dusk descended, firelight from the burning log house showed the raiders off in silhouette. They caught on to the danger moments later, after two had fallen to shots from the forest, and they scattered, seeking Bolan's muzzle-flashes, hunting him instead of simply firing blindly at the trees.

It was the best plan he could think of at the moment, still

outnumbered and on unfamiliar ground. He'd dealt with nearly half the raiders, but a single lucky shot could finish it and leave the rest to carry on with their destruction of the village.

Maybe they'd already done enough, he thought, to drive the tribe away and end their simple life forever. Maybe he'd been too late when the first shots echoed through the forest.

But he couldn't let it go.

He had his sights fixed on a crouching figure, moving through the darkened trees, when suddenly a woman's voice rang out from the forest behind him. She wasn't speaking Portuguese, and while he didn't recognize the dialect, Bolan had grown familiar with the sound of Marta's voice.

Beyond the smoke and leaping firelight, other voices— male and female—answered in the same language. Some sounded frightened, others angry, but they weren't retreating.

Dammit, Bolan thought, she had to get them out of here before—

His target moved and Bolan fired, dropping the shadow man. At once, two more sprang up to take the shooter's place, rushing the spot where they had seen the muzzle-flash from Bolan's AUG. They came on, firing from the hip, spraying the trees on either side of him with bullets.

The Executioner returned fire, saw one of his enemies stumble and fall. The other kept firing, still wide of the mark, but his bullets tore bark from the tree to Bolan's left and sprayed his face with sticky sap.

It burned like acid, sharp pain biting deeply into Bolan's cheeks and eyes. Before the caustic fire could cripple him, he braced his Steyr and held down the trigger, hosing his adversary with the last rounds from the rifle's magazine. He heard the shooter squeal, then more shots from a distance, but his scalded eyes were throbbing, urging him to scream.

Bolan saw nothing but a blur of firelight as he crumpled to the jungle floor.

"IT'S CALLED the manchineel," a soft voice told him, reaching Bolan through a darkness that was streaked with neon rivulets of pain. He might've clawed his eyes, but solid human weight pinned down both arms.

"The tree," Enriquez explained, her voice almost a whisper. "It is fairly common here. The fruit is poisonous, the sap corrosive. Native hunters tip their arrows with it, when they don't have access to curare or the poison frogs."

Bolan remembered gunfire and the spray of burning liquid in his face. "I'm blind?" he asked, dead-voiced.

"We rinsed your eyes," she said, avoiding his direct question. "You have a poultice on them now, the pressure that you feel. It's made from leaves and other things."

"Will I be blind?" he asked again.

"I don't know yet. We need more help. Real medicine."

There was a hollow place inside him, wholly unfamiliar. Bolan had faced death a thousand times, but he had never truly contemplated disability. It was a given, in his mind, that he would someday fall in battle, but he'd never pictured groping through a world of darkness, helpless in the presence of his enemies.

"What happened to the raiders?" he asked Enriquez.

"You killed most of them. Tehuelche did the rest."

"The village?"

"A few huts were saved, but not enough. They will move on. Also, the doctor can't come here."

"Bones?"

"We're taking you to meet him," the woman answered. "Only now you'll be a patient, and we leave tonight."

"How far?" Bolan asked, teeth clenched hard against another wave of searing pain.

"With luck, we should be there by noon tomorrow."

"Right," he said, and tried again to rise. The weight that held him down shifted but didn't yield. "I can't go far," Bolan reminded her, "with people sitting on my arms and legs."

"You won't be walking," Enriquez told him. "It's too dangerous. Before you went a hundred yards, you'd have a broken leg or worse."

"I might surprise you."

"Or," she said, "you'll slow us so much that by the time we reach the doctor, it will be too late to save your sight."

And what if it was too late already, Bolan thought. The way it burned…

"What did you have in mind?" he asked.

"A litter. It's already been constructed…but we'll have to tie you on, for safety's sake."

Blinded *and* bound. A double handicap.

"What happens if we're ambushed on the way?" he asked.

"I have your rifle," Enriquez answered. "You can't use it, anyway. Trust me. Trust us."

He didn't seem to have a choice. The feeling that enveloped Bolan was the closest thing to despair that he'd ever endured. The loss of friends and family was something else entirely, suffering apart, an almost selfish thing. If he was truly blinded, though, life as he knew it would be over. Never mind the mission, Marta, Bones or the Tehuelche. It would take a miracle for Bolan to escape the jungle, much less make his way out of Brazil, back to the States.

And what was waiting for a sightless warrior, there?

Nothing.

He reckoned Hal Brognola would arrange something, "take care" of him somehow, but would it be a life worth living?

Bolan thought of Aaron Kurtzman, married to a wheelchair since a traitor's bullet clipped his spine during a raid on Stony Man. He functioned well enough, but he'd been a technician first and foremost, supreme in a world of keyboards and modems where legs were of marginal value. Kurtzman excelled with his mind, with his hands.

With his eyes.

What could Bolan look forward to in a world of darkness? Braille lessons, perhaps, and learning to navigate rooms where the slightest change in furniture placement would transform living space into a humiliating obstacle course.

Was it worth going on? Would it be better all around if he just bit the bullet now?

A small voice in his head whispered, *Give Bones a chance.*

If they could find him, right.

Find him in time.

Find him at all.

If they weren't ambushed by another mercenary team along the way and shot to hell.

Too many ifs.

"All right," he said at last. "Let's do it."

Whatever happened in the next few hours, Mack Bolan was simply along for the ride.

CHAPTER SIX

Cuiabá

There were advantages to using mercenary troops for certain dirty work outside the government's legitimate domain. As a major in Brazil's security police, Anastasio Herreira recognized the value of competent killers for profit, and he had employed the best available on various occasions.

Sadly, though, sometimes the best weren't good enough.

His latest mercenary effort was a mix of politics and profit. Certain lumbermen had urged Herreira—paid him, if the truth be known—to guarantee that various unwelcome Indians would vacate tracts of timberland where harvesting was scheduled to begin the following month. The tribal elders had been stubborn, clinging to some childish concept of the jungle as their homeland, vowing to remain on soil their ancestors had occupied when any other patch of rain forest would clearly suit them just as well.

Herreira, with the cash in hand and promises to keep, had sought help from a group he'd used before, when clearing out

Cuiabá's drug dealers and street urchins. By some fortuitous coincidence, the tribe first on his list was also one that Robert Downey thought might have some link to the elusive fugitives who has slipped past him in Belém.

Two birds, one stone.

A bargain had been struck. The dogs of war had been unleashed.

But they wouldn't be coming back.

The last word from his contact spoke of slaughter, but it wasn't what Herreira had anticipated. The Tehuelche village had been razed on schedule, it seemed, most of its structures burned, but all the dead remaining at the scene were members of Herreira's raiding party. Most of those, his contact told him, had been shot.

But the Tehuelche had no guns.

In lieu of inquiries and autopsies, the corpses had been stripped and left to rot. The jungle would devour them, erase the evidence of any indiscretion on Herreira's part. Expendability was yet another valuable mercenary trait.

One portion of Herreira's goal was thus achieved. The logging could proceed as planned. His bonus was assured.

But what of Downey's fugitives and Dr. Weiss?

Marta Enriquez was an activist well-known to the security police. Herreira wished now that he had disposed of her before she stirred up so much trouble, but she had seemed insignificant, one of a thousand voices raised in protest to removal of the jungle aborigines. Herreira wasn't psychic, hadn't known that she would be transformed into a player who would frighten Downey and his masters in the CIA.

As for the Yankee, Matthew Cooper, Downey had provided next to nothing in the way of information. Photos snapped in California with a long-range lens revealed a slice of rugged profile under dark hair, neither young nor old. His last-known address—and presumably his name, as well—was false. His one known ally, who remained at home, had been a soldier in the U.S. Special Forces and was now employed as a "security consultant," whatever that meant in the States.

Was Cooper a soldier, as well? Was he a spy?

If so, why couldn't Downey trace him?

Herreira had a sense that events were slipping beyond his control, and it worried him greatly. He preferred simple tasks: tapping phones, breaking strikes, jailing dissidents, contracting removal of thorns from his flesh. Like most policemen in his personal experience, Herreira hated mysteries and problems that he couldn't solve with simple logic or an application of brute force.

He hated Matthew Cooper, even though they'd never met and he knew nothing of the man besides a sketchy physical description. Cooper was an unknown factor, unpredictable, and therefore dangerous.

Was he responsible for slaughtering Herreira's mercenary team? And if he hadn't done it, then who did?

There was a group of rebels in the neighborhood, Herreira knew, led by a peasant named Salvato. It was possible that they had intervened to help the Indians, but once again Herreira had no proof. Salvato's group opposed the present government primarily on economic policies, land ownership, foreign investment and the like. There had been clashes in the past with logging and construction crews, perhaps a dozen deaths per year on average, but nothing on this scale.

Herreira reckoned this was something else.

And at the heart of it, he guessed, was Dr. Nathan Weiss.

Herreira wasn't certain how the doctor figured in this latest incident, but he was nonetheless determined to find out. And to that end, he would be forced to work with Downey's agents in Cuiabá.

Jones and Sutter they were called, a pair of thugs who obviously thought themselves superior to all Brazilians, even though they'd bungled two attempts to snare Matt Cooper in as many days. Herreira knew that much because the mighty CIA was only human after all, and its skulkers couldn't operate in a vacuum.

Jones and Sutter wanted Matt Cooper and Marta Enriquez. More than anything, they wanted Dr. Nathan Weiss. Downey had launched his thugs on a crusade and would accept no more excuses, no more failures.

It was perfect.

All Herreira had to do was to offer his cooperation, strike a helpful pose, while letting Downey's agents take the lead. If they succeeded, he could claim the credit for himself.

And if they failed…well, there was still room in the Mato Grosso for a few more corpses yet. The jungle was insatiable.

It never got enough of human flesh.

"I WISH WE HAD A TEAM of Navy SEALs," Dirk Sutter said. "I don't like working with these wetbacks all the time."

"Pipe down, they'll hear you," Clement Jones advised. "Besides, wetbacks are Mexicans."

"Same difference," Sutter said, scowling behind a sheen

of sweat. His nostrils flared against the mingled stench of smoke and rotting flesh.

"I count fourteen, what's left of 'em," Jones said. "Somebody kicked some major ass."

"Likely a bunch of amateurs," Sutter replied. "I don't see any Indians. Maybe they walked into a trap."

"Who burned the village, then?"

"The hell should I know? We've got two guys missing heads. Are these Te-whatsits headhunters?"

"Tehuelche," one of the Brazilian soldiers said, surprising Sutter. Sergeant's stripes on rolled-up sleeves. The sneaky bastard had to have sidled over for some eavesdropping while Sutter's back was turned. "The Jivaro are headhunters," he said. "Tehuelche, ah, who knows?"

"Thanks for clearing that up," Sutter groused. "I can't tell with the bloating and all, but your boss said most of these were shot."

"Is true," the sergeant said. His open palm glinted with brass that Sutter recognized as 5.56 mm cartridges, the standard round for M-16s and at least a dozen other assault rifles manufactured from Europe to Israel, Singapore and South Africa.

"Your Indians have military hardware now?" Jones asked.

"They didn't, until now. These ones—" the sergeant nodded toward the bloated corpses sprawled throughout the village ruins "—have been stripped of whatever they carried. Weapons, ammunition, everything."

"I get the picture," Sutter told him. "We've got a tribe of maybe-headhunters pissed off and packing military hardware. Do you think they killed this bunch?"

The sergeant thought about it, frowned and shook his head. "Perhaps a few. The short one with the hatchet in his head, I call that the Tehuelche style. Another with no arms, behind the longhouse there."

Jones grinned. "Short-handed, eh?"

"Maybe the headless ones, but they were also shot. I think that someone else has interfered."

"To help the Indians?" asked Sutter.

"Possibly."

"Why else?" Jones asked.

Another shrug. "Maybe revenge or profit. Who can say? If we find out who is responsible, the deed explains itself."

"Terrific. Can we track them out of here?" asked Sutter.

"*Sim,* Senhor. My men have found the trail."

"All right. What are we waiting for?"

The sergeant fanned an open hand across the scene of slaughter. "I thought you desired to study this."

"What for? Dead's dead. Let's wrap this up ASAP, so we can get back to the land of beer and air-conditioning."

"French fries and nachos," Jones echoed. "Big Macs and fried—"

"Jesus, enough! We're in the jungle, not a fucking drive-through window."

Sutter trailed the sergeant, feeling Jones behind him as they crossed the smoking ruin of the village to a point where the Brazilian grunts clustered at the mouth of an apparent game trail.

"This is it?" Sutter asked. "Are we looking at the great escape, or what?"

"Whoever left the village went this way."

Jones checked the compass on his wrist. "Due south."

"Southwest," the sergeant said, correcting him.

"How many are we talking here?" Sutter asked.

"Thirty or forty," the sergeant replied, "more or less. It's hard to say."

"Terrific."

Sutter had an image of himself as Colonel Custer minus long blond hair, fresh out of bullets as a human wave of screaming headhunters came charging toward him through the jungle.

"What's the matter?" Jones asked, prodding him.

"Nothing. Let's go, for Christ's sake, while we've still got daylight."

They'd be camping out tonight, most likely, and he wasn't looking forward to it. Sutter was a city boy at heart, accustomed to four walls, a mattress, running water—all the luxuries, in short. He didn't care for the idea of sleeping rough with inch-long ants, spiders the size of dinner plates and snakes that swallowed native kiddies for a midnight snack.

But most of all, he hated the idea of headhunters with M-16s and hatchets creeping up behind him in the dark.

Jones broke into his reverie, asking, "You think Cooper is with them?"

"How the hell should I know?"

"I'm just asking."

"Well, quit asking, will you? I don't have a goddamned crystal ball. When I know something, you'll know something."

"Yeah. Okay."

His palms were sweaty, where he clutched his CAR-15, and Sutter's pack straps chafed his shoulders painfully. On top of that, his boots were loose and he was working on a set of blisters that would have a fair shot at the *Guinness Book of Records*.

Jesus, it was just like boot camp, all those years ago. He'd put that shit behind him, but here it was again.

The scouts went on ahead, and then the sergeant motioned him to follow. Sutter fell into step behind the man with pale stripes on his sleeves and cursed Blaine Downey's name with every plodding stride.

THE AIRBORNE HUNTERS came at dawn. Bolan could hear the helicopter's rotors slapping air, and even with the poultice on his eyes he knew when sunrise overtook them, from the greater warmth against his skin and the cessation of nocturnal mist.

The other senses taking over, right.

His body knew that he was blind.

Bolan suppressed that thought and used his senses to determine what was happening around him. First, his bearers stopped dead in their tracks and set down the litter. A hush fell over the procession, as if each Tehuelche had frozen in place, immobile and watching the sky.

No, that was wrong. One of them was approaching him with rapid strides. A moment later, kneeling at his side, Marta Enriquez said, "There is a helicopter."

"I can hear it."

"Oh. Of course."

"Sounds like a Huey," Bolan said, meaning the UH-60 Black Hawk that had carried U.S. troops to combat on four continents since the mid-1960s. The familiar sound didn't raise any hopes, though. Bolan knew that thousands of Hueys had been sold to friendly governments and private buyers over time.

That could be anyone up there, and Bolan had no reason to believe the airborne trackers were his friends.

No reason at all.

"They're coming from the village," Enriquez told him.

That was news, the makeshift blindfold having spoiled his normally acute sense of direction. Bolan tensed his arms and legs, testing the bonds that pinned him to the litter, but they didn't yield.

If someone started firing from the Huey now, above the forest canopy, there would be nothing he could do to save himself. If they dropped napalm canisters—

Stop it!

The chopper passed on, moving southward by his awkward reckoning. Still the Tehuelche waited—ten minutes, fifteen— until they heard it coming back the other way. It didn't hover, wasn't working sectors, so he guessed the pilot didn't have heat-seeking gear on board.

Or maybe it was wholly unrelated to his mission and the village raid.

Maybe.

"All right," Enriquez said. "We can go now."

"How much longer?" Bolan asked her.

"Six or seven hours," she replied.

The pain in Bolan's eyes had faded to a kind of constant stinging ache, nothing that made him want to scream out loud, but still enough to keep his mind on tissue damage and the possibility that he would never see again. He didn't know how much relief derived from application of the poultice, versus simple passage of time. Perhaps the worst scenario had already come true, and if he stripped away the crude bandage his world would still be unrelenting darkness.

Bolan flexed his fingers, longing to try it, but his bonds secured him at wrists and elbows, chest and waist, knees and elbows. His bearers weren't taking any chances on the trek to find Bones.

And what good would it do?

Could Weiss salvage his eyesight, as he'd salvaged shattered lives in wartime?

Wait and see, the small, infuriating voice advised.

See what, Bolan retorted silently.

They'd stopped to give him water in the middle of the night, and once again shortly before the helicopter passed. Marta had cupped his head and held a canteen to his lips while Bolan sipped the tepid liquid, taking just enough to quench his thirst without overloading his bladder. Sweating helped in that respect, but it invited flying insects, and he was aware of Marta fanning him from time to time, as they continued on their way.

Bolan imagined how she had to be feeling at the moment. She had traveled all the way to California, seeking help for Nathan Weiss, to extricate him from Brazil by any means available. Now, she was bringing in that "help," a blind man on a litter who was virtually helpless, no damned good at all for what she'd had in mind.

Cruel irony.

The hero was a patient now, and who could say if he'd ever be fit to complete his mission?

At least he'd have an opportunity to speak with Bones, assuming that his escorts knew where they were going and the doctor hadn't disappeared.

And if they couldn't find him, then, what?

Bolan reckoned he would cross that bridge when he came to it, even if he couldn't see it and he had to crawl across on hands and knees.

Belém

BLAINE DOWNEY WASN'T a field agent, never had been, but lately he'd started to think it was time for a change. Perhaps he should try it. Go out in the bush. Get some mud on his boots, dirt on his hands. Buck up the troops a little bit.

And let them know that he was watching them.

Downey trusted Sutter and Jones to do their best, but that was merely adequate. The plain fact was that he'd been saddled with the Company's dregs in Brazil, and with close to a year on the job, he'd had no luck at weeding them out.

Third World postings were like that, sometimes. Unless the station had an covert war in progress, like El Salvador and Nicaragua in the good old Reagan days, Langley often used tropical postings the same way the FBI used Butte, Montana or Juneau, Alaska—as a dumping ground for agents who had fallen out of favor with the brass. It could be politics or plain old everyday incompetence, but those who weren't pink-slipped got transferred to stations where they would theoretically do the least harm.

And where they might decide to quit.

Downey owed his own present posting to a regime change in Washington. It hadn't quite been a night of long knives, but some drastic changes were made at the top and it all filtered down. He'd been yanked from the Russian desk at Langley and packed off forthwith to Brazil, perhaps in hopes that he'd resign or finish out his twenty without making waves.

But Downey's enemies had misjudged their man.

They had also miscalculated the Brazilian situation.

Against all odds, he'd found a handle shortly after his ar-

rival in the country, implications of a Red—well, danger-
ously Pink—uprising in the hinterlands, apparently supported
by a U.S. citizen who had devoted years to helping those less
fortunate. That was to say, the very scum Downey had spent
his entire professional life scrutinizing, subverting, suppress-
ing.

In an age when politicians lived for the next "terror alert,"
when elections were won by condemning an underfed "American taliban" or condemning U.S.-born Muslims as "enemy
combatants," Downey's detractors had handed him a ticket
back to the covert Big Time. Dr. Nathan Weiss would be his
big-game trophy and his lock on job security, all rolled up into
one—if he could only pin the bastard down.

But so far, Downey wasn't having any luck.

No matter what he tried, Weiss eluded him.

Part of that was the hired help's fault, though blaming subordinates for a mission's failure was the bureaucratic kiss of
death. Likewise, his local colleagues weren't the best—no
rocket scientists among them, clearly—but the same was true
throughout the world, yet other spooks still managed to perform without tripping all over themselves.

It never once occurred to Downey that the fault might be his
own. He lived in a world of black and white, Us versus Them,
where the "Us" increasingly came down to "Me." Some quirk
of personality prevented him from placing his own motives
under a microscope, insisting that others were always to blame
for his disappointments, setbacks, failures. Downey's enemies
list was as long as his arm and getting longer all the time.

Sutter and Jones would soon be added to that roster, if they
didn't do something to impress him. Traipsing around the jun-

gle and playing soldier meant nothing to Downey unless his two stooges returned with the scalps he'd demanded.

He'd already predicted success in his bulletins to Langley, skipping over the whole wait-and-see phase to predict a triumph in Brazil that would eclipse any other ongoing black ops in Latin America.

Weiss didn't know it yet, but his campaign to heal the hopeless was about to give Blaine Downey's terminally ill career a big shot in the arm. And best of all, the doctor didn't have to make a diagnosis, didn't even have to lift a finger.

All he had to do was die.

"I think we can arrange that," Downey told himself, smiling. "In fact, I'd bet my life on it."

And if that meant a visit to the field, so what? Heroes smelled better with a whiff of gunsmoke on their clothes. The brass would smell it back in Langley and they'd know Downey was someone to be reckoned with.

One little death, and he was on his way.

THE PAIN in Bolan's eyes had eased enough to let him doze from time to time. The rocking of his litter, coupled with the jungle sounds that issued from somewhere beyond his blindfold, slowly lulled him and he let exhaustion do the rest.

Sleep might not heal him, but it couldn't hurt. A lifetime on the firing line had taught the Executioner to rest when he was able. Hungry, wet or wounded, he knew how to sleep.

Still, he was nagged by doubts and fears as they proceeded on their way. Some people thought that heroes were a fearless breed, but that was a mistake. Some psychopaths were fearless, since they had no grasp of consequences, but hero-ism demanded confrontation and mastery of fear.

A firefighter who braved the flames of manmade hell to rescue children was a hero, while a man who set himself on fire to make some abstract point was just a lunatic.

Bolan had grown accustomed in his life to disregarding fear. Ferocious in battle and outwardly calm in the long wait-ing time between clashes, he presented the appearance of a man who never questioned his own strength or capability. In fact, however, it was questioning that made him strong.

Bolan questioned himself day and night. He examined and reexamined motives, tactics, timing and techniques. No part of his personal or professional life avoided searching scrutiny, nor had it since the day when he'd received the notice of his parents' death that launched him on a long and lonely one-man war.

Those days were far behind him now, but he was still alone. In darkness. There was no one who could promise that his sight would be restored, or, if so, when that might occur. His weapons had been taken from him, Marta rightly recog-nizing that they would be worse than useless in a blind man's hands. If enemies discovered them somewhere along the trail that led to Nathan Weiss, he would be helpless, trussed up like a pig at a luau.

And what could Bones do for him, if they got that far? Was there some potion in his bag of tricks to heal a warrior's scalded eyes? Would Bolan ever see again, or was the loss of sight a blessing in disguise?

Sometimes, Bolan imagined that he'd seen enough of war and suffering. He'd never wished for blindness, but there had been times when he had wished to see no more. That thought, in turn, recalled images of childhood stories about magic lamps and genies, wishes offered that were never what they seemed. Some trap always lay in wait for the greedy and thoughtless, transforming their dreams into nightmares.

But those were fairy tales. This was reality.

A genie hadn't blinded Bolan. That was down to Mother Nature and coincidence, his snap choice of an unfamiliar tree for cover and a bullet aimed just far enough off-target to strike the tree while sparing his life.

Or part of it, anyway.

Did it count as living, without eyes? Millions of people around the world would answer that question with a resounding, *Yes!* But what did it mean to a hard-charging soldier whose greatest handicap in life had been short-term recovery from flesh wounds suffered on the battlefield?

Even as Bolan formed that thought, he knew it wasn't strictly true. His worst wounds were invisible, and some of them would never truly heal. The loss of family and friends, sometimes his fault—at least in Bolan's private view—would haunt him till the day he died.

And what came after that?

Another mystery.

For every loss, though, there was also hope. The present darkness might be only temporary. As the pain was fading, so might Bolan find his sight restored in time.

But time was something that the Executioner could never count on. In his world, all time was borrowed. Fate was always standing by to snatch it back, without a moment's warning.

Bolan's thoughts were wandering on morbid midnight pathways when something he couldn't identify suddenly snapped him out of his dark introspection. What was it?

A sound? A smell? Some sudden tension rippling through the people around him?

Bolan knew that he wasn't mistaken when the column stopped. His bearers halted in midstride and he could feel the tremors where they gripped his litter, stiff-armed.

There was something…

A male voice, unfamiliar, startled him with English from a range of ten or fifteen yards.

"What have we here?" it asked.

CHAPTER SEVEN

"We want no trouble," Marta Enriquez answered quickly.

"But I see your weapons," the response came back, not quite a taunt.

"They are for self-defense," she told the stranger whom Bolan couldn't see.

The unseen speaker switched to Portuguese, but Enriquez stopped him. "English, please."

"Of course. These people are Tehuelche, are they not?"

"They are."

"It's good that you don't lie. I know the tribe's tattoos." A hesitation, then, "Where do Tehuelche get such weapons to protect themselves?"

Enriquez replied without missing a beat. "From enemies. They attacked our village yesterday."

"And you defeated them?" The stranger made no effort to conceal his skepticism.

"We had help," she said, and let one hand fall lightly onto Bolan's shoulder.

"Ah, a fighting man." The voice came closer, topping footsteps. To his left and right, Bolan was now aware of other bodies moving through the forest, encircling the Tehuelche. If they opened fire now...

"Who is he?" the stranger asked. "Not a government soldier, surely."

"I speak for myself," Bolan said.

"Better still. Not British, from the sound of you. I think you are from America."

"That's right."

"Why is he bound and blindfolded?" the stranger asked Enriquez. "Is he a hostage?"

"He was injured in the fight," she said. "Sap from the manchineel has burned his eyes."

"Bad luck, Yankee." And once again, to Enriquez, "Where are you taking him, then?"

"To get help."

"You don't think it's a waste of time?"

"I hope not," she replied. The hand on Bolan's shoulder gave a little squeeze, then withdrew.

"Where would you find this help?"

"I have a friend—"

"Who's a doctor, perhaps?" The stranger probed. "You wouldn't mean *O Médico,* by any chance?"

"I don't know what you mean."

"Ah, *now* you're lying. I can see it in your eyes. You need more practice."

"You insult me!"

"With the truth? I doubt it."

"I suppose you'll want to rob us now. We don't have any-thing to spare."

"Except your guns."

Bolan heard Marta cock the Steyr AUG, immediately fol-lowed by the *click-clack* sounds of other weapons being primed.

"You'll have to take them," she informed the stranger.

"It would not be difficult," the faceless man assured her, "but I have already several wounded men and need no more. As luck would have it, we are also on our way to see *O Méd-ico*."

Full house for Bones, Bolan thought, still not confident that they would profit from association with their new compan-ions.

"You should hurry, then," Enriquez said.

"I think we should stay with you and help protect your he-ro."

"We don't need your help."

"You have it, nonetheless," the stranger said. "And who knows, *we* may need protection."

"Are you bandits?" Enriquez challenged.

"Such a question! I am Primeiro Salvato. Perhaps you recognize the name?"

"Perhaps," Enriquez allowed reluctantly. "You fight the government."

"On some things, yes. It isn't fair that you should know my name, while I remain in ignorance of yours."

"Marta Enriquez."

"And the Yankee?"

"Cooper," Bolan said. "Matt Cooper."

"What brings you to our forest, Senhor Cooper? Are you with the CIA, perhaps?"

Bolan couldn't resist a smile at that. Beside him, he heard Marta's nervous giggle.

"Have I made a joke?" Salvato asked stiffly.

"Indeed you have," she said. "The CIA is hunting us."

"Is it? And why?"

"Because we go to help *O Médico*."

"Marta—"

Her hand found Bolan's shoulder once again, in answer to his warning.

She replied, "Senhor Salvato's not our enemy, Matthew. He fights against the government and corporations who destroy the forest and uproot its tribes. I think he knows already how to find our Nathan."

"If he has wounded men," Bolan answered, "it means there's been a firefight. *That* means he'll be hunted, too."

"It's true," Salvato said. "The devils seek us everywhere. But finding us, that's something else."

"How many wounded?" Enriquez asked him.

"Five, against your one."

"And you would find *O Médico*…"

"Within an hour's march of where we stand."

"Perhaps we should join forces," Enriquez said. "But only temporarily."

It was Salvato's turn to laugh. "I'm not proposing marriage, miss. Only that we walk together for a while."

That said, Salvato stepped away and started barking orders to his troops in Portuguese. Enriquez leaned close to Bolan, whispering into his ear.

"We will be safe," she said. "These men mean us no harm."

As if in answer to her words, Salvato moved back toward the litter, saying, "It's good luck that we met you. Perhaps, when we have reached our destination, you can tell me more about the CIA and why they hunt a fellow Yankee in Brazil."

PRIMEIRO SALVATO—or simply Primo to his soldiers and civilian followers—was naturally suspicious. He had survived the past three years on a diet of wild game, rice and paranoia, dodging government patrols and mercenary killers hired by those whose dreams of wealth beyond imagination he had transformed into nightmares. The day he stopped doubting and let down his guard was the day he would die.

That was a rebel's life, stripped of the curious romanticism that somehow attached itself to living off the land and being stalked by enemies who wanted nothing less than to eradicate the seed of hope itself.

Salvato guessed the myth of a romantic revolution had to go back to Ché, or even farther, to Simón Bolivar. As for himself, the dominant sensation he associated with rebellion was persistent physical exhaustion. Always hunting, fighting or fleeing, never camping anywhere for very long, Salvato couldn't recommend the rebel path to anyone who had a life.

And romance?

He'd had sex exactly twice in the past three years, furtive couplings made in haste, more as a mutual relief from tension than as evidence of real affection. And Salvato was feeling quite tense at the moment, in fact, since his first glimpse of Marta Enriquez.

But what of the Yankee, Matt Cooper, and their strange tale

of being hunted by the CIA? It might be true, of course. Salvato had seen stranger things, and if the Yankee was a spy, it made no sense for him to be blindfolded, bound to a litter. Still, even spies could be injured. And if his story was a lie…

Salvato would have to watch them both closely, as well as the Tehuelche with their unfamiliar weapons. Graduating from bows and blowguns to automatic rifles was a quantum leap in warfare, and he wasn't sure the naked tribesmen even understood the safety features of their captured weapons, much less how to use them in a fight.

If they were intercepted on the last leg of their trek to reach *O Médico,* Salvato would find out.

By which time, he imagined, it would be too late.

He kept his distance from the woman and her Yankee as they marched. There was no idle small talk. Every member of the party stayed alert to jungle warnings—screaming flights of birds or monkeys, sudden silence that betrayed the presence of a predator—and planned how to react if they were challenged on the way.

Salvato's last clash with an enemy had come two days earlier. His men had ambushed a logging crew, killing two security guards and destroying most of the crew's heavy equipment before a flying squad of soldiers burst onto the scene. The battle had been brief, but fierce. Three of Salvato's men were killed outright and had to be abandoned on the field, five others wounded but able to flee with assistance from their comrades. As for the soldiers, they had lost enough men to refrain from pursuit, but reinforcements were easy to summon.

The hunt would go on.

Salvato had done his best to cover their tracks, but he knew that long-term evasion of pursuit was virtually impossible within a limited region. Aerial searches were deadly, trackers equipped with infrared heat-seeking devices and other gear that detected carbon monoxide emissions. Only the dead were relatively safe from pursuers these days, and even they could be found with methane probes.

What did Salvato have to counter that technology?

Two dozen men with the clothes on their backs, plus liberated small arms and an ever-dwindling supply of ammunition. They would have to stage a raid for fresh munitions and supplies before much longer, or they'd wind up fighting hand-to-hand with knives and stones.

Wild men, he thought, and wondered whether it would come to that.

Salvato's war against Big Money and the state had always seemed a hopeless struggle. It attracted souls with nothing left to lose, those who'd been robbed and beaten down so often that the only thing that kept them breathing was the prospect of revenge. From that, Salvato tried to teach them hope—for progress and reform, for justice, maybe even hope for victory.

But hope seemed small and distant lately. It was dwindling by the day. There'd been no fresh recruits in six or seven weeks, and Salvato's jungle band was being whittled by attrition. Combat wounds, snakebite, fever. By one means or another, he was losing soldiers he couldn't replace.

But he wouldn't surrender.

Not even if he was forced to carry on the fight alone.

He had begun as one man raging in the face of stark injustice. So, if necessary, he would finish it, as one man with his back against the wall.

But not today.

Today, at least, he still had soldiers left, along with the Tehuelche and a woman who intrigued him.

And the Yankee, yes.

The Yankee who might still turn out to be a spy.

"THIS SUCKS," Jones muttered as the jungle mud tried once again to strip him of his boots.

Sutter grimaced and said, "Tell me something I don't know."

"How 'bout I tell you this is one colossal frigging waste of time?"

"I'm not the one who needs convincing," Sutter said. "Tell Downey, if you think he'll listen to you."

"Shit."

"You're damned right, 'shit.' That sums it up, all right. He won't listen to shit from us until we bag the scalps he wants, and bitching never helped a goddamned thing."

"You're pissed at *me* now?" Jones retorted, putting on an injured attitude. "That's bogus to the max!"

"For Christ's sake, will you can the valley girl routine?"

"I've had about enough of—"

Sutter rounded on him in the drizzling rain, snarling, hair plastered to his scalp. "You've had enough of what?" he challenged. "Spit it out, why don't you, and we'll settle it right here."

Jones hesitated, fists white-knuckled on his automatic carbine, but he didn't make the move. Another moment and his shoulders slumped. "Forget it, hey? It's nothing. I'm just lipping off."

"Okay." Sutter relaxed a bit, but kept his finger on the trigger of his CAR-15. "We're in this shit together, man. It doesn't help us, getting on each other's nerves."

"You're right. I know. I'm sorry."

"Don't be sorry, bro'. Be sharp. Let's nail these fuckers and get back to someplace where they pave the streets."

"Damn straight."

They'd never been the best of friends, never would be, but Sutter needed Jones to watch his back around the locals, and in case they actually found the people they were looking for. The flip side of that need would be revealed if it turned out their quest was hopeless.

Sutter figured Downey meant it when he said they shouldn't come back empty-handed. Whether Downey had authority to speak for Langley on that subject was a question still unanswered, but they'd definitely have to watch their asses while it was resolved. And if it turned out that the brass supported Downey's judgment, that their days were numbered with the Company, it would be time to strike a new trail and move on.

In which case, Jones would be deadweight, a stone-cold liability. Sutter would drop him like a filthy habit and make sure Jones couldn't turn around and bite him on the ass, from spite.

No comebacks.

Best believe it, friends and neighbors.

"All for one" was fine and dandy, but "one for all" had a short-term warranty, subject to cancellation without notice.

If it all went to hell, he'd be cutting Jones loose. And he'd have to act fast, because Jones wasn't quite as stupid as he

seemed. Like any predator, he had a strong sense of self-pres-
ervation, even if it wasn't always visible on cursory examina-
tion.

Jones would be watching the road signs and ticking off
landmarks himself, just as Sutter was doing. He'd know when
their time had run out and the partnership no longer served
any mutual needs.

When that moment came, if Jones had a clean shot at Sutter, he'd take it.

Unless Sutter dealt with him first.

It was the primeval law of the jungle.

And that's where they were.

At the moment, however, they still had a chance to please
Downey and perhaps redeem themselves with the brass in Virginia. That would depend in large part on Downey's report,
doubtless slanted toward casting himself as the hero, but they
still might do all right.

Maybe.

Well enough to get out of Brazil, perhaps, and one step
closer to something that resembled civilization. Sutter didn't
expect a ticket back to New York or L.A. He'd burned too
many bridges to expect a miracle, one stupid fuck-up after another, but Mexico City wouldn't be so bad.

At least it was closer to home.

Hold on, he told himself. Take it one step at a time.

One muddy step after another.

Toward the payoff that was waiting up ahead.

MARTA ENRIQUEZ HAD MIXED feelings about their new rebel
escort. On the one hand, Salvato's men provided greater pro-

tection against unexpected attack than her Tehuelche kinsman armed with unfamiliar weapons. On the other, they brought trouble of their own to Nathan Weiss at a time when he needed it least of all.

Given a choice, she might've wished them away and left them to deal with their wounded alone, but she also knew that Nathan would've scorned such behavior as cruel and uncivilized. Somehow, the prospect of his anger troubled Enriquez more than any thought of wounded strangers and their suffering.

She saw the way Salvato watched Matt Cooper, fearful and suspicious of Americans regardless of their status or ability to do him any harm. The attitude wasn't surprising, given all that her country—and Latin America at large—had endured based on Washington's whims, but it was simply one more stumbling block in her attempt to rescue Nathan from his enemies.

And from himself.

She'd known at the beginning of her quest that Weiss wouldn't cooperate. For that reason, she'd sought a comrade who could use either persuasion or brute force, as the situation demanded. Matt Cooper had seemed equal to the task, but now he was simply another casualty, one more job Dr. Weiss had to perform before he could even think of leaving the danger zone.

Six jobs in all she would bring him today, and would he thank her for it if the hunters found him with his hands full, too busy with others to help himself?

How would he feel about her, if she brought him to his death?

That thought sparked panic in her mind, and Enriquez almost called the small procession to a halt. She likely would've done so if Salvato's ragged band of soldiers hadn't joined them, but he seemed to know the way without her guidance and would doubtless journey on to find Weiss even if she ordered the Tehuelche not to follow.

If she doomed Matt Cooper to a life of darkness everlasting.

As the thought took form, another question rose to trouble her. Would the Tehuelche follow her commands? Granted, they had agreed to carry Cooper through the jungle when she asked them to, and go with him to Nathan's camp, but that had been primarily because their village was destroyed and they acknowledged a debt to Cooper for saving their lives. Marta, on the other hand—although Tehuelche—was a woman whom they would regard at best as their rescuer's consort. Even with their chieftain murdered, there was no good reason to expect they would place her in charge of their defense and destiny.

Their common blood and language couldn't override tradition spanning several thousand years. It didn't make her male, a battle-tested warrior or a hunter who had fed the tribe with forest game. She wasn't even technically a member of their tribe, although she had shared their hospitality on occasion.

That was ended—and perhaps their way of life, as well—with the destruction of the village. Marta didn't know who'd hired the gunmen, but they had achieved their purpose, even as they died. There were no more Tehuelche in the district now. Whatever scheme the government and its corrupt private supporters had devised was free to move ahead on schedule.

She wished that she could stop them, but she'd leave that task to others. Maybe Salvato could do it, if the ranks of his guerrillas weren't depleted by attrition in the meantime.

Or perhaps no one could stop the tide of "progress" sweeping brutally across the continent from coast to coast, destroying every trace of nature in its path. For all she knew, it was another hopeless cause.

But Nathan Weiss, perhaps, could still be saved.

And doing that, Marta imagined she might save herself.

Assuming that it wasn't already too late.

A week had passed since she'd last spoken to Nathan and agreed to undertake the errand to America. He hadn't planned to move his camp while she was gone, but circumstances might've changed without warning. She might not even find him now.

Or she might find him dead.

Tears stung her eyes and she refused to give that prospect any further thought. If Weiss was dead, she'd know it in her heart. That firm conviction gave her strength to carry on along the trail, surrounded by Tehuelche and guerrillas, watching Cooper on his litter as it swayed between his bearers.

They should reach the camp within an hour, maybe less, and she would see Nathan again. Nothing else mattered at the moment. She would face his disappointment in due time.

And she would find a way, God willing, to preserve his life.

Washington, D.C.

BROGNOLA HAD BEEN on the line all day, first one contact and then another, trolling for the information he required but which was formally denied to him. The CIA was close-mouthed with its data at the best of times, and all the more so with the global War on Terror bogged down in a bloody stalemate. Langley shared with Justice reluctantly, and only then when some snafu required outsiders to clean up a mess.

As far as current operations in Brazil, the Company refused to comment either way.

Strike one.

Brognola was a master of avoiding bureaucratic roadblocks, cutting through red tape and circumventing regulations when it served his purpose—but it wasn't always easy, and the process often wasted precious time.

That was the point, of course.

His adversaries sought to throw up barriers that would discourage interlopers, make the process too exhausting and expensive to reward the effort. No one honestly believed that any single piece of information was secure, these days, but data could be hidden, obfuscated, masked or manipulated to the extent that it became almost unrecognizable to outside eyes.

Almost.

Since Blancanales had alerted him to Langley's interest in Nathan Weiss and his ambassador, Marta Enriquez, Hal had spared no effort turning over rocks and studying what squirmed beneath them. With a full day on the job and several mighty favors called in from the field, he knew three things with ironclad certainty. First, the Company *did* have an operation running in Brazil, targeting Nathan Weiss. Second, it was supposed—or claimed, which balanced out to the same thing—that Weiss had ties with "leftist rural elements" committed to unseating the Brazilian government. And finally, that Langley's interest in the matter was represented by a spook named Blaine Downey, packed off to Brazil after some unspecified problems arose at his last duty posting.

None of it helped Brognola. Nothing he'd learned so far had put his mind at ease. Quite the reverse, in fact. He now knew that Bolan was locked on a collision course with Company agents pursuing an official assignment, and there was damn-all that he could do about it.

If he had sent Bolan south on business for Stony Man, there'd be a process for recalling him, scrubbing the mission on command. They'd pulled the plug on half a dozen operations in the past, when Brognola found his team in conflict with a sister agency or when new information persuaded him that he'd backed the wrong side in confused circumstances.

No problem.

But Bolan wasn't on official business in Brazil. He was helping a friend, and Brognola knew what that kind of commitment meant to the Executioner. Once engaged in the struggle for duty's or memory's sake, there'd be no turning back short of triumph or death.

So now, Brognola was doing the next best thing. He was working on two fronts at once, seeking some way to help Bolan behind the scenes, even as he braced himself and Stony Man for rough weather ahead.

If he could find a weak point in the Langley plan and get that word to Bolan, help the warrior make an end run that would get him out of the jungle alive and in one piece, so much the better.

If he couldn't help on Bolan's end, he had to prepare himself for any fallout from the mission, up to and including official complaints from Langley to the Oval Office. The CIA's director had a hotline to the White House, and he wasn't shy of using it when he perceived that someone had encroached upon his jurisdiction.

Brognola's chief defensive weapon, if attacked on that front, was deniability. The President knew Stony Man's assignment, and he also knew that Bolan, strictly speaking, wasn't on the payroll. If his private mission started to unravel and it jeopardized the larger team, Brognola knew his duty.

He would disavow his friend and cut him loose.

Because it wasn't all for one and one for all in cloak-and-dagger games. Field agents were expendable. They knew it going in, and friendship didn't change that brutal fact.

Brognola would preserve the team at any cost.

No matter if it broke his heart and soul.

Mato Grosso, Brazil

"Soon now," Enriquez whispered to him, bending close, and Bolan waited for the prophecy to be fulfilled. The rocking of his litter no longer lulled him. Sleep was beyond him, the moment approaching when Bones would examine his eyes and deliver a verdict.

Or would he?

Bolan had performed the same silent calculations that troubled Marta Enriquez. He knew the time frame from her departure to the day they had rendezvoused in Cuiabá. She'd had no contact with Weiss for nearly a week, perhaps longer.

And that could be a lifetime in the jungle, with the hunters on his trail.

If Bones was dead or permanently missing, Bolan guessed his fate was sealed. He couldn't ask the Tehuelche to carry him around indefinitely. They would be unwelcome, anyway, in anyplace where he could find alternative medical aid.

And that aid, if he found it, would almost certainly be too late.

It was Bones or nothing, then, and Bolan had even more

reason to hope his old friend was still alive. He saw the irony in the reversal of their situations. Bolan had come to Brazil to help Weiss, and now his eyes—his future—depended on Weiss's ability to work that old battlefield magic.

Bolan smelled the camp before his escorts started whispering in languages he didn't understand. Wood smoke and broiling meat were unmistakable in any setting, all the more so in a world where the dominant odors were moist earth and rotting vegetation.

"Almost there," Enriquez told him, then she spoke urgently to the Tehuelche in their native dialect. The litter bearer nearest Bolan's head replied without breaking stride.

Salvato was there seconds later. "A camp, up ahead," he informed her. "I hope it's *O Médico*."

"Who else?" Enriquez asked him.

Bolan imagined the guerrilla's shrug. "Who knows?" he said. "I smell meat on the fire, but it may not be supper, eh?"

Enriquez made no reply to that, but spoke again to her Tehuelche kinsmen. Bolan heard them shifting weapons, hoping they knew how to use the hardware they'd appropriated from their would-be murderers. If there was trouble, and the Indians fired indiscriminately, he could face more risk from allies than from enemies.

Strangely enough, the idea didn't trouble him.

Somewhere ahead of them, a hundred yards or so, he heard the point men challenged by a guard. Both spoke in Portuguese, their voices quickly joined by Enriquez's as she made her presence known. Salvato joined in the exchange, the opposition folding when the new arrivals had been duly recognized, their mission understood.

Bolan could feel it when his litter bearers cleared the trees and stepped into a clearing, closer to the cooking fire. He fought an urge to strain against his bonds once more, turning his head in the direction of a voice he hadn't heard for years.

"All right," Nathan Weiss said, "show me which one is hurt the worst."

CHAPTER EIGHT

The day had been another long one, as they always seemed to be, for Dr. Nathan Weiss. Since breakfast, meager as it had been, he'd treated one snakebite, a broken arm, a fractured ankle, two burn cases, and half a dozen natives suffering from parasites. Now the war-wounded were straggling in to make his day complete and keep him working well into the hours of darkness.

Perfect.

So far this day, Weiss had recognized only one of his patients. The rest were strangers, drawn to him somehow by the mysterious jungle telegraph system that seemed to announce his presence every time he shifted camp. Almost before his tent was pitched, new patients started to arrive, baring their wounds and souls for *O Médico*.

Someday, Weiss supposed—and most likely sooner rather than later—that same alert system would kill him. One day, perhaps today, the wrong person would find him and he would've come to the end of his run.

But not yet.

The latest camp was crude. One fair-size tent for examinations and operations, with a cot pitched in one corner doubling as Weiss's sleeping quarters. Three smaller tents for the faithful adherents who followed his winding, aimless path through the forest, staying one step ahead of their foes.

So far.

The four who stayed included a Jivaro husband and wife, a Tehuelche survivor of recent ethnic cleansing, and the dropout son of a wealthy family in Rio de Janeiro who could still raise money on the sly from time to time. Together, they formed a kind of ragtag M.A.S.H. unit that no one would credit unless they had seen it firsthand.

But it worked. And that, in the eyes of those who stalked Weiss, was the cardinal sin.

If he'd failed at his self-appointed mission, if the people had rejected him or withered and died at his touch, there would've been no manhunt for *O Médico*. More likely, Weiss supposed, he would've been rewarded by the government and its corporate cohorts. Healing the forest natives, helping them survive another day, was the one unforgivable sin.

And if he also helped rebels from time to time, that only made things worse.

A brief huddle with Marta, back from her short journey to the States, told Weiss his last, best hope for aid had gone awry. The man she'd brought along with her had proved himself in aid of the Tehuelche, but had been injured in the process. On the trail, she'd met a band of rebels bringing wounded in for treatment, and the lot of them were waiting for him now.

"All right," he said to no one in particular, "show me which one is hurt the worst."

"You need to look at Senhor Cooper's eyes," Enriquez said. "The manchineel…"

"Ah, yes." Weiss knelt beside the tall man's litter, resting on moist soil. "Our visitor from the U.S. of A."

"I'd shake hands," the patient said, "but I'm all tied up right now."

"A sense of humor. Good." Weiss took a clasp knife from his pocket, opened it one-handed and began to slice the soldier's bonds. "You must have discipline. Under no circumstances whatsoever must you touch your eyes."

"I hear you, Doc."

The voice teased Weiss, demanding that he recognize it, though he'd never seen the patient's face before. Some auditory trick, no doubt.

"I'm taking off the bandage now. The pain you're feeling may increase with exposure to light. Bite your tongue if you have to, but don't raise your hands. Understood?"

"Loud and clear."

Something about that tone…

Weiss cautiously removed the man's bandage and poultice, gingerly lifting one blistered eyelid, then the other, to explore what lay concealed beneath.

"You've tangled with the manchineel, my friend," he said. "That's *Hippomane mancinella* to the botanists, also sometimes called the poison guava. It has poisonous fruit, caustic sap—all things to all men, in other words. Avoid it whenever you can."

"Now you tell me."

"The good news is, you got first aid in a timely fashion. A

prompt rinse is half the battle, and the poultice has been helping while you traveled, though you likely wouldn't care to know what's in it."

"Everything's damned blurry," the stranger said, wincing as he peered out from between raw eyelids.

"And it will be, for a while. The damage you've sustained is superficial, but it isn't trivial. Infection's a concern, so you'll be getting antibiotics. Any allergies?"

"None that I know of."

"Better still. Some saline rinse and antiseptic drops, a bit of salve to take the edge off. I'm afraid that in the present circumstances, it's the best that I can do."

"Doctor, you haven't said—"

"If you'll regain your eyesight," Weiss interjected, completing his thought. "I believe you will, but there's no guarantee. Marta can get your treatment started while I see about the others."

Rising from his crouch, Weiss scanned the other pained and wounded faces watching him from a respectful distance. "Right," he said. "Who's next."

CLEM JONES WAS SICK and tired of hiking through the jungle, tired and hungry, sweating like a pig and drenched by intermittent rain. He hated mud and bugs and every other goddamned creepy-crawly thing that lived in the jungle, waiting for a chance to bite or sting him, maybe even burrow underneath his skin and lay a batch of filthy eggs.

"We should've tracked them from the air," he muttered as the mud tried once again to leave him barefoot, sucking at his boots with twice the normal pull of gravity.

"You know how well that works," Sutter gruffly replied. "Damned infrared, you think you've got guerrillas and it turns out you've been tracking monkeys through the trees for twenty miles."

"Not with the good stuff," Jones replied.

"Jesus, you think we sell Brazil the good stuff?"

"I'm just saying."

"Save it, will you? This is what we've got. In case you haven't worked it out, we're being punished for the snafu with that Cooper asshole."

Jones had worked it out, all right. Not that he'd needed ESP or anything, the way that Downey ranted on about it. Jones has tried to see it as an opportunity to clear his name and start from scratch, but something told him that would never happen. Not with Downey breathing down his neck and Langley holding grudges over the mistakes he'd made in other postings.

There'd be no tears if he resigned, but Jones had spent too many years in harness to go looking for a new career. He wouldn't get a decent reference from the Company, in any case. Bastards denied they were vindictive, but he knew how that worked. They would damn him with faint praise on paper, while they whispered all his foibles into eager ears.

Jones saw himself working the graveyard shift, some half-assed rent-a-cop despised by everyone who met him, and he figured he could hang on for a little longer, where he was.

Unless they blew this job, of course.

In that case, he'd be plummeting without a safety net.

Downey would see to that, the miserable prick.

"So, how much farther, do you think?" he asked Sutter.

"How'm I supposed to answer that? When you've got the bastard in your sights, you'll know we're there."

"Okay," Jones said. And muttered to himself, "Asswipe."

Sutter half turned to face him, asking with a challenge in his voice, "How's that?"

"I said goddamned mosquitoes here are eating me alive."

"Uh-huh. Just watch it."

Watch my ass, Jones thought, keeping the comment to himself.

As Sutter turned away, a thin green snake streaked right across the path in front of Jones. He raised his CAR-15 reflexively but caught himself before he squeezed the trigger. By the time his right hand found the grip of his machete, the reptile had disappeared.

Fuck it.

He'd probably walked past a hundred snakes since they'd descended from the choppers and begun their crazy jungle trek to nowhere. Jones didn't have a clue how many mosquitoes had bitten him, or what filthy deposits they'd left in his bloodstream. For all Jones knew, worms and flukes were swimming through his veins right now, homing on vital organs where they'd set up camp and eat him from the inside out.

"What do they call that disease," he asked Sutter's back, "where your legs get all bloated and huge?"

"Do I look like a doctor?"

"You know what I mean. With the worms."

"Elephantiasis, for Christ's sake."

"That's it. Do they have it in Brazil?"

"I hope so," Sutter answered. "Downey needs to get some in his balls."

Jones had to smile at that, the image of Downey pushing his scrotum around in a wheelbarrow. The bad news was that Downey would probably turn the affliction to his advantage, bragging that he had the biggest balls in town.

And knowing Langley, someone in the rat's nest would believe him, likely give the bastard a promotion.

It was that kind of world.

Nothing to do but follow Sutter through the jungle, then, and hope they found their targets sooner rather than later. Wrap it up and get back to the city.

But not too quickly.

Asshole Matt Cooper needed to pay for the trouble he'd caused. And paying that debt might take the rest of his life.

IT WAS WELL after sunset, true darkness, and Bolan had finished his supper—a stew with more spices than meat—when Bones came back to see him, doing follow-up.

"How are you feeling?" the doctor asked.

"Better, but the vision isn't keeping pace."

"Give it another day or two. We should have that long, anyway, before we have to move again."

A momentary silence fell between them, broken when Weiss said, "The Politician sent you, did he?"

"More or less. We keep in touch."

"I guess you knew him from the Army?"

"Same as you," Bolan replied.

"There's something… I can't put my finger on it, but you seem familiar."

"Maybe it'll come to you."

"I'm good with names and faces, always have been. Patients, people that I've worked with. Would you think I'm crazy if I said I recognize your voice?"

"Not crazy. No."

"Matt Cooper. Sorry, but it doesn't ring a bell. I knew a Tony Cooper once, in Boston. No relation, I suppose?"

"I wouldn't think so."

"No. But you know Pol from military service, and he asked you to stand in for him because he couldn't come himself?"

"The thumbnail version, right," Bolan said.

"So, who and what are you?" Weiss asked.

"I'm a friend. You can trust me on that."

"I have to tell you, trust is a commodity in short supply around these parts."

"It doesn't look that way to me."

"Meaning?"

"You trusted Marta to bring help, and you trusted Pol to supply it. You trust every stranger who finds you and asks you for help."

"Well, hell, if you put it that way."

"I was hoping you'd trust me to get you out of here."

"Meaning this camp?"

"Meaning this place. This country."

"Wait a second, now." Bones turned to face him squarely. "That's not why I sent Marta to Pol. If I was looking for extraction, it's a four- or five-day hike to the Bolivian frontier. No sweat."

"The other side can read a map," Bolan replied. "You don't think they've been tracking you, plotting coordinates?"

"I think they're busy killing Indians and stealing land," Weiss answered. "I think they've got dollar signs in place of eyes. Your vision has been compromised by accident. They've sold theirs out for profit."

"They see well enough to track you down and kill you," Bolan said. "Unless I miss my guess, there'll be a team coming along behind us, looking for another chance to do the job."

"Brazilian regulars?" Weiss asked.

"Or mercenaries. Maybe CIA. They're in the mix, as well, in case you weren't aware of it. What difference does it make?"

"You're right. Hell, they can only kill me once."

"Is that your goal? Is this about some kind of late-life martyr complex?"

"Right. I'm Jesus of the Mato Grosso. Are you serious?"

"I'm asking."

"Then I'll answer you. I'm not a martyr. I espouse no creed, no party, no religion. I'm a healer. When they kill me, I'll be dead. That's all."

"Better to live and heal another day," Bolan suggested. "Don't you think so, Bones?"

"I don't— What did you call me?"

"Bones. Don't make me sing 'You Must Remember When.'"

"Jesus! Who *are* you, mister?"

"Does it matter?"

"If you're asking for my trust, damn right it matters."

"Trust goes both ways, Bones. I drop a name, it can't go any further. Doctor-patient privilege, am I right?"

"Hell, that's the easy part."

"You think so?"

"I can guarantee it."

"Okay, then. Sergeant Mack Bolan, reporting for duty."

"Bullshit! Is that what you call trust? I knew Mack Bolan, knew his face and—"

"Voice?"

"He's dead, get it? You need to do your homework for a scam like this."

"Well, Bones, there's dead…and then there's dead."

"What are you telling me?"

"Remember the artillery barrage outside Binh Hoa? You had wounded stacked up outside the M.A.S.H. tent, waiting for the knife. Marines and Special Forces, ARVN and civilians. Bolan brought a five- or six-year-old who'd taken shrapnel in the back."

"Sweet Jesus. Sergeant Mercy."

"That was always kind of lame, in my opinion."

Weiss leaned forward, touching Bolan's face. "Somebody did a good job. I can't find the scars."

"They took awhile to fade."

"I guess they would." He paused, then asked, "So what's the deal you came to offer me?"

A THOUSAND MILES of dense jungle and rugged mountains, the heart of Brazil, lay between Belém and Cuiabá. The Learjet Longhorn 55 could bridge that gulf in under two hours, cruising at a constant speed of 523 miles per hour, but Blaine Downey still felt as if the flight was dragging on for days.

His patience, minimal at best, was trembling on the brink of exhaustion. Downey could feel his self-control slipping, the same familiar feeling that had dogged him all his life, from screaming schoolyard battles to the "disagreements" that had damned near flushed him straight out of the Company before he landed in Brazil.

Some might've said his flight to Cuiabá was one more example of reckless behavior. The brass might have said that, if they'd known he was making the trip. Downey, for his part, operated on the theory that forgiveness was easier to obtain than permission. He planned to present Langley with a fait accompli, whereupon his success would make him the man of the hour, a hero of sorts, deserving of a second—or was it third?—chance.

There was a chance the brass wouldn't see it that way, of course. In which case they could can him, finally, but they would still have to explain why they were dumping on a winner.

If he won.

If Downey failed, the question would be academic. Nothing he could do or say would save him then. He'd be job-hunting at age forty-something, with a motley résumé and no serious prospects.

Screw that.

He'd been assigned a dirty job, perhaps selected in anticipation that he'd fail and thus provide the one final, irrevocable excuse to discard him. He'd taken the job because there had been no options, but he didn't plan to fail.

If it meant killing, so be it. A few more deaths would raise no eyebrows in Brazil—or none that counted, anyway. The country was a peaceful paradise compared to Chile or Colombia, but everything was relative. In Latin America, a certain amount of instability and bloodshed was taken for granted, accepted as part of the great status quo. His plan wasn't designed to rock the boat, rather to soothe the waters for parties that mattered.

And if there was blood in the water when Downey was finished, who cared?

Brazil was famous for its piranhas.

Downey felt himself in good company.

Herreira would be waiting when he landed in Cuiabá, standing by with reinforcements for the team they'd already inserted to find Nathan Weiss and his friends. Initially, one faction of Brazil's security police had wanted a show trial for Weiss, to let the world know that an American was helping rebels try to overthrow the country's democratic government, but cooler heads had finally prevailed. A couple million dollars here, a fat arms shipment there, and all concerned had seen the light.

Discretion was the soul of valor.

Silence was golden, et cetera.

Better for Dr. Weiss, Matt Cooper and the rest to simply disappear, as if they'd never lived at all, than for one proud government to embarrass a wealthy and generous neighbor.

The jungle was always hungry.

Weiss and Cooper wouldn't even qualify as a snack.

But Downey—or his men—still had to find the targets, pin them down and make the kill. So far, based on reports Herreira had relayed to Belém, the insertion team had found one burned-out village, populated only by dead mercenaries. Downey wasn't asking whose they were. He didn't care and didn't want to know. But if Matt Cooper had killed them, even some of them, it put a new complexion on the matter.

Taking out the man with no background, no traceable life, was shaping up as one hell of a chore. Downey had lost his confidence in Jones and Sutter as the men to do the job, but they were in the field and it would do more damage to recall them than to let them forge ahead.

Better to field a second team for mopping up and make damned sure none of the targets wriggled through his net. That way, there'd be no comebacks when he told the brass at Langley what he'd done.

What he'd accomplished, right.

They might not like him, then, but they'd respect him. Maybe even fear him, just a little.

Fear was fine with Downey.

At this point in his career, he'd take whatever he could get.

Mato Grosso

PRIMO SALVATO VISITED his wounded men, discovering that each was resting peacefully without complaints. The doctor had dealt swiftly and efficiently with their respective injuries, though he'd run out of local anesthetic on the third of five patients and had to stitch the last two without deadening their pain.

No matter, thought Salvato. Life was pain, a series of hard knocks and losses from cradle to grave. His men were nearly all of peasant stock, raised in a system where their lives and labor were habitually undervalued and taken for granted by rich men and women they rarely saw in the flesh. Today, faceless multinational corporations were raping the very land itself, while the leaders of "democratic" Brazil passed statutes to facilitate the violation, then went shopping for a new Lexus, Jaguar, Mercedes-Benz.

Salvato didn't confuse himself with the hero, Simón Bolivar. He fought today because his homeland gave him no choice, no real opportunity to change the system he viewed as both corrupt and decadent. Debates and demonstrations accomplished nothing, in Salvato's experience, except to clothe an elitist regime with a thin veneer of legitimacy.

Salvato fought because he could, with no prospect of victory. But someday, someone would tear down the walls that hoarded wealth and power for two percent of Brazil's population, while the other ninety-eight percent labored for those who owned them, body and soul.

Enriquez found him as he left the wounded, moving toward the campfire. She was clearly troubled, agitated as she spoke.

"Will you be staying long?" she asked Salvato.

"For another day or two, at least," he said. "*O Médico* says that two of my men shouldn't march until then."

"Leave them here," she suggested, "and be on your way."

"Why so eager for us to be off?" he inquired. "I think your doctor needs protection from the world outside."

"You bring more danger," she retorted. "You'll be followed here and he may die because of you."

"I don't think he's afraid, that one. You should be more like him."

"He thinks of no one but his patients," Enriquez said. "He gives no thought to safety for himself."

"The man's a healer. No one brought him here at gunpoint, did they?"

Fury lit her eyes. "You are supposed to care for people, too," she challenged him. "Yet you would take advantage of his goodness and betray him."

"Take advantage, yes. He offers services my men require. But to betray him, never. There are risks in war. That's all."

"You don't know what he's sacrificed to be here."

"I know him only by his reputation, it is true. We never met before today, but I respect him. Well enough, perhaps, to let him lead his life as he sees fit."

"You only think of fighting, killing. You care nothing for a peaceful life."

"You're wrong," he said. "I fight for peace. My soldiers bleed and die for peace."

"On your terms, I suppose?"

"Who better to impose them than a man of the people?"

"A man who kills for peace."

"And for my country, yes. Is that so strange?"

"But what of love?" she asked.

Salvato smiled. "So that's it. You not only work beside *O Médico,* maybe you warm his bed—or wish you did."

"You pig!"

She slapped his face, a stinging blow that rocked Primo Salvato on his heels. It couldn't wipe his smile away, however.

"What a shame," he said, "for one so young and beautiful to sacrifice herself this way. You ought to be in Rio, living well—or maybe fighting for your people where it matters."

"By your side?" She sneered. "Is that it? In *your* bed?"

Salvato shrugged. "I think *O Médico* frustrates you, Marta. All his time and energy is spent on damaged flesh, when you need healing of another sort. It's very sad."

"I'm warning you to leave before you bring more trouble here," she said.

"And if we stay?"

"Whatever happens next is on your head and on your soul."

"You must know, Marta, I've already made that devil's pact. It comes with leading men to battle, sending them to die. If you lay claim against my soul, you'll have to stand in line."

"You're hopeless then," she said, and turned away, leaving Salvato to himself.

"Not yet," he almost whispered to the night as she retreated out of earshot. "I still hope. I simply don't believe."

"I HEARD YOU CALL one of your helpers Adam," Bolan said. "Is that a mission name?"

Weiss smiled. "Hardly. Adam's a Jivaro. He and his wife are all that's left of a tribe upriver, in Pará. A mining company sent preachers bearing gifts. The clothes and blankets were infected with smallpox. When most of the tribe was down, a mercenary team came in to finish it. Two managed to escape, survive, reach me. I called him Adam, and his wife is—"

"Eve?" Bolan asked.

"Starting over," Weiss replied. "Except there won't be any more. Eve's sterile. Some infection from her childhood, I suppose. The bastards won that round."

"The other two?" Bolan asked.

"Abraham is a Tehuelche shaman. One thing and another, he ran out of people, too. Now we make medicine together and he tolerates me in his world. Ricardo is the wild card. He's a trust-fund baby out of Rio who's been disowned by his family for taking the wrong side on social issues. He's officially cut off, but he still has access to funds through his 'radical' friends. It helps on the supply side, and he doesn't do a bad job with the patients, either. Some kind of penance, hell, for all I know."

The doctor's face swam in and out of focus with the shifting firelight. Bolan thought a measure of his vision was returning, slowly, but he wasn't counting any chickens yet.

"I'm still trying to figure out what brought you here," he said. "The last I heard, you were in Boston."

"And the last *I* heard," said Weiss, "they were sifting your ashes in Central Park."

"You can't trust everything you read," Bolan replied.

"In my case, it was true," Weiss said. "I was in Boston—and Chicago, and New York, Los Angeles—but nothing seemed to fit. They wanted me to pitch in with administration, cut back on my time with patients, and it typically came down to listing reasons why we had to turn more folks away without treatment. I didn't go through med school to be rich and hang with the self-styled elite."

"You're one in a million," Bolan said, not joking.

"Don't sell the profession short," Weiss replied. "There are still plenty of healers out there, getting dirty in the county wards and rural clinics, working where it matters. They're not all writing diet books or playing Dr. Feelgood for the rich and shameless."

"I believe you," Bolan said, "but let's get back to cases."

"You want cases? I treat an average of eight to ten patients per day, seven days a week. Despite what you may think, most of them don't have gunshot wounds and haven't stepped on mines. Indigenous tribes and rural peasants in this country—hell, throughout the so-called Third World—make the worst poverty pockets stateside look like Beverly Hills. They have nothing, Sarge, and people are lining up left and right to take that away from them."

"Sounds like you've found another war."

"It feels that way, sometimes," Weiss granted, "but I only patch them up." He seemed to grimace—something happened to his blurry face, at least—before he said, "No, that's not true."

"What do you mean?"

"I've crossed the line," Weiss said, and briefed Bolan on his flight from the last base camp, the surprise he'd left waiting for those who'd meant to kill him.

"It sounds like simple self-defense to me," Bolan observed.

"Because you never took the Hippocratic oath," Weiss said. "They don't have soldiers vow to 'do no harm.' I broke the big rule. Everything I've done since then seems fraudulent, somehow."

"Maybe it's time to leave," Bolan suggested. "Get a fresh start somewhere else."

"Pretend it never happened?"

"Well…"

"Sorry. It doesn't work that way. I still have dues to pay. And I'm not going anywhere."

"So, why'd you send for help?" Bolan asked.

"Call me crazy. I was hoping somehow I could buy mo time. I'm sorry, for your sake. Looks like I crapped out around."

CHAPTER NINE

Cuiabá

"I hope you had a pleasant flight," Anastasio Herreira said, putting on a diplomatic smile. He didn't offer to shake hands, because Blaine Downey suffered human contact only when it was a mandatory deal-breaker.

"We didn't crash," Downey replied. "That's always more than I expect. Let's hit the road."

Herreira nodded, letting Downey climb into the black sedan ahead of him. He had a fleeting thought of booting Downey in the buttocks, pummeling him on the car's floorboard and driving him somewhere to dump his battered body in the jungle.

Once upon a time…

And maybe once again, someday.

But not just now.

"What's the word?" Downey asked as the car eased into motion.

"No contact, as yet," Herreira answered. "We're in touch,

but they have nothing to report beyond what I've already told you. The Tehuelche village, following a trail. It really wasn't necessary for you to—"

"I want to get involved," Downey announced.

"Excuse me? I don't—"

"In the search," Downey elaborated. "I don't know your men, but frankly, mine aren't Daniel Boone and Davy Crockett, if you get my drift."

"Daniel—?"

"Forget it. Bottom line, I want to get out in the field and supervise the last phase of the mission."

"Senhor Downey—"

"You're about to tell me that I shouldn't do it."

"Well—"

"Don't waste your breath, Major."

Downey's face had taken on a stubborn bulldog aspect. It reminded Herreira of photos he'd seen depicting the late J. Edgar Hoover.

"Senhor—"

"The only thing I need to know," Downey pressed on, "is whether you'll support me or I'm going on my own. There is no if, it's only how and when."

"I tell you honestly, I think this is a grave mistake."

"And that's one reason why I'm not asking permission, see? You have an opportunity to help me out and earn *beaucoup* goodwill from the Company, or you can pout and piss it all away. In that case, I'll go out of pocket for a bush pilot to drop me. All I need are the coordinates."

Anastasio Herreira was a major in Brazil's secret police, but he still cultivated diplomatic skills for dealing with superiors, wealthy civilians and the arrogant outsiders who so often crossed his path. Because that was the case, he didn't sneer when he asked Downey, "Are you trained to survive in the jungle, Senhor?"

"No sweat." Downey grinned. "Langley trains all her chicks before they leave the nest. If Huey and Dewey can handle it—"

"Huey and—"

"Sutter and Jones. Are you with me or not?"

"I can't simply go off and—"

"Relax, brother. Nobody asked you. I need a pilot, some equipment. Maybe backup. Can do?"

Herreira studied Downey's face and saw a possible solution to his problem written there. He could assure "goodwill" by giving this impetuous American some jungle gear, three or four men, and a one-way flight into the kill zone. If Downey succeeded, he would be grateful. If he failed but somehow survived, he might be contrite.

And if he died or disappeared entirely…well, it wouldn't be Herreira's fault.

There would be investigations and protests, of course, if Downey flew into oblivion, but Herreira reckoned that he could minimize his own exposure by helping Downey prepare for the adventure, providing assistance coupled with warnings to desist. The fault then came to rest where it belonged, on Downey's shoulders, and no one in Brazil or in the States could claim Herreira had abandoned a courageous officer to meet his fate alone.

"I think it is unwise, Senhor, but—"

"But?"

"If you wish to see the jungle and assist your agents in their work, it won't be said that I obstructed you."

For one heartbeat, Herreira thought he saw a flash of disappointment or dismay in Downey's eyes, as if the man was counting on Herreira to prevent his escapade, but it was quickly gone.

"Good man!" Downey said. "How soon can we start?"

"We have the gear," Herreira said. "Fitting the boots and clothing, thirty minutes to an hour. While you get ready, I can have a helicopter fueled and pick out five or six men to accompany you. The flight to overtake your men should take another hour, maybe less."

Downey was studying his wristwatch. "If you're right, I could be on the ground by sundown, then."

"I think so, yes."

Smiling with something less than full enthusiasm, Downey said, "All right! Let's move it, men! We're burning daylight!"

BOLAN SAW Marta approaching. Even with his blurry vision, he could recognize her, since the only other female in the camp was Eve the Jivaro, who stood no more than five feet tall.

"Are you all right?" she asked him, settling at his side without an invitation.

"Better," he replied, hoping that it was true. "I feel better at least. The vision still might take some time."

The words "might take forever" hung between them, tactfully unspoken.

"I'm glad," she said. "Do you have everything you need?"

"I wouldn't mind a cold six-pack, but we're a little short on ice."

"And beer," she said, wearing a smile that surfaced more from Bolan's memory than any visible details of Marta's face.

"When is Salvato leaving?" he inquired.

"A few days more." Her voice was troubled, strained.

"It's dangerous for him to stay," Bolan observed.

"I know. But Nathan says his men can't march too soon."

"Nathan" again. Bolan surmised that proximity defeated Marta's best efforts to pretend that she and Bones were merely friends or colleagues. Bolan wondered if she'd share the doctor's bed that night, feeling a small pang of envy that surprised him.

"Doctor knows best," he said, waiting to find out what had brought her from the fire to join him.

Finally she said, "I saw you talking earlier. Did you ask him…I mean…"

"I brought it up," Bolan replied. "He doesn't want to leave."

"I was afraid of that." Her tone was leaden, lifeless.

"He didn't ask for help to get away," Bolan explained. "He wants more time."

"I knew that, too." Marta was weeping now. "I'm sorry, Matt. You've suffered all of this for nothing. I was such a fool to bring you here."

"You didn't bring me anywhere," Bolan reminded her. "I came with open eyes, no pun intended, and I would've done the same if anybody else had told me Bones was up against the wall."

"It's kind of you to say so."

"If you think I'd lie to spare your feelings," Bolan said,

"you still don't know me. We agreed to get Bones out of here, but now I'm not exactly up to it."

"Again, my fault."

"Again, you're wrong. Two inches farther left, the slug that sprayed my eyes would've killed me. You've heard the expression 'shit happens'?"

Bolan saw her nod, the fire behind her.

"Well," he said, "that's true in combat, just like every other walk of life. Sometimes you win, sometimes…"

"All right. If I may not feel honest guilt, then I feel sorry for myself. Is that permissible?"

"It doesn't help us at the moment," Bolan said. "We need a plan to get Bones out of here, before somebody tracks us or Salvato's people and they come down on us like a ton of bricks."

"But how?" she pleaded. "If he will not go—"

"I haven't worked it out yet," Bolan answered.

"When we started, I considered drugging him," Enriquez confessed. "I know the proper drugs and dosage. You were fit to travel then, of course. I couldn't carry Nathan by myself, much less the two of you."

"Suppose his people helped?"

"You mean—?"

"Adam and Eve, the other two. Why not?"

"They're loyal to Nathan, beyond question."

"I don't see a contradiction, necessarily. If they were doing it for his own good, and they could help themselves at the same time."

Against the firelight, Bolan saw her shake her head. "They'd never do it."

"We don't know, unless we ask."

"They'll warn him. He'll be furious."

"Give me another option," he suggested.

"They're as committed to the work as Nathan is, by now. Even Ricardo, with his rich friends in the city. It is not a hobby they'll abandon on a whim."

"If they want to live," Bolan replied, "they'll think about it. If they're all hooked on some kind of death wish, then I grant you, it's a hopeless case."

She hesitated for another moment, then told him, "I'll ask them. But I need some time."

"It's your call, Marta. I'm not going anywhere until the fog lifts."

If it lifts.

"Matt, I—"

"Don't say it." Bolan cut her short. "We need to focus on tomorrow and a plan to stay alive."

"SOFTLY NOW. We have them."

The scout's name was Ernesto Bilbao. He barely whispered to his companion, Vincente Gallardo, crouched beside him in the forest undergrowth and watching bodies moving around the campfire.

"I count twelve, perhaps fifteen," Gallardo said.

"There may be more inside the tents."

"Which is *O Médico?*" Gallardo asked.

"I don't know yet."

They had been sent ahead by Sergeant Alemán and the Americans to find the company they sought, the man they meant to kill and his companions of the moment. Now, watching the camp, Bilbao was surprised to see so many men with guns.

Guerrillas.

All the barracks talk about *O Médico* was proved true, after all. The Yankee doctor *was* in league with elements that warred against the government—if not outright Communists, clearly subversives of one sort or another. Why else were they gathered in the jungle, armed with automatic weapons?

It wasn't a hunting party, not a troop of mercenaries seeking out more Indians to drive ahead of them through the jungle. Even without eavesdropping, Bilbao knew that much.

"We can go back now," Gallardo said.

"Go," Bilbao replied. "I'm staying here."

Gallardo gripped his arm, then pulled the hand away when Bilbao turned to face him. "Why?" his worried comrade asked.

"They sent us for *O Médico,* Vincente. Great will be the praise for he who kills the Yankee doctor."

"Without orders? Have you lost your mind?"

"Go back and tell the others what we've found."

"Ernesto—"

"That's an order." As he spoke, Bilbao pointed to the faded corporal's stripe that marked his sleeve.

Turning away, Gallardo hesitated long enough to say, "They'll kill you."

"Hurry then," Bilbao replied, "before I change my mind and make you stay."

Another moment and he was alone outside the camp. Gallardo vanished into darkness, moving almost silently. He might be insubordinate at times, but Gallardo could move like a wraith in the jungle.

In that respect, he was almost as good as Ernesto Bilbao.

The plan had come to him on impulse, staring through the ferns and creepers toward the firelight. He could creep into the camp and find the doctor, deal with him and have the matter settled by the time Sergeant Alémán and the Americans arrived to mop up the remainder of the rebels. Alémán might scold him, but Bilbao knew his sergeant hated the Americans and would be secretly delighted if they lost their prize to a Brazilian warrior.

Better still, when they were back in barracks, word of his courageous action would inevitably find its way to other ears higher up on the chain of command. Bilbao would be recognized as a commando who could handle delicate assignments with finesse, as one who showed initiative.

Provided that the rebels didn't kill him first.

Taking his time, knowing Gallardo had a good two-hour hike back to the point where the Americans had stopped to rest and wait for word, Bilbao started to slowly circle the doctor's camp. It wasn't large, a simple clearing in the jungle, with tents pressing close against the giant trees.

They made it easy for him.

As he moved, Bilbao left his Uru submachine gun strapped across his back, out of his way. He couldn't sweep the camp with thirty Parabellum rounds and hope to drop all present, much less reload and fire again before the rebels saw his muzzle-flash and cut him down. Instead he pulled the trench knife from his belt, bearing its blackened, double-edged blade. His fingers slipped easily through the loops of brass knuckles that studded the handle, his free hand lightly stroking the sharpened steel peg—designed for cracking skulls—that jutted from the knife's pommel.

One way or another, he would bleed *O Médico* tonight.

The camp layout was simple and straightforward. Bilbao recognized the largest tent as the doctor's workplace and surmised that he might sleep inside it, as well. There were three smaller tents for underlings, while most of the guerrillas ranged themselves around the central campfire, preparing to sleep without cover.

The front flaps of the largest tent were closed, preventing those outside from glimpsing anything that might transpire within. If he was swift and stealthy, Bilbao saw no reason why the others ought to hear him crush the doctor's skull and slit his throat.

Smiling, he crept from hiding toward the rear side of the tent and there paused, listening for sounds of movement from within. When nothing reached his ears, Bilbao ran his long blade through the canvas and began to cut himself a secret access flap.

IT HAD BEEN a long day of surprises for Nathan Weiss. Normal patients and their injuries aside, he had been pleased by Marta's return to the camp, then startled to find her accompanied by Primo Salvato's guerrillas. Continuing that theme, he'd been bemused to find that the "help" she'd brought from stateside was a lone man, partly blinded while en route from Cuiabá. Finally, the capper of all time had been revealed when Weiss discovered that Matt Cooper was in fact Mack Bolan, once a valued friend, now publicly presumed to be deceased.

Weiss lay on his cot in near darkness, trying his best to make sense of the day. He wasn't sure if Marta planned to join him later, or if he had energy enough to make it worth her time.

Thinking of Marta, then, he had to wonder if she'd honestly misunderstood his plan when he'd dispatched her to the States, or if she'd tacked on an agenda of her own without his knowledge. Was she misreading him, or had the feelings shared between them prompted her to act without his knowledge, in what she perceived as his best interest?

In either case, she'd schemed with Bolan—and presumably with Blancanales, too—in a half-baked plot to make Weiss leave Brazil. He would discuss it with her later, calmly if she'd let him, but he wasn't yielding any ground. His work was here, at least until he tired of it or the situation became untenable.

And when would that be?

Maybe soon.

Weiss knew that Bolan could've been a problem, might've tried to take him out by force, against his will, in the name of friendship or plain old sanity. That threat was neutralized, at least for the time being, but Weiss reminded himself to stay on guard, watch his back, take daily stock of those around him.

He could take the jungle at face value, but it wasn't wise. Same thing with friends and colleagues, when the stakes came down to life or death. He had already lost the hangers-on who cared primarily about themselves, but now he had to think about the handful who remained.

The ones who'd pledged themselves to him.

If some or all of them decided they "knew best" and it was time to move him out, he needed to be ready with a counter-argument that would dissuade them. Fair or foul, he wouldn't let them meddle with the mission he had chosen for himself.

Bolan hadn't surprised him with the "martyr complex" line. That phrase had dogged Weiss for years, resurrected by critics each time he stood firm in the face of administrative corruption or ineptitude, speaking out loud and clear for patients who had no voice at legal hearings or in hospital boardrooms.

But the critics were wrong.

Weiss had known martyrs and didn't care to join their ranks. But if the choice came down to healing those who needed him the most or sitting at a stateside desk and lobbying a bunch of fat-assed politicians, Weiss already knew the path he'd choose.

No matter where it led.

Even if it might get him killed.

A footstep in the semidarkness made Weiss perk up his ears. Marta? He hoped so, hoping, also, that she didn't want to talk right now. He'd missed her, missed their stolen moments, and he hoped they could postpone The Argument until tomorrow. If she was bent on fighting, though, they'd have to step outside, because—

A shape loomed over Weiss's cot, too broad across the shoulders for a woman, and the smell was wrong. Man-sweat, gun oil and clinging odors from the jungle made him think one of Salvato's men had wandered in to seek advice about some private ailment.

Weiss sat up and thereby dodged the knife thrust meant to pierce his jugular. He grabbed the outstretched arm, remembering a little of his Army training and a great deal more he'd learned from grappling with drug-crazed patients in low-rent emergency rooms.

The blade man cursed and kicked him, missed his groin and bruised his thigh. They fell together, Weiss slipping free of the cot, sprawling on dirt with his would-be killer straddling his waist.

The blade poised for another lunge as Weiss shouted, "Somebody! Help!"

THE SCUFFLING SOUNDS roused Bolan from a troubled dream of darkness, wide awake and searching for the source when Bones called out for help. Weiss had suggested that he sleep inside the operating tent, but there'd been no reason to think Bones needed bodyguards.

For two full beats, rising and moving toward the violent sounds, Bolan forgot that he was nearly blind. A flap of canvas brought him back to here-and-now reality, slapping his face as Bolan blundered into it.

Careful!

He'd never truly seen the inside of the operating tent, and so he had no floor plan in his mental data bank, no map he could refer to with his eyes closed. Compromising speed and caution, Bolan groped his way around the canvas curtain and across the dark space separating him from Weiss's cot. He heard the cot tip over, bodies tussling on the bare dirt floor.

What if it was Marta?

No. Bones wouldn't call for help in that case, even if their passion literally swept him off his feet. Although he couldn't understand a word it said, the second grunting, hissing voice that Bolan heard was definitely male.

No Marta, then. No Eve.

One of Salvato's rebels?

Stop him first, then sort it out!

Bolan followed his ears, using his blurry eyes as backup, homing on the corner where Bones slept, and where someone now seemed intent on killing him. When he was ten feet from the grapplers, Bolan took a risk and called in his most commanding voice, "Back off!"

The wrestlers separated and he saw a dark form rise, turning to face him. From the crouching stance and lack of muzzle-flashes, Bolan guessed it would be martial arts or blade work. When the man lunged at him, steel hissing through air, he had the answer.

But he had no knife.

The Ka-Bar lay with Bolan's rifle and Beretta, stacked beside his sleeping bag. He'd left them in his haste, and in the knowledge that he couldn't be relied upon to send a bullet where he wanted it to go.

Bare-handed, then, he faced the circling figure in the darkened tent. Bolan wondered how much his adversary saw, and whether that advantage was about to be the death of him.

Behind the prowler, Weiss had found his feet and moved to intervene, but he was laid out by a roundhouse kick that struck his head with a resounding *thwack!* Bolan moved in as the attacker spun away from him, and almost took the blade beneath his ribs before he seized a sturdy wrist in his left hand.

His right struck at the prowler's face, connected with a nose and flattened it before a knee slashed toward his groin. Bolan turned sharply, took it on his hip and drove his shoulder hard into his adversary's chest. The man snapped at him with his teeth, foul breath in Bolan's face, and then the creeper's free hand clamped on Bolan's hair.

There were no rules or referees in combat to the death, and Bolan recognized his present situation as a struggle to the bitter end. Voices outside the tent told him that Marta and Salvato's men were coming, but he didn't know whose side the rebels would be on, and he could only cope with one assassin at a time.

Groping, he found the stranger's crotch and turned his fingers into talons, clamping down with all his might. The prowler squealed, a higher pitch than any he had used so far, redoubling his attempts to plant his blade in Bolan's flesh while ripping at the tall man's scalp.

Bolan lifted, twisting, and as the hand released his hair, he drove his forehead into the bloody face poised inches from his own. His enemy lurched backward, Bolan moving with him, and they both tripped over Bones. Falling, Bolan had time to twist the upraised knife away from him, taking a shallow cut along his ribs instead of skewering a lung.

The Executioner raised his right elbow, driving it hard into his enemy's larynx as Bolan fell on top of him, two-hundred-plus angry pounds behind the blow. He felt the prowler's voice box crumple like a turkey's wishbone, but the man still had sufficient strength to thrash and buck beneath him, probing with his knife, clawing with his free hand.

Bolan hung on, closing his eyes and averting his face from the fingers that sought it, desperate to inflict some final damage. He pinned the creeper's knife arm to the earth and rode his death throes as the man strangled, shivered and finally went limp.

The others were around him now, and there was light enough for Bolan to make out parts of the blurry face beneath him. Details still eluded him, but Bolan wasn't sure how much of that was damage from the manchineel or blood smeared on his adversary's visage.

Rising, Bolan kept a firm grip on the dead man's knife, his fingers slipping through the knuckle-duster slots, in case he needed it against Salvato's men. They made no move against him, though, and Marta broke the silence seconds later, asking anyone who'd listen, "Oh, my God! Who's this?"

PRIMO SALVATO PUSHED his way through the cluster of bodies, moving into pallid lamplight, hearing similar questions on everyone's lips.

"Who is he?"

"Where did he come from?"

The body lay a few feet from *O Médico's* crude operating table, facing upward, dead eyes staring at a point somewhere beyond the tent's ceiling. Beside it stood the Yankee with a wicked combat knife in hand, facing the tight ring of Salvato's soldiers who surrounded him. Off to the Yankee's left, Marta Enriquez was examining *O Médico* for injuries, the doctor trying to prevent her probing search.

"I'm fine, Marta," he said. "A little shaken up, that's all."

Salvato recognized the tall American's concern that one or more of his guerrillas might attack without warning. Cooper still hadn't seen the faces of Salvato's men, except in blurry clusters, and he wouldn't know what should be obvious to every other person present.

"I don't know this one," Salvato said, speaking in English

for the Yankee's and *O Médico's* sake. He pressed his men. "Does anyone among you know him?"

As he scanned the ring of weary faces, each in turn denied it with a curt reply or head shake. Salvato believed them, unable to think of any reason why a movement ally would attack the doctor or his aides.

The corpse was dressed in standard-issue jungle camouflage fatigues, web gear and combat boots. The face, though naturally dark, was painted for additional concealment in the forest. Slung across the dead man's back, a loaded Uru submachine gun forced his spine to arch in death.

"His gear all looks official," Salvato said, "though of course it could be stolen. We raid government supplies whenever possible."

"I felt a chain around his neck," the Yankee said. Crouching, he felt inside the dead man's shirt with his free hand and pulled a set of dog tags free. Holding them out to no one in particular, the tall man asked, "What do they say?"

Salvato took the tags, noting the rubber edges fitted to prevent their clanking when the soldier moved. He squinted at the topmost tag, reading out loud.

"Ernesto Bilbao. He's regular army—or was."

"So they've found us," Bolan said.

"One man?" Enriquez clearly didn't grasp the situation yet. "But if you've killed him—"

"He's a scout," Salvato said. "No gear to speak of, meaning that he left it somewhere close enough to reach on foot. He carries a machine pistol, less weight than the standard-issue combat rifle and better for speed. That knife—it's his?"

Bolan nodded.

"A quiet killer, this one. He was either sent to kill *O Méd-ico,* or else he went beyond his orders. Either way, where there's one scout, there should be more—and troops not far behind."

"He's right." Bolan had turned, addressing himself to the doctor. "We need to get out of here, Bones."

"Right now?" The healer sounded weary, still shaken and winded from the attack. An oblong bruise was forming on his right cheek, where he had received a heavy blow.

"Since we cannot defend the camp," Salvato said, "we should go soon. Immediately would be best."

The doctor's shoulders slumped. "Dammit. I thought, maybe this time—"

A little cry from Enriquez interrupted him. She moved toward Bolan, reaching for his side. "You're hurt," she said.

"It's just a scratch."

Salvato saw blood seeping through the tall man's shirt on the left side, where steel had penetrated fabric, finding flesh. The Yankee registered no pain, a fact that raised him one more notch in Salvato's estimation.

Still...

Salvato knew that Washington supported the Brazilian government with military aide, advisers and the like. He found it curious that the attack upon *O Médico* would come within a few short hours of Cooper first arriving in the camp.

Of course, they had arrived together, meaning anyone could say the same of him. And Cooper *had* stepped in to deal with the assassin, not the sort of action he'd expect from an accomplice.

"Let me take a look at that," the doctor said, moving to Bolan's side. And then, reluctantly, "As soon as you're patched up, we'll pack and leave."

"I hope it's not too late," Bolan replied.

Salvato felt the same, but with a twist.

As they prepared to go, he would be on alert for enemies both outside *and* inside the doctor's camp.

CHAPTER TEN

"Speak English, dammit!"

Heat, rain, lousy food and lack of progress since he'd joined the field team all combined to grate on Downey's nerves. Now one of the two scouts they'd sent out hours earlier was back and jabbering in Portuguese to Sergeant Ally Something, pissing Downey off.

"Come on, for Christ's sake, what's he saying, Ally?"

"Sergeant Alémán."

"Whatever. Can you translate that palaver, or is it supposed to be a secret?"

Blank-faced, Alémán replied, "They found the doctor's camp. It's nine kilometers southwest, approximately."

"Where's the other guy?" Sutter asked, horning in.

Downey shot him a scowl, reminding Sutter who was now in charge, then turned again to Alémán, asking, "So, where's the other one?" he asked.

"He stayed behind," the sergeant answered.

"Why? What for?"

"To kill *O Médico,* I think."

Downey saw red. "Son of a bitch! Who told the stupid bastard to do that? Who was it?"

"No one told him, Senhor Downey." Aléman was cool, verging on icy. "It is called initiative."

"Oh, yeah? Where I come from, they call it goddamned insubordination, sonny. I'm supposed to question Weiss, not drop him in a hole before he has a chance to say word one."

"Senhor—"

"How good's this little prick, the one with the *initiative?*"

"One of our best," the sergeant said.

"Terrific. That's just fucking fabulous. One of your best can't follow orders, so chances are this whole damned exercise was a colossal waste of money, time and energy. I hope you're happy, Private."

"Sergeant Aléman, Senhor."

"You think so? I'll be laying out the details of this screwup for your superiors. Don't count on having stripes this time tomorrow, pal."

"Yo, Mr. D."

He turned toward Sutter. "Who the hell are you supposed to be, Vanilla Ice?"

"No, sir." Contrition didn't suit him. "I was thinking, sir, that we should drop in on the camp regardless, maybe find that Cooper and the woman. If the doc's already dead, there's nothing we can do about it, but at least he's done. Maybe the others still can tell us something. Sir."

Downey hated surrendering his fury. He could rant for hours when the mood came over him, but now, reluctantly, he understood the wisdom of what Jones proposed. Still angry, waspish even in defeat, he turned on Alemán once more.

"All right," he snapped, "let's get this shit packed up and hit the trail. I want to see that camp before your *best* scout ruins everything. And then I want his head, you hear me? On a fucking stick."

Watching the others stow their gear, Downey had time to realize that what had happened might not be the worst thing in the world. Of course, he had been looking forward to a private chat with Nathan Weiss, after Herreira's crack interrogators tenderized the pinko prick. That chance might now be lost to him, unless Matt Cooper or the doctor's other aides were quick and tough enough to stop Alemán's scout from getting through and pulling off his smart-ass stunt.

But even if the smart-ass dropped the doctor, Jones was right about one thing. The others—Cooper, the Enriquez woman, anybody else who hung around with Weiss—were a potential motherlode of raw intelligence that Downey might turn to his own advantage.

Weiss presumably had contacts in some of the rebel groups, and maybe in the government, as well. If Downey could prove that, name names and bring down the traitors, it would be no small coup.

But he was after something more.

He wouldn't rest until he found out who Matt Cooper really was, and where he'd come from. What his ties were to a high-security PI in San Diego, and where the links might go from there. He was onto something, even if he didn't know precisely what it was, yet. Someone in the States was meddling in his business, trying to run rings around the Company, and if he could discover who that was…

It would be payday, right.

If Downey saved the Langley brass a major headache, maybe even critical embarrassment, it would reverse the long decline of his career. They might not let him write his own ticket, precisely, but he'd damn sure get out of the doghouse where he'd been sequestered for the past few years.

"Come on," he told the whole damned bunch of them, "let's get this circus on the road! Places to go, people to see!"

Glad now that he'd been too fatigued and lazy to unpack, Downey stood waiting for the others to collect their gear, stamp out the modest campfire, shoulder packs and weapons, all the rest of it. He checked his watch and tapped his foot, like a schoolteacher waiting for a tardy pupil to appear.

Downey knew any one of the Brazilians could've killed him in a heartbeat, probably bare-handed, but he didn't care. They wouldn't touch him, wouldn't balk or bitch when he unloaded on them, because he was the big spook, top dog, and the man in charge.

Brazil's ambassadors might criticize the U.S.A. from time to time, strike poses for the press and for the peasant types at home, but most of them still showed the proper deference in private. And none deferred more readily that the commanders of the state security police.

Downey could shit on everyone around him, and he'd come out smelling like a rose. But he was thinking far beyond Cuiabá and Belém right now, beyond Brasilia, back to Langley where his file had worn a loser's flag for too damn long.

The wind was shifting, Downey thought, and when a new day dawned, his enemies would all be blown away.

DESPITE HIS FUZZY vision, Bolan still made himself useful breaking camp. He joined Adam and Abraham in rolling up the operating tent after Salvato's men had torn it down. He helped them bind the sections of the tent securely, leaving loops of rope that each in turn would shoulder when they hit the trail.

Marta and Bones were busy packing up the medical equipment, meanwhile, parceling it out among the various Teheulches who had joined them in the camp. It didn't have the feeling of a permanent arrangement, but the tribesmen had no other sanctuary at the moment, and the hunters tracking Weiss were also their enemies.

Salvato's guerrillas had barely unpacked, and most of them traveled light as it was. They took less time to get read, and Salvato volunteered several men to help carry *O Médico's* gear. The rebel leader didn't seem to care where they were going at the moment, as long as they stayed one jump ahead of the trackers and his wounded had access to medical care.

That left Bolan the odd man out as he hitched up his pack and slung the Steyr AUG over his shoulder. The movement sparked a brief echo of pain where the prowler's knife had grazed his side, but Bones had stopped the bleeding with a styptic pencil, bandaged it, and there was no more to be done.

Enriquez found him, standing alone and off to one side, when the campfire was finally extinguished. He recognized her form and scent before she spoke.

"How are you, Matt?"

"I'm getting by."

"With the tents, equipment and the other wounded men," she told him, "I'm afraid we have no litter bearers left. You'll have to walk."

"That's a relief," he answered, meaning it. "I'll take rear guard and track you by the noise. Come sunrise, I can probably see well enough to make my own way."

"You've improving that quickly?"

"I'm getting there," Bolan replied with more confidence than he felt. "When are we pulling out?"

"Soon," Enriquez said. "Another ten or twenty minutes, I believe."

Sooner the better, Bolan thought. He was concerned about the second army scout, how long the dead intruder had postponed his penetration after they split up. He didn't know how far away the reinforcements were, how many men were coming, when they would arrive.

You don't know squat, he told himself, trying in vain to shrug it off. The weight was settled squarely on his shoulders and refused to budge, exacerbated by the sense of helplessness that dogged his every halting step.

Killing the prowler should've reassured him that he wasn't useless, but the way it had gone down did little to restore Bolan's confidence. If he'd been sleeping anywhere except the operating tent, he never would've reached the scene in time to help Bones, and he'd nearly botched the play at that. Dumb luck had made the difference, stumbling over Weiss's prostrate form and finishing the fall atop his enemy.

Another couple inches with the knife blade when he fell, and Bolan would be dead, instead of standing with his gear on, waiting to begin the worst march of his life. He owed life to that tiny margin, to an accident, and still he didn't know if it would be a life of murky shadows, fumbling aimlessly through the remainder of his days.

"I don't want you on rear guard, as you call it," Enriquez said. "You may get lost or fall along the way, and we won't know until it's already too late."

"Marta—"

"No argument!" she ordered, stepping closer to him, slender arms encircling Bolan's waist. "I'll tie this rope around you and the other end I fasten to my belt. Four feet between us is enough, I think. You follow me, and I will guide your steps."

"A nursemaid."

"No," she said. "A friend. You've done enough already, saving Nathan's life."

Bolan refrained from spilling the dumb-luck scenario. Instead he told her, "If they overtake us on the trail, release the rope."

"We'll see."

He clutched the strand of hemp and jerked her close. "Promise," he said, "or I untie it here and now."

Bolan could feel her watching him, could almost see her eyes, imagining the mixed emotions there. At last she said, "All right. If they catch up with us, I'll drop the rope."

"And stay out of my way." He smiled and gave the AUG a pat. "My marksmanship's not what it used to be."

SUTTER WAS STEAMING as they marched through darkness and another drizzling rainfall, but he kept it to himself. He would gain nothing by antagonizing Downey, even if he thought his supervisor was a first-rate horse's ass.

Why did he have to show up on the trail, for God's sake, when they had it covered and it would've been so sweet to bag the doctor without having brass breathe down their collars? One last chance to make up for the trouble in Belém, and now Downey had snatched it from their hands, meaning to claim the glory for himself.

Bastard.

Sutter imagined all the different kinds of fatal accidents that could befall a city boy in the Brazilian jungle. He imagined Downey plunging into quicksand, smothered by an anaconda, brained by a falling tree and stripped to the bone by piranhas. Sadly, none of those things were likely to happen with Sergeant Alémán and his commandos along for the hike, but there were always means of circumventing Mother Nature.

Sutter could stumble and fall on the trail, for example, triggering an accidental gunshot that would send a bullet speeding toward the back of Downey's head. Making the slip look natural could be a problem, though, and while Jones might not rat him out, Sutter surmised that the Brazilians would bag two gringos for the price of one.

Okay, no accidents while they were on the trail.

But what about the doctor's camp?

Alémán's scout had reported a dozen or more armed guerrillas protecting the target, ready to rock if someone came trying to snatch him away. And if the other scout had managed to get past them, maybe even capped the quack before they nailed him, Sutter knew the rebels would be in a righteous snit. That meant his team would have to fight their way in past the guards, all blasting anything that moved.

When it was over, who could say which bullet put out Downey's lights? It wasn't as if a CSI team would be flying in to run ballistics tests, dig bullets out of trees and match them up to gun barrels.

Something to think about, for sure.

One lucky shot, and any glory accruing from the operation would go to those who deserved it. Glancing briefly back at Jones, slogging along behind him as they marched in single file, Sutter considered making it *two* lucky shots, but he thought that would be stretching things too far.

Langley might be suspicious if two agents bought the farm on the same operation, and capping Jones would make it twice as likely for one of the natives to catch him red-handed.

Speaking of natives, Sutter wasn't sure how the Brazilians might react with only one lone gringo in their midst. For all he knew, *they* might arrange an accident for him and make it a clean sweep.

No, thanks.

He'd watch for chances to get rid of Downey, stay alert, no playing fast and loose to get himself in any further trouble. All he needed was—

Jesus!

From out of nowhere, something fat and scuttling on too many legs dropped onto Sutter's bush hat, made the short leap to his shoulder and ran scrabbling toward his open collar. With a snarl, Sutter slapped at it—once, twice, scoring on the third time with a *crunch* that spattered warm juice on his neck and ear. His trembling fingers came back dripping yellow.

"Shit, what was that?" he asked Jones.

"What's what?"

"Forget about it."

Sutter clenched his teeth and turned away. Another angry swipe cleared most of the warm offal from his neck and shoulder. Passing by a giant tree, he wiped his sticky fingers on the bark, then rubbed them vigorously on his cammo pants.

Behind him, Jones said, "Yo, you got an itch or what?"

"Fuck you!"

"Shut up back there, you two!" Downey commanded without breaking stride.

Perfect.

A lucky shot for sure, first chance he got. Put the prick out of my misery, he thought, smiling for the first time since Downey had joined the patrol.

Another hour remained before they reached the target—maybe more if the scout had misjudged the distance. It gave Sutter time to work up his nerve, getting ready for the second fatal shot he'd ever fired. The first one hardly counted, having been a true and proper accident in Bangkok.

Second time's the charm.

Now all he had to do was watch and wait, get through the next few klicks without more vermin dropping on his head, and he'd be in what his old man used to call tall cotton.

Nice and easy.

Going for the gold.

NATHAN WEISS SURVEYED the campsite, barren now, and satisfied himself that nothing had been left behind. There was no way to hide the fact that he'd been here, although the jungle would begin to work on that as soon as he departed. In a week, perhaps, the clearing would be overgrown once more.

But Weiss didn't believe they had a week.

He didn't think they had a day's head start, this time.

It might be hours, but at least he wasn't fleeing under fire. There'd be no further corpses on his conscience—for a while, at least.

Moving had turned into a habit, never planned that way, but something that was forced on him by circumstance which then somehow became a way of life. It had begun when he was in the Army, shifting with the tide of war, dispatched wherever men were being maimed and killed for goals he never really understood.

The pattern had continued stateside, as he proved himself "inflexible"—a fat administrator's choice of terms—at one hospital, then another and another. Things were always fluid on the urban clinic scene, more so when he had wound up in Brazil, searching for something that he couldn't find back home.

Instead of *it*, he'd found himself.

Weiss couldn't turn his back on that, no matter what it cost.

"We're ready, Doctor," Enriquez called to him. She still tried to be formal when they were in public, so to speak, making him smile sometimes.

But not tonight.

"Coming," he said, and walked to where she stood with Bolan, the pair of them roped together like mountain climbers about to scale Everest. Pausing at Bolan's side, he said, "Just sing out, Mr. Cooper, if the pace is too extreme."

"I should be fine," Bolan replied.

Fiction preserved, Weiss joined his other people in the column. Ricardo flashed a grin that lacked sincerity, while Abraham, Adam and Eve stood stoically with heaps of gear strapped to their backs.

"You've got too much," he told them, but they shook their heads in unison, rejecting any sympathy.

Strange bedfellows, these were. Before he'd left the States, even while he was still in Rio de Janeiro, Weiss would've laughed hysterically at anyone who'd told him he would someday be a jungle gypsy, trekking endlessly from camp to camp with a Tehuelche shaman, two Jivaros and a rich kid who'd reinvented himself in the crucible of radical politics. It would've seemed impossible, beyond ridiculous.

But it was true.

Weiss cherished no illusions about changing the world, Brazil, or even the province where he pitched his tent. All he could hope for and aspire to was another day of healing strangers—some of them poor farmers, others forest-dwelling aborigines, still others rebels on the run. He drew no lines, rejected no one, living only by the oath he'd sworn so long ago.

First, do no harm.

In fact, Weiss knew he'd failed at that. Forgetting the trap he'd laid for his enemies last time around, when they'd come hunting him, he sometimes thought that he damaged his patients simply by trespassing in their lives. Granted, a few of them might die without his help, while countless more would suffer needlessly, but that help carried a price for all concerned.

How many innocents had been detained, interrogated, even

killed because authorities suspected they might know where Weiss had gone? He'd never know, but it would haunt him to the moment when he drew his final breath.

How many suffered *more* because he tried to help them, in his Yankee-arrogant belief that only he could make their world a slightly better place?

It was too late to change that now. He was committed to the course of action he had chosen, and there was no turning back. The jungle road led forward, but he knew that it was coming to an end.

The next day or the next month, what difference did it make?

When he was gone and creeping things reclaimed his body for the Earth, who would remember him and what he'd tried to do?

Marta, of course. Some of his patients, while they lasted, though he knew the rigors of their daily lives distracted them from idle reminiscence. Pol Blancanales would remember, since Weiss had horned into his life after long years away.

And Mack Bolan, back from the dead against all odds and logic. He'd remember for a while, if he survived the futile journey that had nearly claimed his eyesight.

So much pain and death.

Weiss sometimes wished he'd listened to his father, studied law instead of medicine and kept the fresh blood off his hands.

But what about his soul?

The night sounds of the jungle soothed Weiss as he followed a group of Salvato's guerrillas southwestward. Behind him, his people kept pace with their burdens, Marta and Bolan almost literally joined at the hip, then more rebels with their wounded on litters.

What a picture they had to make, the long march.

Going where?

Weiss wasn't sure, but something told him that he'd know when it was time to stop and lay his burden down.

THE MARCH WAS EASIER than Bolan had expected—and harder. Marta took her time, alerting him in whispers to the many changes in topography, creepers and roots that could've tripped him, low-hanging branches and sharp-jutting stones. The good news was that Bolan could see some of it by filtered moonlight, several times anticipating her alerts when objects in the path were large enough to catch his blurry eye.

The hard part was surrendering a portion of his fate to someone else's hands, knowing that if she chose to drop the rope and melt away into the forest he would never find her. That kind of dependence had been alien to Bolan since his early childhood, and he didn't like relearning it as an adult.

Too bad.

He always played the cards as they were dealt to him, though he wasn't above reshuffling if he saw an opportunity. This time he couldn't discard, couldn't draw and couldn't fold. The only thing Bolan could do was bet the limit, hang on to his cards and hope that they'd be good enough.

"We have a steep slope here," Enriquez said, and he heard her boot heels scuffing at the mud. "There are vines to both sides you can use for support."

He found them, waited while her dark form seemed to drop from sight in front of him, the waist rope going taut as

GET FREE BOOKS and a FREE GIFT WHEN YOU PLAY THE...

Just scratch off the silver box with a coin. Then check below to see the gifts you get!

SLOT MACHINE GAME!

YES! I have scratched off the silver box. Please send me the 2 free Gold Eagle® books and gift for which I qualify.
I understand I am under no obligation to purchase any books, as explained on the back of this card.

366 ADL EEZ3   **166 ADL EEZR**

FIRST NAME	LAST NAME

ADDRESS

APT.#	CITY

STATE/PROV.	ZIP/POSTAL CODE

7 7 7	Worth **TWO FREE BOOKS** plus a **BONUS** Mystery Gift!
🍒 🍒 🍒	Worth **TWO FREE BOOKS!**
♣ ♣ ♣	Worth **ONE FREE BOOK!**
🔔 🔔 🍒	**TRY AGAIN!**

(GE-L7-06)

DETACH AND MAIL CARD TODAY!

The Gold Eagle Reader Service™ — Here's how it works:

Accepting your 2 free books and mystery gift places you under no obligation to buy anything. You may keep the books and gift and return the shipping statement marked "cancel." If you do not cancel, about a month later we'll send you 6 additional books and bill you just $29.94* — that's a savings of over 10% off the cover price of all 6 books! And there's no extra charge for shipping! You may cancel at any time, but if you choose to continue, every other month we'll send you 6 more books, which you may either purchase at the discount price or return to us and cancel your subscription.

*Terms and prices subject to change without notice. Sales tax applicable in N.Y. Canadian residents will be charged applicable provincial taxes and GST. Credit or debit balances in a customer's account(s) may be offset by any other outstanding balance owed by or to the customer.

If offer card is missing write to: Gold Eagle Reader Service, 3010 Walden Ave., P.O. Box 1867, Buffalo NY 14240-1867

BUSINESS REPLY MAIL
FIRST-CLASS MAIL   PERMIT NO. 717-003   BUFFALO, NY

POSTAGE WILL BE PAID BY ADDRESSEE

GOLD EAGLE READER SERVICE
3010 WALDEN AVE
PO BOX 1867
BUFFALO NY 14240-9952

NO POSTAGE
NECESSARY
IF MAILED
IN THE
UNITED STATES

she descended. Bolan half turned, leading with his left foot, clinging to a sturdy vine as he began to navigate the steep decline.

They had been going slowly downhill for an hour, more or less. Bolan recalled the maps he'd studied in Belém, now folded in his pack and temporarily illegible. They were following the drainage path of the Rio Cuiabá, more or less, which meant a gradual descent until they reached the Rio Paraguai that formed Brazil's southwestern border with Bolivia. They were headed toward Butch and Sundance country, but Bolan had no clue as to their final destination.

He wondered if Bones knew, himself.

The mud slope was treacherous, but Bolan slipped only twice, and his grip on the vine saved him from tumbling down on top of Marta. The Steyr slapped against his hip, and the Beretta's armpit rig was snug against his ribs, six inches above the cut from his enemy's knife.

All dressed up, he thought, and nowhere to go.

That wasn't strictly true, of course. He was going somewhere at a fairly good pace. He just didn't know where that was, when or if he'd arrive, who'd be waiting to meet him or running up close on his heels.

Enriquez rested for a moment at the bottom of the slope, pulling Bolan closer to her so that some of Salvato's guerrillas could pass, softly rustling in darkness.

"How are you?" she asked.

"I'm all right," he said. "Really."

"I don't know how long we'll be walking."

"No problem."

"Okay. We should go."

"After you."

The forest was alive, as always after nightfall. Birds and frogs and insects all had songs to sing, stories to tell, species to propagate with mating calls. The night sounds stilled at their approach and then resumed when they had passed, producing the illusion of a reverse Doppler effect that defied the laws of physics.

Bolan wondered if pursuers could use the effect to predict their movements, then decided any hunters would experience the same sound warp. Likewise, the night would hide their tracks unless the stalkers came equipped with floodlights.

But tomorrow they'd be plain to see.

For anyone with eyes.

And when morning came, Bolan wondered if he'd be fit to fight, or simply one more invalid the others needed to protect. Grappling hand-to-hand in the dark with a prowler was one thing, but it didn't stack up to a firefight, defending a camp. Bolan could load and fire all right, but in his present state he couldn't guarantee who'd be on the receiving end.

One thing at a time.

If they were jumped on the trail, he'd do his best and hold fire if there was the slightest doubt about his target. Once they pitched camp again, wherever that might be, Bolan would reassess his situation and devise a plan that wouldn't do more harm than good.

How long?

Not yet.

He concentrated on the rope around his waist and Marta's silhouette in front of him, the night sounds and the gentle downhill slope beneath his feet. The last thing that he needed now was sprained or broken ankles.

Trouble—maybe Death—would find him in its own good time.

All Bolan could do now was try to be prepared.

CHAPTER ELEVEN

Blaine Downey thought he'd known fatigue before, but nothing in his life prepared him for a forced march through the jungle in the middle of the night. He'd tripped and fallen half a dozen times, hearing Sutter and Jones behind him trying not to laugh.

Bastards'll pay for that, he thought.

Oh, yes.

It was his own damned fault, though, thinking he could help by hopping on a plane, then on a helicopter, plummeting into the midst of a world so alien he didn't recognize most of the plants, much less the rank fungi and creeping things that covered every tree trunk, every log and stone. It seemed to Downey that the whole damned place was rotting from the inside out.

He longed to ask if they were getting close, if they were getting anywhere at all, but talking seemed to be a mortal sin. The sergeant had already hissed at Downey twice, not caring who it was who paid the bills and was supposed to call the shots.

Damned insubordination, but there wasn't much that he could do about it for the moment. If he braced the sergeant, tried to call him down in front of his troops, Downey might find himself in an Alamo-type situation where losing was a lead-pipe cinch. It was smarter to take the rude shit for a while, then complain to Herreira when they were safely out of the boonies, back in the real world of concrete, tinted glass and air-conditioning.

Blaine Downey's world.

And he'd be moving up in that world, with Nathan Weiss's scalp on his belt. If he could bust Matt Cooper in the process, trace him back to some outfit opposing the Company, so much the better.

But Downey would settle for Weiss, his head on a platter.

How much longer?

His feet and legs ached, his back hurt, and now Downey was getting a headache. A couple of stiff drinks would straighten him out, but liquor—like everything else worth a damn—was beyond his immediate reach, a chopper flight away in Cuiabá or hell-and-gone back in Belém.

What a country, he thought. What a world.

They'd been walking for hours, it felt like, with Downey's boots and belt and pack straps chafing him despite the so-called "professional" fitting he'd gone through with Herreira's people.

Damn Herreira, anyway. He had to have known it would turn out like this, the misery Downey was going through. One big laugh at the arrogant gringo's expense he'd be having— that was, until Downey brought in the man who'd been ducking Herreira's "elite" commandos for over a year.

My score, Downey reminded himself with each painful step, counting cadence. All mine.

But how much longer could it take to find the god-damned camp?

Same scout, same trail. What was the problem?

Downey was no trailblazer, granted, but if these were what passed for elite troops in Brazil, he understood why they couldn't find a gringo in a haystack. It was like some kind of Keystone Kops routine.

Downey wasn't impressed, and when he had the big man's ear at Langley, after they had duly celebrated his achievement, he might drop a hint that too much money had been wasted on Brazil's security police. Perhaps the purse strings should be pulled a little tighter until things were sorted out and quality improved dramatically.

Something to think about.

But he couldn't begin to cash in on that score until he made it, and the way it looked right now, they might keep marching through the goddamned jungle all night long.

Ten minutes later, glum and soggy and increasingly pissed off, he heard a small commotion and the column halted. Downey took a chance and pushed ahead, to find the sergeant and his weary-looking scout huddled in conversation.

Portuguese, of course.

Not shy of interrupting them, he asked, "What's wrong this time?"

The sergeant turned to face him, putting on a smile that could've been relieved or just sarcastic. "Nothing's wrong, Senhor. We've reached our destination."

Downey thrust his head forward, peered into darkness. "I don't see a goddamned thing. Where is it?"

Pointing through the trees, the sergeant said, "That way. Two hundred meters."

Downey felt the smile fierce on his face. "It's about fucking time. What are we waiting for?"

"The camp is gone, Senhor."

"What do you mean, it's gone."

"It seems we've come too late."

The smile on Downey's face had turned into a snarl. "Show me," he said.

DIRK SUTTER WASN'T sure if he should be relieved or disappointed. Standing in the middle of the forest clearing, with a dead man sprawled beside the ashes of a campfire, he tried looking at the scene in different ways but couldn't find a take that made him happy.

One way he could look at it, his chance for capping Downey had eluded him, at least for now. Whether he got another opportunity depended on what happened next, if they pushed on in search of Nathan Weiss or dropped the whole damned thing.

Another way of viewing it, he might've missed his shot or someone could've seen him take it, either dropped him where he stood or given Sutter up to the authorities. Pulling a dead-end tour of duty in Brazil was bad enough, but Sutter didn't want to die here, much less rot in a cage.

So it was good and bad, depending. And he had a chance to reassess the plan, whatever Downey and the sergeant finally decided in regard to pushing on or turning back.

A Huey ride was sounding better by the minute, but his interest focused on the drama even now unfolding by the stiff and cold, dead fire.

"This is your guy, I take it?" Downey prodded Sergeant Alémán.

"It is."

"Looks like he blew it, huh?"

Stiffly, the sergeant said, "We must assume he failed to reach his target."

"And by that," Downey replied, "I know you mean to say his *self-appointed* target, since the stupid bastard had no orders to approach Weiss, much less take him out."

"It was an act of faulty judgment, I acknowledge."

"Faulty judgment?" Sutter recognized the tone of Downey's voice. The chief was winding up to an explosion. "Faulty fucking judgment? Look around you, Sarge. What do you see? Nothing! We're standing in the middle of a goddamned vacant lot because your man was too macho to follow simple orders. He blew this, and it reflects on *you*."

The other troops began to mutter, cutting hostile glances back and forth among themselves. Downey was stirring up the natives, and he didn't seem to care. Sutter nudged Jones and took a firm grip on his carbine, getting ready.

Just in case.

"What would you have me do?" Alémán asked. "I'll gladly file a charge of insubordination, but the funeral may delay his court-martial."

Downey was livid, posturing. "We're getting smart now, is that it? One of the men most wanted by your government and mine, who aids the rebels fighting to destroy our way of life, escapes because *your* man fucked up, and your great answer is a stand-up comedy routine? Amazing. Do you want to sing a song, or can we try to salvage something from this mess?"

"What do you have in mind?" the sergeant asked.

"Oh, I don't know. Maybe we ought to find the bastard, like you were supposed to do in the first place. How's that for an original idea?"

"You would pursue him, then?"

"I don't imagine he'll be coming back here to surrender."

"We are running out of rations, Senhor Downey. It was not expected that the search would take so long."

"We've got a saying in the States, Sergeant. Expect the unexpected. I don't guess that rings a bell down here?"

"The men are near exhaustion."

"They're supposed to be elite professionals," Downey retorted. "You want to get Major Herreira on the horn and tell him that your boys are tired?"

"We need supplies."

"Too bad you can't just eat excuses, eh? Here's a suggestion—either buzz your people for an air drop, or quit bitching and get busy on the job your man screwed up."

"We need to bury him before we go," Sergeant Aléman said.

"Oh, hell, why not? These weary boys of yours won't mind a little digging, while the enemy increases his headstart. No problem. I believe I've got a hymn book in my pack."

The sergeant's tone was dangerous. Sutter released the safety on his CAR-15.

"To leave him here, like this, is unacceptable," Aléman said.

"Then leave another message with headquarters. Tell them where to find him when they're finished dropping breakfast. Simple. Can you think of any other reason why we don't haul ass right now and try to catch our man before he goes sightseeing in Bolivia?"

Sutter surveyed the troops, feeling their heat. Most of it focused on Downey, but if they blew, Sutter supposed there would be wrath enough to go around. He didn't raise the carbine yet, to cover them, but any second now—

"All right," the sergeant said. "I'll call."

"Good man," Downey said, backing off his hyper tone. "We'll get the bastard yet."

Behind Sutter, Jones whispered, "That was too damn close."

Tell me about it, Sutter thought.

And then, One chance. That's all I need.

JOAQUIN SANTOS WAS tired of crouching in the shrubbery. His legs and back ached from remaining in the same cramped posture, without moving, for one hour and three minutes. He could see his watch, to gauge the passing time, but he dared not reach up to slap the insect that was gnawing busily on sweaty flesh behind his ear.

The men in front of him, an easy pistol shot away, might see him if he moved, might hear him if he struck the vicious little monster from his head. Better to wait and watch, unnoticed, until he was certain what they planned to do.

Mostly they stood around a dead man's body in the middle of the clearing, staring at the corpse, discussing it. The man was known to them, Santos decided, for they didn't search or loot the body. After half an hour or so, one of the soldiers had produced a shelter half and covered it, the dead man's feet protruding as if he was now a dirty secret swept under the rug.

The corpse aside, Santos saw nothing in the clearing that

required an hour's scrutiny, but still they lingered, studying the ground as if it might surprise them and reveal some precious secret. Near the corpse, a sergeant and a foreigner—perhaps American—stood arguing, presumably about where they should go from here.

Santos couldn't care less which way the soldiers went, as long as they went soon. The muscles in his calves and thighs now felt as if they had been doused with kerosene and set on fire, while both his feet were numb. If he was forced to fight or run right now, Santos knew he would lurch about and stagger like a drunkard, if he didn't fall flat on his backside in the mud.

He beamed the silent order toward his enemies, but they didn't receive it. How much longer could he wait?

Not long.

He had been sent ahead to tell *O Médico* that patients were en route to see him, nine men injured in a clash with soldiers east of Cáceres. Five of them could walk, albeit slowly. Litter bearers had the other four, assuming they survived the ten-mile jungle trek.

But now, he saw, *O Médico* was gone. Instead of tents and surgical tools, he saw only soldiers and guns. Santos would have to meet the party, warn them to turn back.

And he would have to do it soon.

Santos couldn't predict how Adriano Blas would take the news. Volatile at the best of times, Blas was most explosive in the face of disappointment—and the past few weeks had offered little else for leftist rebels in the Mato Grosso. Twice they had encountered soldiers in the forest, and both times they had been forced to run away, leaving their dead and dragging the wounded behind them. Blas raged at the survi-

vors over minimal infractions, and he seemed to take no plea-
sure from the news that his chief rival, Primo Salvato, had suffered the same kind of setbacks.

Santos didn't believe that Blas would literally kill the
bearer of bad news. But still…

The closer their wounded came to the enemy, the greater
the risk for all concerned. But if Santos ran to warn them now,
alerting the soldiers to his presence, they would pursue him,
thus force him to lead them away from his friends if he could.

And in his present state, they'd likely capture him. Inter-
rogation would proceed, and Santos cherished no illusions
that he could withstand torture indefinitely. When he broke—
and he *would* break, that much was certain—then he wouldn't
have to worry about Blas.

Because his comrades would be dead.

At last, the soldiers in the clearing seemed to have arrived
at some decision. There were no more arguments. The sergeant, stormy-faced, apparently had knuckled under to the
foreigners. He ordered two men off to the southwest, then
barked the others into ranks, holding his final order while the
three sunburned outsiders found a place in line. That done,
they left the clearing, following their scouts.

The corpse remained to welcome scavengers.

Rising was every bit as painful as Santos had feared it
would be. Grimacing, he powered through it, limping for the
first few yards, until his muscles started to relax and feeling
came back to his feet. At first he walked, then he began to jog
at double-time.

He had more news for Blas, all of it bad.

O Médico was gone, and now the soldiers had his scent.

BOLAN'S FIRST SUNRISE after his encounter with the manch-ineel had been pitch-black, hidden somewhere beyond the poultice covering his eyes. The second was an exercise in sub-tlety, night's velvet darkness lightening by slow degrees be-neath the forest's looming canopy. As light intruded on the world around him, so the jungle's background music changed slowly from nightsong to the chirping sounds of day.

In front of Bolan, Enriquez's form was more distinct than it had been by moonlight, clearer than it had been the previ-ous day. His eyesight was improving, but there'd been no sud-den miracle, no turning back the hands of time to how he was before the accident.

Bolan wondered if he'd ever find that clarity again, and si-multaneously heard the small voice whisper, *Wait and see.*

Bad pun or prophecy?

The long night was behind them, and as if in celebration of that fact, the column straggled to a halt.

"What's happening?" he asked Marta.

She slipped the rope free from her belt and handed the loose end to Bolan. "I'll find out. Wait here."

"No nature walks?"

"I'll be right back."

He heard the rebels speaking Portuguese, Tehuelche tribes-men talking softly in their native dialect. No one from either group approached Bolan or spoke to him. He was the ultimate outsider in this primal landscape, separated from aborigines and guerrillas alike by language, politics and pigment. He stood apart, burdened with gear and weapons he could barely use.

Enriquez returned five minutes after leaving him. "They've

found a place to camp," she said. "Another hundred meters, more or less."

"Camping so soon?"

"The injured need their rest. We all do."

Bolan didn't argue. He had no rank here. "I'm in your hands," he said.

She took it literally, removing the loose rope from Bolan's left hand and grasping his fingers in hers as the column moved forward again. The trail was wider here, as if generations of tapirs and jaguars had trooped to the clearing before them, to bask in its sunlight or worship the moon. When they reached it, Bolan stepped aside, out of everyone's way, and turned his face up to the sky.

Sunlight lanced at his eyes and he closed them, enjoying the glare that still shone through his eyelids. Red curtains screening his optical nerves from white light that could finish the job caustic sap had begun.

"Don't overdo it, Mr. Cooper."

Bolan turned to find Weiss at his elbow. The erratic sounds of soldiers pitching camp had covered his approach. "Don't worry," Bolan said. "I'll take it easy."

"That'll be the day."

"It's early to be stopping, Bones."

Weiss shrugged. "Maybe we lost them."

"Are you gambling with your patients now?"

It sounded worse than Bolan had intended, but Weiss didn't flinch. "Of course," he said. "I gamble every time I stitch one up or set a broken bone. My bet is that the damned fool will have sense enough to watch his step next time. I nearly always lose."

"They won't just let it drop."

"Relax. We're resting here, not building houses."

Bolan let it drop. He was in no position to insist they keep on moving. As for any extrication plans, he guessed that Marta hadn't spoken to the others yet. In any case, they couldn't make a move under Salvato's nose, in broad daylight.

"How's the vision?" Weiss inquired. "Be honest."

"It's improving. I can likely read a billboard, if you've got one handy."

"Not today. But you should take it easy while you can. Sleep couldn't hurt."

"Noted."

"How do you like our chances, Sarge?"

"I'll answer that as soon as someone tells me what we're doing."

"I'd say we're retreating—or advancing to the rear, if you prefer."

"With what in mind?" Bolan asked.

"I told you, I'm not giving up."

"It's not a crime to save yourself."

Dawn's light revealed the fuzzy outlines of a frown on Weiss's face. "I guess that all depends on who picks up the tab."

And to that sentiment, so like his own, the Executioner made no reply.

Cuiabá

MAJOR HERREIRA listened to his aide in stony silence. When the young lieutenant finished his report, Herreira asked, "How long ago was this request broadcast?"

"Ten minutes, sir. No more."

"They're asking for supplies."

"Yes, sir. Specifically, field rations."

"Food for two more days."

"Yes, sir."

Herreira could reject the plea if he was so inclined. It lay within his power to recall Sergeant Aléman and the remainder of his men, less one already dead. He could recall the three Americans, as well, have Aléman extract them forcibly if they refused to leave the jungle.

But instead he asked, "You have coordinates, Lieutenant?"

"Yes, sir."

Without further hesitation he instructed, "Make the drop."

"Yes, sir."

"Dismissed."

Herreira had no interest in the lieutenant's salute, but he returned it as he did most things, from habit. Only when the door closed and he was alone could he relax and slump back in his chair.

So, they had missed *O Médico* and lost a scout, but they were pressing on. That would be Downey's brainstorm, trying to discover victory within defeat.

Herreira wished him luck.

Downey was like a coral snake, never letting go of an idea once he had sunk his fangs into it. Sadly, also like the serpent, he injected most of what he touched with crippling venom. Everywhere he went, the CIA man poisoned hearts and minds and attitudes. He had no friends, to the best of Herreira's personal knowledge, but the power of his agency still made him a formidable adversary.

Let him go, Herreira thought. And may the jungle claim him for its own.

Unfortunately, he supposed it wouldn't come to that. Herreira didn't know how Aléman had lost the scout. There were a thousand ways to die downriver, in the wilderness, but from the tone of Aléman's message he guessed it hadn't been an accident.

That meant they had engaged an enemy, and yet had nothing else to show for it. Their payoff was a corpse, but Downey was unwilling to abandon the pursuit.

Herreira tried to guess how his superiors would judge his choice to let the team proceed. Against the risk of further casualties, there was the possibility of bagging Nathan Weiss, plus the fringe benefit of mollifying Downey and the CIA. That was no small thing in itself, Herreira realized, and might count in his favor if the mission ultimately came to grief.

That wouldn't be Herreira's fault, since he'd received advance permission from the brass and wasn't on the scene, but he knew how responsibility was rationed out on the police force. Downey had approached him with the project, he had sought approval for it, and approval had been granted on the basis of Herreira's personal assessment. That, in turn, was based on Downey's claim that he could find Weiss in the jungle, find and kill or capture him.

It would be down to Herreira then, his judgment, his advice, his capability. His fitness for the rank he held. He would be judged and very possibly found wanting, based on actions that occurred outside his presence, over which he had no physical control.

Abandoning the mission after they had lost a man, one man, would seem to be an act of cowardice. The men he served would want Herreira to avenge that insult to the service, to their country. If it cost a few more lives to punish those responsible, the dead would be described as heroes and Herreira would be cast in their reflected glory.

But if he should lose them all…

He shrugged that thought away. They were hunting a doctor, not some revolutionary mastermind. He was accompanied by peasants, at least one of them a woman, and a lone American whose role remained obscure. How deadly could they be?

Major Herreira might've asked the scout, but he was dead. Herreira didn't even know the soldier's name, an oversight he should correct as soon as possible.

But first, he needed to prepare himself for failure, in case Downey's luck was running true to form and jeopardizing those around him. If that was the case, Herreira would be doubly glad that he'd declined an invitation to the hunt.

Downey could chase his fellow countryman to Hell and back, for all Herreira cared. The major was concerned with more important business at the moment.

He was busy looking out for Number One.

Mato Grosso

ADRIANO BLAS DIDN'T take the news quite as badly as Joaquin Santos had feared. It was many times worse.

Blas led the Fist of Freedom by sheer force of personality and by strategic acumen. Upon receiving word that *O Médico* had fled for parts unknown without so much as a goodbye, it was his rage that made his officers and soldiers run for cover.

Cursing, bellowing, Blas quickly found the confines of his

tent too limiting for the explosive anger welling up inside him. Out into the camp at large he stormed, scuffing the soil with heavy boots and swinging meaty fists at enemies nobody else could see. He had presence of mind enough to leave the firearms in his tent, but Blas enraged was fierce enough to kill a man bare-handed, and the others scattered from in front of him.

All but one.

Lucidio Chama was barely half the size of his commander, wiry, long of face with sunken cheeks—the very opposite, in fact, of Blas the raging bull. Strangers might wonder how he managed as the Fist of Freedom's second in command, but all doubts would be banished if they peered inside his cunning mind, his ruthless soul.

He stood in front of Blas now, directly in the cyclone's path, and said, "My friend, you're wasting time."

"What did you say?" Red-faced and snarling, Blas appeared as if he might be on the verge of apoplexy.

"You're wasting time," Chama repeated. "Time we can't afford to lose."

"How dare—"

"You must decide," Chama said, heedless of his comrade's fury, "whether you will seek *O Médico* or let him go his own way."

"Let him go?" Blas raged. "Go where. We need him. Every week we have more sick, more wounded. If the Yankee bastard thinks he can just fold his tent and leave, he must be—"

Chama interrupted him again. "In that case," the small man said, "we must leave at once. He has a good lead and the soldiers are behind him. They will make him hurry. He'll be difficult to catch."

"I'll catch him," Blas promised, "and deal with the damned soldiers, too."

"We must hurry, my friend."

"Hurry. Yes."

That swiftly, in the time it takes a thought to form, his rage was transformed into purpose, aimless action into hurried preparation for departure. Blas and his guerrillas led a life in hiding, ever ready to evacuate their humble quarters on a moment's notice if the enemy came calling, and that lifestyle served them well as Blas moved through the camp, commanding every mother's son with two legs and a weapon to be ready for the trail within ten minutes.

Chama followed him, was at his elbow asking, "What about the wounded, Adriano?"

"Wounded. Yes."

Blas ordered that the men who couldn't walk unaided should be brought along behind them, under guard. That pulled a dozen fighting men out of his ranks and left him twenty-seven for the all-out rush to overtake *O Médico*. Santos had told him there were fifteen soldiers and three Yankees pursuing the doctor. Blas would eliminate them, take their gear and weapons, then persuade Weiss that it was a bad idea to leave his friends untended, without so much as a by-your-leave.

The rebel leader recognized an inconsistency in his thought process, namely that if Weiss hadn't packed up his camp, he would by now be either dead or taken prisoner. Blas understood that his own outburst was an aberration, wholly inappropriate, but that volcanic rage had plagued him all his life. He'd come to terms with it and made it work for him, long years ago convinced himself that it wasn't a handicap but simply part of who he was.

If Dr. Weiss was properly contrite, if he confessed to fleeing out of fear alone and not some urge to get away from Blas, he might be spared from punishment. Confession was good for the soul, they said, and Blas never felt happier than when some underling confessed that he, Blas, had been right about some point or other all along.

Surely *O Médico* would see the light of reason when it was explained to him. Chama could take the man aside and counsel him, even provide a script if that was what it took.

But Blas wouldn't allow *his* doctor to desert him, to forsake the Fist of Freedom at a time when he was needed most. It simply wasn't happening. That fact above all others occupied his mind as Blas strapped on his gear and watched two of his soldiers break down his tent.

They missed his deadline by a minute and a half, but Blas ignored the failure. He could be magnanimous at times, particularly when other targets occupied his mind.

O Médico.

He hoped the doctor was prepared to plead for mercy. Otherwise…physician, heal thyself.

CHAPTER TWELVE

Another march.

Bolan was ready when they started, feeling strong, if not rested. Tethered to Marta, he resumed his place in line, reminded of a trained bear in a circus, a deep-sea diver, an unborn child.

A blind man.

He gave his bleary, aching eyes no rest, shifting incessantly from one mark to the next, testing himself to see if this or that leaf was more clearly visible, if he could make out more details of one guerrilla or another.

It was coming back, slowly, but each new measure of improvement troubled Bolan, made him worry that this might be the best it ever got. That he might never see any better than this, for the rest of his life.

And then—what?

Suicide? Bolan wasn't the type, didn't fold in a crunch and surrender.

What, then?

He couldn't just go knocking at the Old Soldier's Home and expect to be welcomed. He had a dead man's service record, and besides, the care was minimal at best. Brognola might suggest he spend some time at Stony Man, but how long could he stand to feel the Stony operatives and the rest handling him with kid gloves, regarding him with thinly veiled pity?

It may not be a problem, Bolan thought, smiling as he kept pace with Marta on the jungle pathway, following her lead and picking out a few of the more blatant obstacles himself.

The strike team that was hunting Bones might solve his difficulty for him. If they had a tracker worth his salt, trailing the column from their recently abandoned campsite shouldn't be too difficult. Salvato's men would fight, but they weren't numerous and some of them were injured. Any force of decent size could overrun them. If the enemy had air support...

"Step down, here," Marta warned him.

Bolan took the hand she offered him, not really needing it, and saw a shadow where the trail had been deeply eroded on the back side of a buried log. He stepped down, found his footing and moved on.

Like that, a human being learned to make accommodations. Bolan had no doubt that he could learn to find his way around a small apartment, maybe even a small neighborhood. He'd count steps back and forth from the couch to the kitchen, and then from his door to the mom-and-pop store on the corner.

For what?

To "survive" in the sense that his heart kept on beating, while his brain churned with thoughts of lost opportunities, goals he would never achieve?

It's improving, Bolan reminded himself. Wait and see.

No sweat—except that his enemies might have another idea. They might want to eliminate him, or perhaps they would put him on trial.

And that would be a problem.

Living half-blind in a low-rent flat was one thing, but a Brazilian prison was something else entirely. Bolan had already proved he could fight one-on-one, hand-to-hand, but he wouldn't last long in the lockup, grappling with inmate wolf packs.

A new low, Bolan thought. No smile this time.

A first, fat raindrop struck his scalp and spattered. Seconds later, it was pelting down like bullets and he wondered what it had to be like above the forest canopy, with no shield from the downpour.

"Careful of the slope here," Marta cautioned.

Bolan saw her starting to descend in front of him, as if the earth had opened up to swallow her. He grazed the nearest tree trunk with his fingertips and found a dangling vine that felt like slender knotted rope. Gave it a yank to satisfy himself that it would hold a portion of his weight.

The soil was almost moist here, no such thing as drought, and fresh rain made it doubly slippery. Bolan dug in his heels, began to slide regardless, but the bristly vine and Marta down below prevented him from falling. Three feet down, the trail leveled again and he was on his way, already soaked through to the skin.

Rain forest, right.

It could be any jungle in the world now, anyplace the Executioner had ever hunted men, and Bolan wondered for a fleeting instant if his disability was cosmic payback of some kind. He jettisoned the thought at once, because it presupposed a sentient universe *and* one where bad guys had the final laugh.

If that was true, and he'd been fighting on the wrong side all his life, he didn't even want to know it.

Not in this life or the next.

The warrior turned his face up to the rain and let it flood his open eyes.

Show me, he thought.

But nothing came.

"MORE RAIN," Downey muttered. "Just what we need."

"Saves taking showers, anyway," Sutter said, plodding on his heels.

"That's so damned funny I forgot to laugh."

His answer got a snort from Jones, then both of them shut up before the sergeant could fall back and scold the pair of them for making noise. He wouldn't challenge Downey, but his glare alone might be enough to trigger Downey's anger.

On arrival in the forest, he'd expected to discover that the hunting party had located Weiss and his companions, staked them out and kept the lot under surveillance for the main event. Instead he'd stepped into a mess that made a Chinese fire drill seem well-organized, and now he had to chase Weiss through the stinking jungle in the goddamned rain, playing a bitterly exhausting game of hide-and-seek. It pissed him off and made him want to strangle someone—anyone—at the first opportunity.

Of course, he'd never strangled anyone at all. Not yet. But the idea of it was satisfying, somehow. Downright therapeutic, in a way.

Something to think about, if Dr. Weiss was still alive when Downey reached him. Maybe he'd be all choked up.

Or maybe I'll just blow his brains out, Downey thought. That ought to do the trick.

He'd never done that, either, never had occasion for real wet work, but if he was ever primed to try it, Downey felt the urge right now. First Weiss, then Cooper, then the woman who'd brought them together.

Make a clean sweep of the lot. Why shouldn't he?

This was a hunting trip, no matter how they tried to dress it up with talk of national security, the War on Terror, this and that. Downey had come out hunting human beings, just as others waited all year long to get out in the woods and stalk a deer, a bear.

He'd come this far, and he wouldn't be denied his trophy, even if he couldn't hang it on the wall.

Downey wanted to ask if they were gaining on their quarry, but he knew the sergeant wouldn't answer him. How could he? They were on the right track, anyway, assuming that the scouts were any good. The food drop had required a detour and delayed them twenty minutes, but the extra weight in Downey's pack made him feel better, even as it chafed his shoulders raw.

They wouldn't starve, they damn sure wouldn't freeze, and if they didn't lose the trail he would inevitably overtake the doctor's team.

A dozen guns at least, the scout had said. Downey had no idea if he was right or not, but it would be the nearest thing to a pitched battle that he'd ever seen, up close and personal. Downey hoped that he wouldn't piss himself and run for cover, but he wouldn't really know until it happened.

Grim resolve, he thought. That's all you need.

The will to fight was two-thirds of the battle, he imagined. After that, it all came down to sweat and gunsmoke.

Downey had begun composing his report to headquarters while he was slogging through the rain and mud. He would acknowledge Jones and Sutter without giving them a major boost, and there would certainly be room to mention that one of the native team had nearly blown it, trying for a solo hit on Weiss. That would explain the extra time and effort Downey had expended, not his fault in any sense, and it would make his triumph that much more impressive. One man against the elements, against all odds, against incompetence on his own team.

It was the sort of thing they liked to read at Langley. Downey knew that from experience. They wanted field reports that made the Company look good and cast its Third World sister services in roles that they were suited for—like doing background searches, fetching coffee, taking out the trash.

It wasn't honest, strictly speaking, but it greased the wheels and made the brass happy. What more could Downey ask, for his comeback?

They had a motto inlaid on the lobby floor at Langley that had always made him smile: The Truth Shall Set You Free. Sometimes, in fact, it made him laugh out loud.

Give me a little science-fiction every time, thought Downey. Just as long as I come out on top.

THE RAGGED COLUMN stopped again at midday, for another rest break and a hasty meal. The wounded were in need of care and everyone was weary, though Salvato's men tried not to let it show. Marta couldn't remember if she'd ever been this tired before, bone-weary to the point that she could sleep wherever she lay down, on soil or stone, and only wake again when she had reason to welcome the day.

Cooper sipped water and sat by himself after she loosed the rope that bound them, freeing her to move around the camp. She saw Ricardo talking urgently to Dr. Weiss and passed them by, looking for Adam, Eve and Abraham. Marta found them together at the clearing's southeast corner, huddled as if they'd always been the best of friends and Jivaros had never stalked Tehuelches for their heads.

They greeted Marta with a silent nod that rippled down the line from left to right. Kneeling in front of them, she was suddenly reminded of the classic monkey statues—see no evil, hear no evil, speak no evil.

Would it be the same when she asked them to listen?

"I must ask you something," she began. They waited in their fashion, none asking what she desired of them. She said, "I know you're loyal to Doctor, as I am, but I must ask if you would break that trust to save his life. Would you?"

Abraham frowned. Eve blinked. Adam retained a bland expression on his face, as if he didn't understand.

"If something isn't done," she tried again, "Doctor may not survive another week. His enemies are close behind us. They may strike tonight, maybe tomorrow, and destroy us all."

Adam surprised her with a shrug, as if to say, What can be done?

She took the silent ball and ran with it. "We must help Doctor get away from those who would destroy him. Far away, he needs to go, where they can never find him."

"Doctor is a wise man," Abraham reminded her. "He knows this."

"Yes, he does." Any response encouraged Marta at this point. "But he won't leave because he loves his people."

All three nodded understanding on that point. They understood the love of family, of tribe, and how it felt to have that snatched away by brutal enemies.

She had to play connect-the-dots and try defeating simple logic with emotion. "If he stays to help his people, Doctor will be killed or sent to prison," Marta said. Her throat tightened around the ugly truth. "The people will be scattered far and wide."

"The same thing happens if he goes away," Abraham said.

"Perhaps," she granted. "But if Doctor lives, he can help other people. He can also tell the world outside what happens here, to the Jivaro and Tehuelche."

"Do they care?" Eve asked.

"Sorry?"

"This other world you speak of. Do its people care what happens here?" It seemed to be an honest question, not a challenge.

"Some care, yes," Marta replied. "I think many would care, if they were told."

"You tell them," Abraham suggested.

Marta shook her head. "It's not the same. They know Doctor. He is a famous man in that world." That was overstating it, but Marta thought the lie might be forgiven. "They will listen and believe him."

"White men," Adam said disdainfully.

"Like Doctor, yes."

"He isn't white inside," the former headhunter observed.

"You see his heart," Marta said. "The world outside will see his skin and think him one of them. They may believe him, then."

She hoped so.

"And believing," Abraham inquired, "what would they do?"

"They have influence with the government," Marta explained. "Their words and money are important to our enemies."

"Will they protect our people?" Adam asked.

It was a trick question, she thought. His people were already dead.

"Perhaps." She wouldn't guarantee it, couldn't take that extra step beyond persuasion, toward betrayal.

"Why help now," Eve asked, "and not before?"

"Some things are difficult to learn," Marta answered. "Some people take more time to learn."

"If they believe Doctor, will he come back?" Sly Abraham, baiting the trap.

Again she said, "Perhaps."

He recognized the lie. She saw it in his eyes, but he did not accuse her. On the contrary, he asked, "Sister, what must we do?"

THE MARCHING HELPED, but Adriano Blas was still enraged, still heard the angry pulse throbbing against his eardrums like a tom-tom. His jaw ached from clenching at the mental image of *O Médico* deserting him, leaving his men to suffer without care.

Blas understood that Dr. Weiss had never joined his army and didn't espouse the cause per se, but *he* decided who should come and go. As field commander of the Fist of Freedom, that was his prerogative.

Blas meant to punish those who'd driven Dr. Weiss out of his camp, but that was only part of the equation. Weiss could easily have run to him, Blas, for protection in his hour of need. It would've shown respect and loyalty, two qualities that Blas required from all who served him.

Now, *O Médico* would have to be chastised for showing faulty judgment in a crisis, thinking he could save himself and Blas would never know.

Slogging along the trail, it crossed his mind that Dr. Weiss may never have considered him at all, as either a protector or potential enemy. That notion stoked the fires of rage inside him until Blas felt fierce heat in his cheeks.

Insults demanded a response, but it was infinitely worse to be ignored. An enemy's vituperation proved that he remembered and assigned importance to the target of abuse. Forgetting signaled that a person—Blas, in this case—had no substance worth considering. He mattered neither as a friend nor foe.

Blas turned and saw his soldiers straggled out behind him, plodding steadily through mud that clutched and caked their boots, making them lurch as though their feet were set in blocks of concrete.

"Hurry up!" he stormed. "You're like old women in the market."

Furious, Blas tried to double-time and nearly fell instead. He kept his balance with an effort, ears straining for any hint

of laughter, but his men weren't suicidal. When he shot another glare at them, Blas found their eyes downcast, focused
on what lay underneath their feet as they picked up the pace.

Better.

In Blas's view, fear was the basis of authority. When people said that they respected strength, it was another way of
saying they were frightened into paying homage. Loyalty
was earned by demonstrating that no rival matched his
strength, ferocity or cunning. If he let a mortal insult pass un-
punished, it was the beginning of the end for Adriano Blas.

Granted, he'd have to watch his temper when the doctor
stood in front of him. Executing Weiss would be a self-de-
feating act and could make Blas look foolish. Likewise, if he
injured Weiss so badly that the doctor couldn't work his
magic, the whole exercise would be in vain.

How could he wound *O Médico* without disabling him?

Of course.

Weiss had an entourage he treasured, people who assisted
him and whom he treated as his family. The woman, Marta
Something, Blas assumed to be the doctor's lover. There were
others, too. Three Indians and a pathetic youth who'd scorned
a life of luxury to feel superior. All trusted friends and colleagues of *O Médico*.

Blas pictured how Weiss might respond if one or all of
them were threatened. If the men were shot, for instance, or
Blas gave the women to his soldiers for an afternoon's amuse-
ment. Then, perhaps, the doctor would experience a grand
epiphany and understand that Adriano Blas was not to be ignored.

Such thoughts, Blas realized, weren't becoming to a liberator of his people, but what of it? He was only human, after all, with feelings just like anybody else. In the mission school he had learned that a British poet once wrote "If you cut me, do I not bleed?"

Blas was prepared to modify that verse. Whoever cut him should prepare to bleed, and if retaliation on the object of his anger posed some inconvenience, Blas would gladly bleed the object's family, friends and neighbors.

Given time, his people would assimilate that rule and Blas would have the honor he deserved. No matter how many ungrateful peasants he must kill to make it happen.

For the first time since he'd heard the scout's report about *O Médico*, he smiled. It might turn out to be a good day, after all.

"Faster!" he barked again, and focused on the point men, barely visible ahead of him, testing the trail.

Blas had a message for *O Médico* that couldn't wait.

He meant to teach Weiss the meaning of fear.

WEISS SETTLED on a log whose coat of spongy moss would add a new shade to his camouflage fatigues and asked his patient, "How's it going?"

"Better," Bolan said. "In this light, I could tell if you were smiling."

Weiss made the attempt. "How's that?"

"You wouldn't get an acting award."

"I'd settle for a couple hours' sleep."

"You have a fix on where we're going yet?" Bolan asked.

The smile went south. "Salvato knows a place, he says. Cover and altitude. If it works out, we could stay there awhile."

"With him?"

"I told him I'm not choosing sides," Weiss said.

"You have a choice?"

"I've made it clear. If I don't like the layout, we keep moving."

"And by 'we,' you mean…?"

"Whoever cares to join me. Sarge, I wouldn't blame you if you chose to stay behind."

"I didn't come to join Salvato's army," Bolan said.

"I know. You came for me," Weiss replied, "but I can't give you what you want."

"I asked you to survive, Bones. Nothing else."

"You could take Marta with you. Set her up somewhere safe in the States. I still have friends—"

"She wouldn't leave you," Bolan said. "That's why she came to Pol and me."

"I'll make her understand."

"Good luck with that. Meanwhile, how far away's our destination?"

"If we camp tonight, Salvato says we ought to be there before noon tomorrow."

Weiss watched Bolan do tne math. "I'd guess we're covering two miles an hour, tops," he said at last. "Say fifteen miles or so by sundown, if we don't hit any snags. Maybe the same tomorrow, that much closer to the border."

"No," Weiss told him flatly.

"All I'm saying, it's an option."

"We've already had this conversation. I'm not leaving. When the heat dies down, I'll head back north and east. Make for the Amazon."

How far was that? A thousand miles?

No sweat.

"You're smiling now," Bolan observed.

"You caught me."

"Something funny?"

"Everything, from some viewpoint."

"Enlighten me."

"I came down here to heal myself, as much as anybody else. Fed up with bureaucratic bullshit, apathy, red tape—whatever. Maybe I imagined it would be some kind of tropical vacation. Nate does Rio. Remember what that joker said about the best-laid plans?"

"It rings a bell," Bolan said.

"Right. So, here's my tropic getaway. Most mornings, I wake up and wish my ass was back at County General in Chicago."

"No, you don't."

"Excuse me?"

"I don't need my eyes to see through that one," Bolan said. "You're conning both of us with that BS, and I'm not buying it."

"So, what, you read minds now?"

"That's right. They teach it at Fort Benning, on a weekend course."

"Okay, what am I thinking?"

"You're afraid. That's only natural. Who wouldn't be?"

"Are you?" Weiss asked.

"Absolutely. Today more than most."

Almost afraid to hear the rest, he asked, "What else?"

"You wish you had more time, resources, opportunity to

do what you do best. That's why you came, not looking for a spot of shade under a palm tree. What you've got, though, is a slice of hell that's getting hotter by the minute, and you don't know how to let it go."

"Suggestions?"

"Just let go," the Executioner replied.

"It's not that simple, Sarge."

"I know. It never is."

"What would you do?"

"If I was duty-fit, you mean?"

"Let's say."

"Okay. I'd send the rest on to the border, then hang back and throw a little party for the trackers. Shake them up enough to be discouraging and give them second thoughts."

Weiss knew what that meant. "It's not me," he said.

"No."

"In *my* place, what would you do?"

"Try for the border, Bones. I'd move as fast as possible and hope that it was good enough."

"Just leave."

"That's it."

Weiss thought about it for another moment, knowing what he had to say.

"I can't. I won't."

BOLAN WATCHED Primo Salvato leave the cluster of his men and cross the clearing, coming closer. For an instant the rebel's shadow fell across Bolan, then he crouched at Bolan's side, two feet of empty space between them.

"You see me now?" Salvato asked as Bolan turned his way.

"I see enough."

The rebel nodded. "So, you know the doctor from a long time, yes?"

Bolan considered what else Marta might have told Salvato, calculating that this one slip wouldn't hurt. "A long time," he conceded.

"You were soldiers?"

"Once upon a time."

"I think you're still a soldier, Senhor Cooper."

"I'm retired."

"Still with the uniform, the weapons. Still a jungle fighter. You don't seem retired to me."

"I came to help a friend, that's all."

Blurry or not, Salvato's face wore a suspicious frown. "You know about my country, I suppose," he said, "and all of South America."

"I know some things," Bolan replied. "What did you have in mind?"

"Your country, U.S.A., often behaves as if it owns this continent. Your government sends agents, armies, gunboats. Here and there, they tell us who should rule, how we should make our living, what we may and may not do."

"That isn't me," Bolan said.

"No?"

"You have my word."

"That's no small thing, Senhor. Unfortunately, I don't know you. I don't know if you're an honest man or someone sent to cut my throat while I'm asleep."

"You think I came for *you?*"

Salvato shrugged. "Who knows?"

"I hate to burst your bubble," Bolan answered, "but I'd never heard of you before you met our column yesterday. I still don't know exactly who you are or what you're fighting for, but I can tell you this—if I was after you, I wouldn't have been traveling with Marta to find Dr. Weiss, on the off chance that you'd run into us sometime. Does that make any kind of sense to you?"

Salvato was quiet for a moment. Bolan couldn't tell if he was digesting his words or sulking over the knock to his ego, but he finally nodded. "You're right," he said. "I may be— what do you call it?—paranoid?"

"You may as well hold on to that," Bolan said. "Even paranoids have enemies, and in your line of work you're bound to make a few."

"You speak the truth, Senhor. Two years ago, police arrest my sister in Diamantino, where she learns to be a nurse. They ask her where to find me, but she doesn't know. She doesn't lie to them, you understand. I've told her nothing."

Bolan knew the story wouldn't have a happy ending, but he made no move to interrupt.

"My sister tells the truth. She hasn't seen me in almost a year. They threaten to expel her from the nursing school, but she can't tell them what she doesn't know. I'm wise, you see?" Salvato tapped his temple with an index finger.

Bolan waited for the rest.

"At last, they tell her it will take some time to process her release. They go away, but she is not alone. Three men in masks come to the cell a short time later. Shall I tell you what they do?"

"I get the picture," Bolan said.

"Is funny you should say those words, Senhor. *I* got the picture, too. There was a camera in the cell. They film my sister's rape and sent the...cartridge?"

"Videocassette."

"They send it to our mother. As a gift, with shiny wrapping paper. You enjoy a good joke, yes?"

"Not that kind," Bolan said.

"They make one bad mistake, though. One man in a mask has a tattoo, right here." Salvato tapped the back of his left hand. "I see it still. A snake, crawling inside a skull. It takes some time, but finally I find the young policeman with the snake tattoo. He tells me everything I want to know. That also takes some time."

Bolan had been there, more or less. He knew the rage that burned, the icy calm that followed after it.

"The young policeman begged for death, Senhor. When I grew tired and had the other names, I granted his request. I visited the others, then. Two rapists of my sister and the officer who told them what to do. All gone, now. I'm a murderer, they say."

"What happened to your sister?" Bolan asked.

"She took her own life, to erase the shame. It is a mortal sin, we're told. She burns in Hell forever now, because of what was done to her."

"Do you believe that?"

"It's one reason why I fight," Salvato said. "To give them all a little taste of Hell on Earth."

"But not the only reason."

"Sometimes I believe the fight may do some good."

"Sometimes it does," Bolan agreed.

"Please understand, I tell this story of my loss not for your sympathy, but so you understand how I reward those who would steal part of my life."

"The only thing I hope to take away from here is standing over there." Bolan nodded toward Bones, huddled in conversation with Adam and Eve.

"And if he will not go?" Salvato asked.

"I guess we'll see," the Executioner replied.

CHAPTER THIRTEEN

Marta Enriquez knew they had begun to climb, because her legs ached in a different way than the previous day. Going downhill used muscles at the back of her legs, pulling behind her knees. Climbing worked the larger muscles in front of her thighs, producing the same burn she sometimes felt while running.

Nathan had named the muscles, smiling, when she'd complained about it. Gastrocnemius and peroneus longus in back, adductor magnus and quadriceps femoris in front. Smiling, he'd told her that the hiking kept her gluteus maximus in rare form.

Matt Cooper offered no complaint, whether they marched uphill or down. He didn't slouch beneath his pack and weapons, kept his head up, always scanning with the eyes that he assured her he could perceive more with each passing day.

She hoped that was the truth, because Marta would need him soon.

The others had agreed, at least in principle, to help her take

Nathan away from danger. They didn't seem shocked when she described the process of sedating him, but reading native faces could be difficult. They were with her, regardless, and that made the difference.

As long as Matt Cooper could more or less fend for himself.

She hadn't told Ricardo of the plan because the young man was cut from different cloth. He came from money, dispossessed now, and this time was an adventure for him. Marta didn't know where he would go when it was over, what he'd do next, but she feared that here and now he might warn Nathan to preserve the status quo. Rescue the fantasy.

Marta hadn't decided whether she should tell him at the last moment and hope he'd go along, or if she ought to plan on two syringes for the big night. If she had to drug Ricardo, he wouldn't be going with them. Better that he take his chances with Salvato and an honest plea of ignorance than slow them with more deadweight and possibly betray them when he woke.

Salvato was another problem, or potential problem. Marta didn't know if he would follow them, try to retrieve the doctor for his men, or if he'd simply shrug and let them go. He had to have reasons for conveying Nathan and the rest of them to what he called a safe location, and she guessed it wasn't simply from the goodness of his heart.

If he pursued them, she would have to deal with it. There was a chance they could outrun Salvato, though he might not be put off by crossing the border. She would fight, if necessary. Cooper could help her, and Marta knew the others would defend Nathan at any cost.

To the death, if need be.

And what would be her great accomplishment, in that case?

It won't come to that, she told herself. Salvato wanted Nathan for his prowess as a healer, not as a hostage caged under guard. Coercion was counterproductive, but it wasn't, she realized, beyond the realm of possibility.

Salvato lived by warrior's rules, in a world where violence was often the first, last and only resort. The fact of his survival after two or three years being hunted in the bush proved him a ruthless man, and cunning. He would do whatever he perceived was necessary for himself and for his men.

Hence Marta's plan to smuggle Nathan out of camp in darkness, without being seen. It would be difficult, of that she had no doubt. But waiting for the enemy to overtake them, knowing what it meant to Nathan—either death or prison—was intolerable.

She would save him if she could, or die in the attempt. Marta believed she owed him that, and much, much more.

She broke stride, turned to check on Cooper, and she found him watching her.

"Still here," he said.

They hadn't used the rope today. Cooper insisted that he could see well enough to follow her without it, and she took him at his word, still warning him of sudden changes in terrain. The climbing trail was easier for him, it seemed, though scattered showers made it slippery in places. Sometimes she saw Cooper groping for a vine or sapling to support himself, missing the first attempt, but she could tell his vision was improving.

Was it good enough for creeping through the jungle after nightfall, fighting soldiers who were clear of eye and well familiar with the battleground?

The answer to that question waited for the actual event.

And by the time she learned it, Marta knew, it would be too late for a hasty change of plans.

THERE WAS A HAZE across the morning, seen through Bolan's eyes, but he could pick out shapes and colors better than he had the day before. He had begun to recognize some of Salvato's men by sight, although he didn't know their names.

He thought of one man as Alfalfa, for the way his hair stuck up on top. The chronic sloucher, he called Stoopy. One who often swung his weapon toward the source of common or imaginary sounds was Nervous. The machete-wielder, Bolan knew as Blade.

He hadn't named the others yet, fixing on those who walked most often close to Marta and himself. Were they assigned as guards, or was their placement in the column mere coincidence?

It didn't matter in the daylight, while they marched. He knew from Marta that the move on Bones would come in darkness, after they had pitched their tents on higher ground. Salvato's "safe" place in the hills was still somewhere ahead of them. And while it might be relatively safer than their last two camps, Bolan had no illusion that it offered them long-term protection.

Bolan had no proof they were being followed at the moment, but he would've called it a safe bet. If hunters weren't pursuing them right now, with a clear trail to follow, then their enemies had dropped the ball big time.

But they would still be coming after Weiss. If not today, then certainly tomorrow or next week. He knew the bible of guerrilla warfare inside out. Counterinsurgency required proactive attitudes. An army constantly on the defensive was as good as beaten, for it had surrendered the initiative to its opponents.

Based on prior events—two raids on Weiss's camps within a week or less—Bolan had no reason to doubt the hunters were pursuing them with all deliberate speed. The loss of one scout shouldn't slow them down significantly, but he wondered why they hadn't summoned air support.

Two possibilities occurred to him. The first, that the hunters had fallen out of touch with headquarters somehow, was so unlikely that he deemed it virtually impossible. Even assuming that they only had one radio and that was somehow lost, the brass would send search teams to locate the patrol.

The other option hinged on personality, but Bolan felt that it was closer to the mark. If Blaine Downey was working with the hunters, much less in direct command, Bolan surmised that the CIA man would regard Weiss's capture as a personal victory. It would be something to write home about—the home, in this case, being Langley, from which rank and favors flowed. Failure, by the same token, would mean personal defeat, unless Downey could fob it off on the Brazilians.

Either way, he wouldn't want to share the capture—or the kill—with native pilots. They could mop up afterward, but Downey would want Weiss's scalp, and likely Bolan's, for himself.

Bolan wasn't concerned about the effect that his death or capture would have on Stony Man Farm. The necessary firewalls were in place and well-established. Hal Brognola had long since burned any bridges between the late Mack Bolan and Matt Cooper, or Bolan's alternate identity as Colonel Brandon Stone. Both names had dossiers in place behind them, but those covers—"legends" in spyspeak—would vanish with a keystroke, on command.

Bolan dead was no liability at all to Stony Man.

The Executioner caged was a risk only if his captors broke him, forcing him to spill his guts—and that wouldn't happen as long as he could spill blood instead. He could always go down fighting, take one for the team.

He owed them that much, anyway.

"Bit of a cliff here," Marta warned him, snapping Bolan's full attention back to the here and now.

It wasn't what he'd call a cliff, but it was steep enough to pose a challenge. Half a dozen steps in front of him, the ground rose sharply—Bolan guessed it would be fifty-odd degrees—then seemed to level off again, a dozen feet or so above eye-level. The trail was a zigzagging scar across the earthen slope.

Those who had gone before were dropping, roped to help the litter bearers with their burdens. Bolan didn't envy them, having to hoist and drag the wounded up that hill, but he stayed focused on the problem of his own ascent. One careless slip would send him tumbling back downhill, snowballing into others and perhaps plunging to further injury.

Watching Marta, reaching for the nearest rope, he dug his heels in and began to climb.

MORE RAIN.

The next time I start chasing some asshole, Downey thought, I'll make sure it's in the desert.

But there wouldn't have to be a next time if he got it right *this* time. That thought was all that kept him going with too many bugs, too damned much rain and mud, too little food and rest. If he could make this score, the rest was history.

Cooper was history, along with Dr. Weiss and everybody else in his pathetic half-assed entourage. They never should've pissed him off this way, Downey thought, defying him when it might've been so easy.

Bad mistake.

The last one they would ever make.

That was, if he could ever find them.

Every hour on the trail spiked Downey's anger quotient that much higher, even as it drove him further into mind-numbing fatigue. A hike was one thing, but this trek was starting to remind Downey of the Bataan death march.

Not that the native troops were suffering, as far as he could tell. Bastards. They'd probably grown up in places just like this, helping parents lug sacks of coffee beans around the god-damned jungle all day long. Downey could almost feel them smirking at him now, because he wasn't Jungle Jim, but if they had a pool going on when he'd call it quits and chopper out, the lot of them were in for a surprise.

His parents hadn't raised a quitter, even if Downey was somewhat out of shape and didn't know which native plants were edible versus the killers that would put unwary nibblers in the ground. That's why the Lord made native guides and porters, so that well-fed city boys could take it easy and enjoy the scenery.

But not this time.

Whatever Downey brought away from this little adventure

would be well and truly earned. The brass would recognize that, back at Langley, and he'd be rewarded for his guts as much as his accomplishments.

Another Wild Bill Donovan, he thought. That's me.

Trailblazing through the jungle in pursuit of enemies who threatened not only America's prestige south of the border, but its long-established friendship with Brazil. Downey was sweating on behalf of diplomats who doled out promises and trusted others to fulfill them in a pinch.

Fat bastards.

He was marching through the jungle on three hours sleep to prove the point that he had been misjudged by those above him in the pecking order and deserved another chance. This *was* his second chance, in fact.

And probably his last one.

Any consolation Downey felt just now derived from Jones and Sutter, huffing on the trail behind him. They weren't snickering at Downey now, on those occasions when his boots slipped in the mud or dangling creepers slapped him in the face. They had enough to think about, just keeping up, plodding in Downey's footsteps with their muttered curses music to his ears.

Smart bastards thought they'd steal his thunder, take the lemons that he'd handed them and churn out lemonade, but they were learning their mistake the hard way. Every step he took, they had to follow. Each time one of them stumbled, Downey smiled.

Laugh *that* off, bastards.

Downey had rehearsed what he would say to Weiss, if there was any chance for them to speak. He'd considered and rejected the formal approach—*Dr. Weiss, I presume?*—while a simple, *Hey, asshole, you're dead!* lacked the special something he was striving for.

Spooks in the movies had the best lines, but Downey was no Pierce Brosnan, and he didn't have a staff of writers standing by to punch up his dialogue. He would think of something when the time came, and if it wasn't Pulitzer material, so what? Weiss wouldn't be critiquing him, and the two overpriced gorillas trailing him would have more important things to think about.

Like saving their jobs.

Or their lives.

Mess with the bull, you get the horns.

And Blaine Downey was in a mood to gore someone for keeps.

ADRIANO BLAS TILTED his head back, opening his mouth to catch a sip of rain. It tasted green, in his imagination, after streaming through the forest canopy above to find him waiting, but earthy flavor didn't bother Blas. He'd tasted worse, and might again, before he overtook his enemies.

And when he caught them, he might taste their blood.

Why not?

The Mayans, Incas and the mighty Aztecs had been man-eaters. They were part of his heritage. Perhaps a few drops of their blood flowed in his veins, along with that of Portuguese invaders and the slaves they brought to till their fields.

There was a savage side to Blas that made him primitive, and he could feel it struggling to emerge, to have its way with those he tracked.

His scouts told him that they were gaining on *O Médico,*

but that the trail was now confused by others who had followed after Weiss. Blas guessed those were the soldiers Santos had reported, with their Yankee masters. If he overtook
them first, Blas would be pleased to slaughter them and leave
them in the forest, food for scavengers.

Meanwhile, he told his scouts to stay alert and watch for any
sign that Weiss's party had eluded those who followed them.
The doctor might not know that he was hunted, but it wouldn't
do for Blas to track the soldiers while his real quarry escaped.

So far, there was no sign of anyone from Weiss's column
deviating from the course they'd set, southwestward from
the last abandoned camp. Blas didn't know where they were
going, maybe pushing on into Bolivia, but he expected to
catch up with them before they went that far.

And when he did…

Only *O Médico* held any interest for him. Blas cared nothing for the hangers-on, unless they had some skill that made
them vital to the doctor's work. Unfortunately, there might
be no time to find out which ones were expendable. No insubordination would be tolerated. Any gesture of resistance
would be met with crushing force.

The way Blas liked it.

On the other hand, submission—preferably with tears and
groveling—might be rewarded with a show of generosity. If
Weiss and company had run in panic, fearing for their lives
and heedless of direction in their haste, Blas might reward
them with the gift of life.

Perhaps. But if he had to teach them all a lesson…

First things, first.

The other team of trackers was his problem at the moment.

If they beat Blas to his quarry, if they killed *O Médico*, his effort would've been for nothing. Blas might punish them, but there'd be no one left to treat his wounded.

On the other hand, if the pursuers captured Weiss alive, then Blas could rescue him and make himself the doctor's hero. That, combined with certain threats, would certainly convince Weiss that he shouldn't stray.

And if it didn't, for some reason, then *O Médico* could serve the cause in other ways, as an example of what happened to those who defied Adriano Blas and the Fist of Freedom. The Yankee had chosen Brazil, injected himself into the country's problems with a claim to love and serve the poor. It was too late, now, for the man to change his mind and say the whole thing was a big mistake.

Chama was suddenly beside him, speaking softly, his voice barely audible over the tramp and slosh of boots in mud. "The men are very tired," he said.

"Are they?" Blas checked his watch, discovering that it had stopped again. "Ten minutes, then. No more."

Chama hurried along the line of march, his soft voice hissing orders. Everywhere he passed, the men stopped in their tracks, some kneeling, others slumping against trees to ease the burden of their gear. Blas didn't care if they were dying on their feet, except that weary men slowed down involuntarily, and what he needed in the bid to overtake his enemies was speed.

Ten minutes' rest was nothing, in the scheme of things. The doctor's band would be on its last legs by now, with hunters coming on behind. So much the better then, for Blas, to overtake them when they least expected it.

And teach them all a lesson they wouldn't forget.

"THIS IS THE PLACE," Salvato said, beginning to relax for the first time since they had fled the doctor's camp by night.

"Right here?" Bolan asked. "I admit my vision's been a little blurry lately, but I don't see anything resembling a defensible position."

"Up there." Salvato pointed to the summit of a broad plateau that rose out of the forest greenery, a hundred yards ahead. "Cover and high ground, all in one."

"How many angles of approach?"

Salvato turned to face the Yankee. "For a mountain climber, there are many. But for poorly trained Brazilian soldiers, there is only one."

"Meaning there's only one way out," Bolan replied.

"No one is forcing you to join us Senhor Cooper. If you wish to wait below and find out how many are tracking us, please be my guest."

"I don't mind heights," he said. "It just feels better if your hidey-hole has a back door."

"Come, then, and we shall see."

Salvato knew it was a waste of time and energy to bandy words with the American. Having agreed that Cooper could accompany them, he should ignore the man—or better still, observe him closely, being ever ready to retaliate at the first sight of treachery. He was a long way yet from anything resembling trust, where Cooper was concerned, and he had cause to question Weiss's judgment, if the doctor had invited an American commando to his camp.

Maybe *O Médico* was tired of playing Dr. Schweitzer in the jungle and had summoned help to extricate him from his folly. That appeared to be the woman's—Enriquez's—goal, whatever Weiss might think. Salvato had been watching her, noting the way she whispered privately to the Tehuelche shaman and the Jivaros. Unsure what they were planning, he resolved to wait and see.

"It seems," Enriquez said, speaking for the first time since they'd stopped to rest, "that we'll be trapped up there. You say one trail to reach the top. How many soldiers would it take to camp below and guard that path? I call it being caged, not safe."

"It's where we go," Salvato answered her, "when there is nowhere else. They've never found us yet."

"Maybe they never followed you this close before."

Salvato frowned. "My best men will be covering our tracks from this point on," he said. "Again, if anyone desires to stay behind, it's better if you leave the column now and choose a new direction."

Dr. Weiss stepped forward, asking, "How will patients find us in your secret place?"

"It's not a permanent retreat," Salvato said. "I think you have enough to treat, for now."

"And how long are we staying here?"

"Until it's safe to leave, Doctor. Again, if you prefer to stay behind…"

Frowning, Weiss said at last, "A few days can't do any harm."

"A wise choice, Doctor. Shall we go?"

The trail was steep but passable, with earthen steps cut at the steepest point, before they reached the lip of the plateau. Enriquez produced her rope and tied herself to Bolan once again, ignoring his objections with a woman's single-mindedness. With wounded men to carry, it took almost ninety minutes for the last of them to reach the summit, but they made it.

They were safe.

At least for now.

Enriquez had scored a point, though, with her questions down below. She was correct in guessing that Salvato hadn't passed this way before, with hunters stalking almost on his heels. The men he'd tasked to hide their trail were good, but were they good enough?

The fact was that he couldn't think of any safer place to go. The plateau was a geographical anomaly, thrust upward from the jungle floor, two hundred feet or so, yet forested on top. It was as if a giant's thumb had pressed against the Earth's crust from below, raising an oblong patch two hundred yards across and some three hundred yards in east-west length. Above, the forest flourished, but without some of the creeping predators whom isolation had deprived of prey for several million years.

When all had reached the top, Salvato led them to the clearing where his soldiers camped from time to time. Netting was hung between the trees there, twenty feet above the ground, sagging with leafy camouflage designed to screen them from a search by air. The leaves were dead and withered now, Salvato saw.

"My men will fix the nets tomorrow. In the meantime, we can risk fire until dark."

"Hot food?" Weiss asked. "Sounds good to me."

"I'd like to look around a bit," Bolan said, "if nobody minds."

Salvato managed not to smile. "Be careful, Senhor. Don't step off the edge."

"I'll see he doesn't," Enriquez answered, glaring razors at Salvato.

"As you wish."

Salvato watched the two of them go off together, noticing that Cooper didn't seem to need much guidance anymore. He wondered if the Yankee would be useful in a fight, or if he'd simply grown more dangerous. In either case, he needed watching.

And if he proved false, Salvato vowed there would be one less blind man in the world.

"HEAR THAT?" Bolan asked, when they'd walked some fifteen minutes due east of the camp.

"The birds, you mean?"

"Behind the birds. Their background music."

"What? I don't—" She hesitated then, and Bolan thought she closed her eyes. "You're right. There *is* something."

"This way," Bolan said. He could make out vibrant greens on every side, the looming boles of trees. If forced to quantify the comeback, he would've said that he'd regained some two-thirds of his vision since the night he had been carried into Weiss's camp.

Was this the best he could expect?

There was no time to think about it now. They'd almost reached the source of the pervasive sound he had been following, familiar and yet alien in those surroundings.

Running water.

"It's a river!" Enriquez said, excited, as they stood upon the bank.

"There's more," Bolan informed her, turning to his right. He tracked the river's course, using the water's shine and sound to guide him, letting the woman sound the warning if he missed a jagged stone or rotting log along the way.

The river's sound was changing, growing louder, as they traveled toward the eastern edge of the plateau.

"What is that?" Enriquez asked him, clutching Bolan's hand.

"A little farther," he instructed her.

At last, they cleared the tree line and the long drop lay in front of them. Bolan couldn't make out details of the forest canopy below, although he ventured perilously near the edge. Enriquez clung to his hand and held him back.

Part of the problem with his view was blurry vision, but the rest was rising mist, shot through with rainbows from the sun above. To Bolan's left, a waterfall plunged out of sight, its torrent raising spume that settled brisk and cold upon his face.

"It's beautiful," Enriquez said. "Can you see it?"

"Colors," Bolan said. "We need to see what's down below."

"Can you...?"

He shook his head. "Not yet. You'll have to tell me."

"It's important, this?"

"It could be life or death."

"Explain."

"You heard Salvato say there's only one trail leading up here, right? I don't know if that's true or not, but if we're cut off from below, we'll need an alternate escape route."

"What? You mean to jump?"

"I'm sizing up the possibilities. If we have time, later, we'll search for other paths. Now, will you help, or not?"

"I don't like...looking down," she said.

"Just take your time on the approach, then peek over the edge."

"Santa Maria." Glaring at the precipice in front of her, she said at last, "All right. Wait here."

"Yes, ma'am."

Enriquez got down on hands and knees, then wriggled on her stomach to the brink, straining her neck to peer beyond the overhang. She spent a moment there, then wriggled back, retreating ten feet from the drop before she stood.

"It falls into a pool or lake below," she said. "Maybe one hundred feet."

"Did you see rocks?"

"I couldn't tell."

"Okay. Something to think about."

"I couldn't do it. No." She shook her head for emphasis.

"When the alternative is certain death, you'll be surprised what you can do. Meanwhile, let's hope it doesn't come to that. You want to do some more exploring, on our way back to the camp? We need to know this ground."

"Yes, please."

"Maybe we'll find another way."

"But you don't think so," she replied.

"We won't know till we walk the ground."

"And if the army doesn't find us?"

"We still need a way down, for Bones," he said. "Unless you've given up your plan."

Her answer sounded grim, determined. "We'll search as you said, on the way back to camp."

CHAPTER FOURTEEN

Nightfall was fast approaching when the scouts returned and huddled with their sergeant for a conference in breathless Portuguese. Blaine Downey crowded in on them, clutching his carbine to his chest, and asked the noncom, "What is it this time?"

"There is another column moving toward us," Sergeant Alémán replied.

"What do you mean, another column?" Even when they spoke to him in English, Downey felt as if he had to crack some arcane code.

"Soldiers," Alémán said. "Maybe guerrillas."

"Soldiers means our side, right? You think Herreira's second-guessing us?"

"You've heard my only contact with the major," Alémán replied. "But I don't think so. No."

"Where are these guys?" Downey demanded.

"Westward." The sergeant pointed vaguely into forest shadows. "They'll intercept us in another hour, maybe, if we hold our present course."

"It can't be Weiss, then?"

"No. His group is still ahead of us, moving southwest-ward."

Downey was silent for a moment, pondering what he should do with the new information. Reinforcements from Cuiabá couldn't reach them in time to be useful, assuming Herreira agreed to another air lift. That left Downey to choose from one of three options.

He could retreat, give up the chase and let Weiss go.

He could change course and try to miss the new players, whomever they were.

Or he could forge ahead to meet them and find out.

The first option was unacceptable. He was on thin ice now, with both Herreira and the Langley brass. Further humilia-tion wouldn't get him anyplace but out the door.

The second choice was too damned hit-or-miss, a haphaz-ard scheme with disaster written all over it. One misstep, and he might blunder into an ambush laid by the very war party he sought to avoid.

"How many in the other group?" he asked.

Alémán shrugged. "They heard, saw glimpses, but they couldn't count the men."

"You're sure they aren't just Indians?"

"Men armed with modern weapons. Speaking Portuguese."

"Okay. I say we take them out."

Behind him, Sutter grumbled something Downey couldn't understand.

"What's that?" he challenged.

"We're supposed to bag the doctor, not jump everyone we meet along the way."

"So, you're in charge now? Taking over, are you?"

"All I'm saying—"

"In the field we call that mutiny," Downey said. "It's a capital offense."

"So, what, you're gonna *shoot* me now, for having an opinion?"

Downey's index finger tingled on the trigger of his CAR-15. "Keep your goddamned opinions to yourself," he snapped, "or turn around and march your sorry ass back to Cuiabá."

"All I'm saying—"

"That's enough!"

The shrill tone of his voice surprised Downey almost as much as it shocked Sutter. The larger man retreated, lowering his eyes. "Okay," he said. "Jesus."

"I didn't hear that, soldier."

"I said, 'Yes, sir, Mr. Downey.'"

Better. Downey turned on Jones to nail it down. "Something you want to say?"

"Not me. Sir."

"Right." Downey swung back toward Alemán, feeling the others eyeball him with new respect or fear. Right now, he'd take whatever he could get and run with it. "Where can we intercept them? How much farther?"

Sergeant Alemán exchanged more rapid dialogue with the scouts. At last, pointing again, he said, "A half mile that way, if we hurry. But it takes us off our course."

"We'll hurry, then, and pick up the trail when we're finished. I want to teach these guys the golden rule."

"What's that?"

"Do unto others," Downey said, "before they can do unto you."

The sergeant didn't answer. He was busy giving orders to the scouts, then speaking to the other uniforms. If anyone complained about the change of plans, it was lost in translation. A moment later they were double-timing through the gloom of dusk, leaving the now familiar trail and veering due westward.

Might be a mistake, Downey thought, but he couldn't change his mind and overrule himself. Instead of second-guessing his command decision, Downey tried to think who might be marching toward them on a hard collision course.

Most likely rebels, though it could be smugglers, maybe bandits. Any way he sliced it, they'd be doing the Brazilian government a favor, taking out another bunch of malcontents and scum.

But what if they were friends of Weiss, marching to join his column? Weiss already had guerrillas with him, in addition to Matt Cooper. It was best to head off any reinforcements now, while there was time.

Downey was panting after he had jogged a hundred yards, Sutter wheezing behind him in the shadows. Doggedly, he pushed for greater speed, until he started crowding Sergeant Alemán.

Do unto others, right, he thought. Let's get it done.

THEY RISKED a fire, trusting the forest and the cammo nets to cover it, but there was no fresh meat to roast. Some of Salvato's men found tubers and wild onions, boiling them together in a kind of vegan stew whose taste reminded Bolan vaguely of potato soup his mother used to make.

Adam told Enriquez something in their common dialect, and she translated for the Executioner. "He said tomorrow, he'll hunt monkeys for the pot."

"I never thought I'd pine for MREs," Bolan replied.

"What's that?" she asked.

"Army rations," he explained. "Meals, ready to eat."

"Are they delicious?" Marta teased.

"I wouldn't go that far."

Bones, seated on her other side, broke in. "The food I always think about when I see olive drab is SOS."

"SOS?" Marta echoed.

"It's chipped beef on toast," Weiss explained, "but the troops—and the cooks, if my memory serves—called it shit on a shingle."

"It wasn't bad, most of the time," Bolan said.

"But to have it for breakfast, three days out of five? When I think—"

The first shot could've been an illusion, some natural sound of the jungle, distorted and muffled by distance. That hope disappeared as the snap, crackle, pop of small arms fire erupted, full-automatic and semiauto weapons spitting death in the forest below the plateau.

Bolan dropped his mess kit and scooped up the Steyr AUG. On his feet by the time those around him responded, he turned toward the sounds and made off through the trees. Moonlight guided his steps past the dark forest giants, while the sounds of mortal combat acted as a homing beacon. Yards short of the precipice, on open ground at last, he slowed, proceeding cautiously while others overtook him.

Staring down onto the moonlit forest canopy with bleary eyes, he couldn't pick out muzzle-flashes in the night. Salvato's soldiers had no better luck, but some of them were pointing in the general direction of the sound. It wasn't science, even in the vaguest sense, but Bolan estimated that the shooters were at least two miles from the plateau.

Salvato, gliding up beside him, said, "I think someone has trouble."

"So it seems," Bolan replied.

"Maybe they don't come for us, after all," the rebel leader said.

Bolan thought that was wishful thinking, but he kept the glum opinion to himself. Whoever was involved in the firefight below, they were distracted for the moment. Maybe it would terminate their mission, but he wasn't counting on it. They still needed to prepare for uninvited visitors, and for evacuating Bones when it was time.

"How long can it go on?" asked Enriquez, on his right.

"Until there's no one left," Salvato answered, "if we're lucky."

It had occurred to Bolan that the sounds might indicate a slaughter rather than a skirmish. "Are there villages down there?" he asked.

"Nothing that close that I'm aware of," Enriquez said. "No more Tehuelche. Too far south for Jivaro."

"Hope for the best," Salvato said. He turned away, back toward the fire. "The more who die tonight, the fewer we must kill tomorrow."

Enriquez waited until Salvato was beyond earshot, then said, "I don't know how he lives with so much hate."

Bolan wanted to say, It isn't hate, it's practicality. Instead he told her, "Think of it as a survival mechanism."

"It's such a waste."

He wouldn't argue that point with the lady. "Salvato has guards posted. We should get some sleep."

"With that noise going on?"

"It won't last long," he answered, speaking from experience. "It never does."

As he retreated toward the campfire, slower steps this time, Bolan couldn't escape a sense that they were running out of time—for Bones, and maybe for himself. They hadn't found another exit from the high ground yet, and from the sounds rising to Bolan's ears, it seemed entirely possible that they would soon be under siege.

Unhappily he found himself agreeing with Salvato, wishing injury or death on men he'd never met. The timing and location of the skirmish might be pure coincidence, but Bolan didn't think so. They had been followed, hunted, and now hell had broken loose along their back trail.

Let it be.

His mind echoed Salvato's words.

The more who die tonight, the fewer we must kill tomorrow.

THE FIRST WARNING of danger was a rifle shot, too late for Adriano Blas to rally his guerrillas and prepare a sound defense. He didn't see the bullet strike, too busy diving headlong for the nearest cover as a storm of automatic fire erupted all around him.

Squirming on the ground, Blas found a tree to hide behind

while bullets swarmed overhead, seeking flesh. His men were returning fire without orders, instinctively—and damned lucky, too, since Blas seemed to have lost his voice for the moment.

Blas raised his Imbel autorifle high enough to clear the ground and fired a wild, one-handed burst into the darkness in front of him. His scouts were up there, somewhere, if they lived, but Blas needed the racket and recoil to ground him, restoring a measure of his shaken courage.

Another burst, and Blas could feel the more familiar rage replacing unaccustomed fear. He hadn't glimpsed the enemy yet, had no idea who was trying to kill him, but two possibilities quickly came to mind.

The ambush party might be soldiers, either those who followed Weiss or a patrol dispatched on some mission completely unrelated to his own. The government declared all-out offensives on guerrilla bands from time to time, then lost interest and retreated into a defensive posture. This surprise might be an unhappy coincidence of time and place.

But, on the other hand...

As Blas squeezed off another aimless burst, watching as six or seven muzzle-flashes answered him, he wondered if the ambush party was composed of rebels allied with *O Médico*. Someone had killed the dead man left behind in Weiss's camp, and while it might have been the Jivaros who lived with Weiss, Blas didn't think so.

Rebels made more sense. A rival group, perhaps, that had encouraged Weiss to pull up stakes and go in search of somewhere else to ply his trade.

That thought angered Blas as much as the slugs streaming

over his head. Spewing a whisper-stream of curses, he rolled and crawled around the giant tree that sheltered him, seeking another angle of attack against his hidden enemies.

Prolonged firefights were doubly perilous, not only for the risk of being shot, but for the danger that their racket might attract other hunters through the darkened jungle, following the sounds to spring upon any combatants who survived. If he *was* dueling with rival guerrillas loyal to Weiss, there still might be a troop of regulars within earshot, advancing even now to close the ring around their rebel prey and slaughter all within it.

Blas wished that he had a hand grenade, to speed things up, but they were presently in short supply. Likewise, he yearned to break the stalemate while his men had ample ammunition left for their primary mission. If they used it all fighting with strangers in the night, what weapons could he wield against *O Médico* and his companions when they finally were face-to-face?

One problem at a time.

Blas spied a muzzle-flash that seemed to be directed toward his soldiers, aimed and squeezed off half a dozen 5.56 mm rounds in answer. In darkness, at an estimated range of sixty feet, he couldn't tell if any of his bullets found their mark, but there was no immediate response from that position.

Blas took it to be a hopeful sign, advancing further on his belly through the mud and stinking vegetation of the forest floor. It had been drizzling rain a short time earlier, and now his camouflage fatigues were fouled with slime. Some bastard had to pay for that, the stench and filth that Blas endured to save himself.

Another muzzle-flash, and yet another, to his front. Blas sought for a position that would grant both decent cover and a field of fire, cursing as his left elbow struck a slab of stone and sent pain lancing through his shoulder.

There! He'd found another tree that granted him a fair view of his enemies' position in a snarl of undergrowth. Scowling, Blas sighted down the barrel of his Imbel MD2 and squeezed the trigger slowly, with a lover's touch.

THE AMBUSH WENT like clockwork, right up to the moment when the shooting started. Downey, lying prone behind a log furry with moss and God knew what else, had been braced and ready for it, yearning for a chance to pour long days of anger and frustration through the barrel of his CAR-15. Having demanded the first-shot privilege for himself, with Sergeant Alemán reluctantly agreeing, Downey'd waited while the shadow shapes took form and closed the gap before he squeezed the trigger.

Gently…gently…

It was only one shot, aimed dead-center at the silhouette that was a man he'd never seen before, but instantly the world around him rang with thunder, blazing with muzzle-flash lighting. The din was horrific, instantly reminding Downey that he hadn't fired a weapon in decades without first donning earmuffs.

Downey flinched involuntarily and spoiled his next two shots, triggered by reflex well above the head of anyone downrange who still might be standing upright. Worse yet, when Downey raised his head to scan the battlefield, he found that many members of the ambushed column weren't only still alive, but also firing back.

A bullet smacked the log six inches to the left of Downey's face and he recoiled in panic, triggering another wasted shot that wouldn't pass within ten feet of the sniper who'd spooked him.

What was this shit?

Downey knew he was a novice when it came to jungle combat, but he had a vision in his mind of how an ambush should proceed. The hidden gunmen fire in unison, their targets drop and die. Case closed. The bastards weren't supposed to lay down cover fire and generally tear the landscape all to shreds.

Downey was having major second thoughts about his plan, but it was too damned late to back out now. Assuming he could make the others listen, somehow order all of them to turn and flee in unison, they'd run the risk of being shot down in their tracks or followed by the men they'd failed to kill first time around.

It would be simpler if he fled alone, but what would that accomplish? If he managed to survive the first few deadly moments, Downey knew that he'd be lost within the hour, wandering disoriented through the trackless jungle until something killed him or he simply starved to death.

Incredibly, Downey was caught in his own trap. Last time I call the shots, he thought, and realized that it was very likely true.

Unless...

On either side of Downey, twenty feet apart, Sutter and Jones were busily returning fire, blazing away at phantom enemies. From where he lay, they almost seemed to be enjoying it, if that were possible. Downey was watching Sutter when the big man paused to feed his piece another magazine, and Sutter glanced up from the task, meeting his eyes.

What was that look? Darkness obscured the nuances, but

if he hadn't known better, Downey might've suspected Sutter was annoyed to see him still alive.

Most likely just confused, thought Downey as he beckoned Sutter to his side. Sutter played dumb or cagey, pointing to himself, then Downey, with a questioning expression on his face, as if to say, *Who, me?*

Dumb bastard.

Downey cycled through the gestures once again, with more exaggeration this time, so they could've been interpreted by someone in a coma. Grudgingly, Sutter nodded and started crawling through the muck toward Downey's nest, behind the massive log.

Now he was getting somewhere. Downey turned toward Jones, raising a hand to signal him, but having to wait while Jones fired off another six or seven rounds into the night. Willing the man to glance his way, Downey was on the verge of calling to him when a bullet struck the log a hairbreadth from his ear.

But, Jesus, it was on his side!

Recoiling, Downey spun around to face the only possible direction where the shot could've originated. For a frozen heartbeat, he saw Sutter poised, his rifle shouldered, aimed at Downey's face. He waited for the bullet, cursing silently— until the back of Sutter's head exploded and he toppled forward, dead.

Behind him, Sergeant Alemán crouched with a semiauto pistol in his hand. Wasting no time, he clambered over Sutter's corpse and closed the gap to Downey's side.

"That's one," he said, and glanced behind Downey, toward Jones. "You need to think about the other one."

"I will," Downey replied. "Thank you."

"Thank me if we get out of here alive," Alemán said. "I think we need to leave now, if you don't object."

"No," Downey answered. "You're in charge. Just say the word."

Alemán smiled and raised his left hand, fingers wrapped around a dark metallic egg. "The word," he whispered, "is 'grenade.'"

THE FIRST EXPLOSION startled Adriano Blas. He'd almost grown accustomed to the back-and-forth of gunfire, crawling through the mud and rot between wild fusillades, rising to fire, then dropping back to crawl some more. Blas couldn't swear that he'd accomplished anything, but he was still alive and fighting.

What else was there?

The grenades changed everything.

First one blast in the darkness, then another and another. There was no real pattern to them, members of the ambush team lobbing their lethal gifts at random, but the blasts wounded morale, as surely as their shrapnel lacerated flesh.

Worse yet, he couldn't trace the silent arc of a grenade in flight, to kill the man who threw it. Blas reckoned his enemies could sit back in the trees and lob grenades all night, without revealing where they were.

Blas knew he had to retreat, but quietly, without alerting his opponents to the move. While they made noise with their grenades, he had to pull his soldiers back, salvage as many as he could.

But first, he had to find them.

Scattered at the first reports of gunfire, hemmed in at the

column's point by enemies, his men were scattered randomly across a killing ground some forty feet wide and sixty feet long. Blas started creeping through the undergrowth, hissing and calling softly as he went, pronouncing names at random, punctuated with his own.

Each time he found one of his men alive, Blas whispered orders to withdraw, take anyone discovered while retreating and fall back for half a mile. He had a place in mind, described it, and admonished each survivor not to make a sound in passing through the field of fire.

It seemed to take forever, crawling on his belly while the earth heaved underneath him and a crisscrossed latticework of gunfire swept the air above. It took an aching lifetime, nudging corpses when he found them, moving on in search of others still alive. Blas persevered, retreating even as he searched the smoky forest, until finally he'd reached a point where he could safely stand erect.

From there, he ran.

There was no shame in it, a raw survival mechanism. Fighting to the death for an objective was one thing, but dying in the dark for nothing was a mindless waste of manpower. Blas still didn't know who had beaten him this time, but with any luck at all, he might find out one day.

And when he did…

Blas ran the best part of a quarter mile, then slowed to a walk, chest heaving as he fought for breath. The odors emanating from his body as he walked included cordite, jungle rot, fresh blood and rank fear-sweat. Blas wondered if the other troops would smell him coming and suppress a spasm of disgust at his approach.

He had been tricked, his column nearly slaughtered, but he wasn't giving up.

Not yet.

He found the others where he'd told them to regroup, milling around a slab of stone thrust skyward from the forest floor by some ancient upheaval, or perhaps imbedded in the soil when it came plummeting from outer space. They stood or crouched with weapons trained on Blas until they recognized him, then the muzzles lowered slowly, with an almost visible reluctance.

First, before he spoke, Blas counted heads. Five of the men he'd started with were missing, and he knew that two of them, at least, were dead. He'd found their corpses, shrapnel-torn and bullet-punctured, on the killing field. Their blood was on his hands.

Five dead or missing left him twenty-two combatants, three of whom he saw were slightly wounded but still fit to march and fight. Blas chose his words as he addressed them, knowing that if he could hold them now, they'd follow him to Hell itself.

"We started out to find *O Médico*," he said. "That hasn't changed. We need him for our comrades, now and in the future. We can find his trail again and track him down, tomorrow or the next day, at the latest. When we have him, then we'll track and punish those who interfered with us tonight."

Blas hesitated, felt them watching.

"For your friends, alive and dead—who's with me?"

Slowly one hand raised and then another, until all of them had signaled weary, mute agreement. They were his.

And they had just begun to fight.

BOLAN HAD NEARLY turned back toward the cliff's edge when he heard the hand grenades, but what would be the point? He didn't know who the combatants were, except to say with iron-clad certainty that none of them were allies. If they hunted Bones, they hunted him, and anything that hurt them or compelled them to waste ammunition was a point in Bolan's favor.

On returning to the fire, he sat alone with private thoughts. The sounds of combat from the rain forest had ceased, and he wasn't distracted by the conversations held in Portuguese or native dialects. Bones had already slipped into his tent, and Marta, likewise, was nowhere to be seen.

They couldn't leave this night, he realized, because they hadn't scouted all the possible escape routes. If the following day brought no interruptions, he would try to circumnavigate the rim of the plateau with Marta, seeking a path of retreat that Salvato had missed, or else kept to himself. Failing that, they would have to avoid or dispose of the sentries he posted and make their way down after nightfall, avoiding detection until they secured a fair lead.

A piece of cake, he told himself with bitter sarcasm.

Bolan went through the steps that were required to make their plan succeed. Sedating Bones was the first stumbling block, a task for Marta if she had the nerve to pull it off. If she could catch him already asleep and slip the needle in, so much the better. Less chance, that way, of an altercation that would rouse the camp and spell disaster for their plan.

Step two was getting out of camp with Bones an inert burden, skirting any late-night ramblers from Salvato's troupe.

No guards were posted on the camp itself, Salvato being satisfied that only one approach required lookouts, but that didn't insure that every man would be asleep when they began their flight through darkness.

Flight.

The more he thought about it, Bolan wished they had hang gliders and could take their chances on the wind, but fantasy was unproductive and he let it go.

Step three, if they got out of camp with no alarms raised, was the relatively short hike to the point where they'd ascended on arrival. Guards *were* posted there, and Bolan hoped they could be overcome without fatalities, if only to reduce Salvato's anger when he found out they were gone. Again, a warning cry or shot would bring the others down upon them and destroy whatever hope they had of putting miles between themselves and the guerrillas.

If they made it to the foot of the plateau, their true ordeal still lay ahead of them. Hiking to the border would take several days, whether they carried Bones or herded him along involuntarily. Would he resist, on waking to discover he'd been kidnapped? Once the deed was done, would his intransigence collapse?

Too many questions.

Bolan knew he couldn't plan for all eventualities. His own ability to carry out the mission was distinctly compromised, although his vision at the moment was the clearest it had been since the initial accident. Still, he couldn't deceive himself into believing he was fit to lead the party, blaze the trail and pick out early warning signs along their route of march.

Useless, in fact, a small voice in his head declared, but

Bolan had no time for doom and gloom. The exercise he'd planned with Marta would be challenging enough without defeatist attitudes at the beginning.

Time enough for that later.

One key to their success or failure was Salvato's response to their exit. If he shrugged it off, so much the better. In that case, they'd only have to think about the dangers ranged ahead of them and any hunters who'd been after Bones before they teamed with the guerrilla band.

If he decided to pursue them, though, the odds would quickly go from bad to worse. Their chances of survival would be cut by half, by Bolan's own best estimate.

But there as nothing to be done about it now.

They had to forge ahead and take their chances, or remain on the plateau indefinitely, trapped until the army found them and unleashed sufficient force to take them down.

Given a choice, Bolan would rather trust the jungle.

It had never let him down before, never defeated him, but he would not mistake it for a friend.

The jungle didn't care who lived or died. It simply *was,* and always would be, unless people came along and cut it down.

Before discouragement could take a grip on him, Bolan gave up and spread his bedroll on the ground. Above him, through the trees, his eyes made out the fuzzy light of distant stars, some of them dead a thousand years before their glimmer reached Earth.

He slept then, his last waking thought a fierce determination that the next day wouldn't be his last.

CHAPTER FIFTEEN

It was officially the worst night of Blaine Downey's life. Before that day, he would've pinned that honor on his sixteenth birthday, when he'd wrecked the old man's Volvo on a joyride and the cop who'd taken the 9-1-1 call had recognized his playmate as a hooker with a rap sheet twice the length of Downey's academic transcript.

That was bad, but this was Hell on Earth.

After routing their unknown enemies, they'd counted heads—fifteen still breathing—and then marched two hours from the battle site, pausing at frequent intervals to strain their ears for any sound suggesting that they'd been pursued. When Sergeant Alémán was satisfied that they were clear, he called a rest stop but forbid a fire or any conversation louder than a whisper. So they sat and waited for sunrise, a group of battered losers drenched with the sporadic, pelting rain.

Throughout the final hours of darkness, Downey brooded over Sutter's treacherous attempt to kill him. He'd been shocked, initially, and hated owing anything to Alémán—

much less his life—but there it was. The more he thought about it, the more angry he became, wishing that he'd been quick enough to shoot Sutter himself.

Too late for that.

The best he could accomplish now was grilling Jones in whispers, badgering his agent for assurances that Sutter's move had been a one-off aberration, nothing they'd cooked up together with an eye toward getting rid of him. Jones fervently denied knowledge of Sutter's plan, and while he picked up nothing to suggest the frightened man was lying, Downey still resolved to watch him constantly for the remainder of their sojourn in the jungle.

Easily said, but when fatigue kicked in at last to override his fear and anger, pulling Downey's eyelids down like blinds on dirty windows, he surrendered grudgingly and slept until the sounds of his companions breaking camp roused him to dawn's gray light.

Breakfast was two granola bars that tasted more like cardboard dipped in sorghum, but they stilled his grumbling stomach for a while. Downey hadn't unpacked the night before, so merely had to grapple on his pack and he was ready for the trail.

Downey wasn't a woodsman. In the city, he used street signs to determine the direction he was traveling. As far as blazing trails, forget about it. When he was eight or nine years old, he'd read that moss grew on the northern side of trees, but that hadn't prevented him from getting lost on a hike through the New Jersey Pine Barrens, where he could've sworn the goddamned trees were ringed by moss on *every* side. Now, in Brazil, the rules for North America went out the window and he knew that he'd be lost again in nothing flat without a native guide.

So he was stuck with Alémán and company, who clearly hated him. His only ally, now that Sutter had revealed himself and paid the price, was an incompetent whom Downey didn't trust as far as he could throw.

Perfect.

The sergeant had been all for turning back, calling a whirlybird to pick them up, until Downey reminded him how close they were to Weiss, and how a score like that could wipe out any stain of failure attached to Alémán's command of the detail. It wasn't blackmail, not exactly, and the other troops went for it when he mentioned payback for their friends.

Jones was the solitary holdout, whining that they'd lost too much already. He was muttering, "Game over, man," when Downey faced him nose-to-nose and gave Jones the alternatives. He could snap out of it and fall in line, or he could stay behind with Sutter, fertilizing Mother Nature. That was all it took to close the deal, and they were on their way.

But where in Hell were they going?

Southwestward, Alémán told him, following *O Médico's* original route of march, more or less. They hadn't struck the trail again, but Alémán assured him they were close. Downey accepted it on faith, no choice left but to follow now, and he was trudging wearily into the fourth hour since sunrise when the sergeant called another halt.

Ahead of them, an island seemed to rise out of the forest, reaching for the sky. Wooded on top, it glowered down at them from steep, bare cliffs.

Beside him, Jones asked, "What the hell is that?"

Downey ignored him. At the plateau's summit, he'd already seen what had attracted Sergeant Alemán.

A plume of white smoke wafting on the breeze.

MARTA BEGAN the last phase of her treachery by estimating Nathan's weight. He seemed thinner, poor dear, since her departure for the States, but she couldn't be sure. She hadn't felt his body pressing down on top of hers since then. There'd been no time, no privacy to speak of, since the night a stranger tried to kill him and Matt Cooper intervened to save her lover's life.

Would they be lovers, after this?

It was a calculated risk, but Marta valued Nathan's safety above her own feelings. If he despised her for trying to keep her alive, if he cast her aside, pushed her out of his life, then so be it. She couldn't be responsible for self-destructive choices that he made in days and weeks ahead.

But she could fight to save his life right now.

The medicine was never closely guarded. There were no addicts or thieves in camp, no risk of waking up the next day and discovering that this or that had vanished from their small supply of drugs. Marta knew where the stash was kept, as did the others. Any one of them could pick up a syringe and fill it, but she'd volunteered because she had a bit more knowledge, and because she wanted any anger Nathan felt after the fact to fall on her.

The plan was hers, and she would take responsibility.

She waited until Nathan was engaged in conversation with Matt Cooper, on the far side of the camp, then slipped inside the tent that served him as a combination operating room and sleeping quarters. It was empty at the moment, all wounds tended, patients resting peacefully. She knelt at the drug locker and opened it, selecting a familiar rubber-capped bottle and checking the label for safety's sake.

She had pegged Nathan's weight at 160 pounds, with a ten-pound margin of error. Allowing for the higher weight wouldn't pose any threat to Nathan's life, and if it rendered him unconscious for a longer period of time, so much the better. There might be nausea when he awoke, perhaps a headache, but she meant to have more medicine on hand for that.

And if he fought them, struggled to reject their help, what then?

Marta plunged the hypodermic's needle through the tiny bottle's rubber cap, inverted it, and pulled the plunger back to fill it. Pale liquid flowed into the syringe, creeping past hash marks calibrated on the side. When she had filled it with a dose sufficient for a man weighing one hundred and seventy pounds, Marta capped the syringe and placed it in the left breast pocket of her shirt, flap buttoned for security. The bottle, still half-full, went into her pants' pocket.

Just in case.

No matter how Nathan reacted, once they carried him away from camp, she was prepared to see it through and bear him far enough from danger that his next choice would at least be free of threats from rebels or the army. If he chose to turn around and plunge back into danger, that would be his choice.

But she wouldn't be there to watch him die.

Emerging from the tent, she glanced quickly around her, wondering if she looked half as guilty as she felt. Betrayal wasn't easy for her, but she'd come to think of Nathan as a man possessed, an addict who required strong intervention in his life to save him. If he thanked her for it later, that would be a happy day.

If not, at least she'd know that she had given him a fighting chance.

Staring across the camp, she watched Nathan and Cooper, deep in conversation. Cooper spent more time looking at Nathan's face, she realized, and once he turned to find her from a distance, eyes locked on her own. It startled her, and Marta realized he was improving faster than she'd realized.

Would he be ready for their flight that evening?

As if in answer to her silent thought, he nodded, then turned back to Nathan.

It was down to hours now, she knew.

Ready or not, they had no other choice.

"YOU THINK THEY WENT up there?" Blas asked his chief lieutenant.

Chama shrugged. "Someone is up there," he replied. "You saw the smoke."

He had. That much was fact. A pale trace rising like a levitating threat above the treetops, swiftly blown away. If Blas had blinked, or glanced the other way for just a second longer, he'd have missed it.

"Why not Indians?" he prodded Chama.

"It may well be Indians," the smaller man admitted. "But we won't know that until we go and see. The trail leads here."

"It leads in this direction. Perhaps they went around the mesa."

Nodding, Chama said, "That's possible. We'll know within the hour, if we push on."

"But if they went up there…" Blas left the thought unfinished.

"We must either climb or let them go."

That was the problem, and they both knew it. Adriano Blas, despite his fearsome reputation as a warrior, was afraid of heights. He hid the weakness when he could, called on younger subordinates when there were trees to climb for fruit or scouting wild terrain. Chama had known him long enough to recognize the phobia, but he had never let it slip. Now he was giving Blas the option to save face by calling off the manhunt for *O Médico*.

"The doctor has too much to answer for," Blas said. "I can't ignore it."

"In that case…"

"We go," he said. "See where the trail takes us."

Chama rallied the soldiers who had fallen out to rest after a grueling night. They closed around him silently and listened to the order. None protested or complained about the brief rest stop. When Chama chose the point men, they moved off into the forest without looking back.

Now that the smoke was gone, Blas fought an impulse to pretend that he'd imagined it. Mist could've looked the same, or steam escaping from a thermal spring. Blas likely would've done it, but he hadn't been the only witness. Chama and a couple of the men had also seen the smoke. If Blas tried to ignore it or pretend it was a quirk of his imagination, he'd be branded as either a fool or a coward.

Neither was acceptable to Blas.

If they determined that *O Médico* and his companions had ascended the plateau, then he would have to climb.

But in the meantime, he would pray it wasn't so.

The mesa wasn't far ahead, perhaps a half mile as the parrot flew, but it took longer on the ground. A murky river blocked their path, with swampy ground on either side that teemed with snakes and leeches. By the time they cleared that obstacle, Blas and his men were filthy, sopping wet and near exhaustion. Lukewarm rain at their next rest stop only made it worse.

Blas cursed the day when he'd first met the turtle.

But it was down to honor now. If he was forced to scale the heights alone and strangle Weiss with his bare hands, Blas knew he couldn't let the matter drop. He was compelled to see it through, if only for the right to call himself a man.

At last, nearly three hours after he had seen the wisp of smoke on high, they stood in front of a cliff that seemed miles tall to Blas, although he guessed its height was closer to a hundred feet.

"They didn't climb this wall," he told Chama. "I'd bet my life on it."

"Fan out and find the trail," Chama ordered the men. "It's here, somewhere."

Please, Jesus, let it go around, Blas thought.

They set off following the tracks that marked their quarry's passage. At some points, it seemed to Blas that there were more tracks, as if Weiss had somehow gained a larger following in transit from the last place they had found his trail. Blas couldn't see how that was possible, and while it troubled him, his main anxiety was focused on the cliffs that towered overhead.

It almost seemed as if his prayers had found receptive ears on high. The trail led him halfway around the plateau's base, through trees and scrub brush, never coming within twenty feet of the sheer wall until—

"Another trail!" one of his point men called.

Blas hurried forward, silently beseeching Providence to make the new track veer away from the plateau, but he'd run out of luck.

"This one goes up," Chama said, pointing to a narrow track more fit for mountain goats than human beings. And bending closer, he remarked, "These scuff marks on the stone look fresh."

Blas felt hard knots forming in his stomach. Feigning interest, he asked Chama, "How can you tell that?"

"They haven't faded from exposure. See?"

More pointing, and Blas bobbed his head as if he understood. "Still, we don't know it was *O Médico* who climbed up there."

"We ought to check it," Chama said.

The little bastard had him there. Refusal made him seem both cowardly and foolish, to have chased his prey this far, then stop when he was this close to the kill.

"You're right," Blas said at last. "We climb."

BOLAN AND ENRIQUEZ had completed one-fourth of their trek around the plateau's brim before they stopped to rest and sip from their canteens.

"It's bigger than it seems from below," she said.

"A matter of perspective." Bolan watched a butterfly flitting erratically among the trees ahead. He had the shape and colors down, but finer details of the swiftly flapping wings eluded him.

"Better?" Enriquez asked.

"Better," he conceded. "We'll see how I do tonight."

"I'm worried," she confided.

That was understandable, but Bolan didn't want to let her dwell on it. "You've covered all your bases, Marta. Some of it comes down to nerve and luck. If we can find another way off this plateau, without passing Salvato's guards, we'll have it made."

He was exaggerating, trying to increase her confidence, but what he said was partly true. If they could find an exit from the flat-topped mountain that Salvato and his soldiers didn't know about, they would gain valuable time before pursuit— if there was any—could begin. That kind of lead could make the difference between escape and death.

"And if we don't?" she asked.

"You know the plan," Bolan replied. "We get around the sentries, one way or another."

"I don't want to harm them. They've been friends to us."

"That's why we're looking for another out," Bolan reminded her.

"I understand. But when the time comes—"

Bolan turned to face her squarely, interrupting. "When the time comes, if you have to choose between Weiss and Salvato's men, who will it be?"

"Nathan, of course."

"Hold that thought."

They walked in silence for a while, birds and small mammals scattering at their approach. Bolan wondered, briefly, what it had to be like to inhabit an isolated world less than one square mile in area. The birds could range at will across the jungle canopy below, but what of smaller creeping things? Did rodents and the like feel trapped on the plateau, or was it simply all they knew?

Bolan trusted his healing eyes enough to get him off the mesa, one way or another. Whether they could see him through the midnight forest was another question, one whose only answer lay in the attempt. He wouldn't know until he tried.

And he was bound to try this night.

Halfway around, they found a deep cut in the mesa's rim and moved in closer to survey a deep scar angling across the cliff face, terminating twenty feet or so above the forest floor. It would be passable with climbing gear, maybe bare-handed for a seasoned rock-climber, but Bolan didn't like their chances when it came to dragging Bones along on that descent. If no one dropped him, Bolan thought the odds were good that Weiss would pull his bearers free and send them plummeting to Earth.

"No good," he said, turning away.

By the time they reached the waterfall, their turn nearly completed, Bolan knew Salvato had been right. The only readily accessible approach was that which they had used to reach the summit, and the rebels had it covered now. Two men on watch around the clock, in rotating four-hour shifts.

"We'll have to think about the timing," Bolan told her. "If we can't sneak past the sentries unobserved, we need a good lead on the shift change, or we may as well forget it."

"I'm hoping we don't have to fight," she said.

"It doesn't hurt to hope," he granted. "But you'll need to bring a weapon, anyway."

"How long do you plan to stay here?"

Weiss studied Salvato's face as the guerrilla leader pondered a response. "I don't know, yet," Salvato said at last. "We're safe here, for the moment."

"I understand it's not your problem," Weiss pressed on, "but I have work to do, patients to see. And I can't do that work perched on a mountaintop."

"My men are patients, Doctor."

"And I've done my best for them. They're on the mend. If you can manage changing dressings once a day, they should be fine."

"This time," Salvato said. "But what about the next?"

"You know I don't turn anyone away."

"Doctor, it's only been two days since soldiers tried to kill you in your bed. Have you forgotten? Are you so determined to provide them with another opportunity?"

"I'm not forgetting," Weiss replied. "But if they drive me into hiding where I can't do any work, it means they've won."

"You're only beaten if they break your spirit. You already live in hiding," Salvato said. "One camp or another in the jungle, always running, never time to rest."

"That's medicine," Weiss said.

Salvato frowned. "Why are you here, Doctor? I don't mean on this mountain. In Brazil."

Weiss smiled. It was the same thing Bolan had asked, and Marta before him. How many times had he heard and deflected that question in the past two years? Fifty times? A hundred? More?

"You want the bottom line?" he asked.

"Is that a truthful answer? Yes, the bottom line, by all means."

"Right." Where to begin? "Sometimes you hear about people who want to make a difference, do some good?"

"I hear such things," Salvato said, "but rarely see them."

"Well, I was the very opposite in med school. Doctor's son, affluent childhood, yada-yada. All I really wanted was the path of least resistance to a nice, fat bank account. My father did all right. I wanted to do better. In a word, I wanted to be rich. I had my eye on plastic surgery."

Salvato seemed bemused. "What changed?"

"Turns out my family had *two* traditions. One was medicine, the other was a patriotic tour of duty in the military. I could probably have ducked it, but I figured, what the hell? It's good experience, a sop to conscience, and with that out of the way I could get down to the important stuff—like money, sports cars, flashy women."

"Capitalism."

"Whatever. It didn't quite work out."

"You saw something, perhaps," Salvato said.

"Or something saw through me. It turns out there were people really suffering. Not bummed because their parents didn't get them rhinoplasty or a tummy tuck for Christmas. People *dying* all around me, shot to hell or riddled with disease that made the plague look like a summer cold."

"A world you'd never seen before."

"And then some. It reminded me of all those Save the Children ads on television, but I couldn't change the channel. Pretty soon, I realized I didn't *want* to change it. I was helping people, and it felt better than washing a Jaguar, better than counting my money."

"You left the army, though."

"Another revelation," Weiss replied. "It turns out there were people sick and suffering at home. Who knew? I didn't need to go halfway around the world to work with people who'd been starved and brutalized. You find them in the ER, every day."

"In the United States."

"All over."

"Yes. And yet, you left your country. Here you are, in mine."

"We call that hubris. I got tired of butting heads with people in the States who didn't share my vision, so I asked myself one morning, 'Why not save the world, instead?'"

"Beginning in Brazil."

"Call that a fluke. I always wanted to see Rio during Carnivale, but when I got there, all I saw were street kids suffering from God knows what. Just call me Don Quixote. Any windmill in a pinch."

"I think you are a revolutionary, in your way," Salvato said.

"I wouldn't bet the farm on that."

"I have no farm to bet."

"Your life, then. I don't like the odds."

Salvato shrugged. "Perhaps I'm wrong, but you should think about remaining here. Take the last step toward truly changing one part of the world, at least."

"I'll think about it," Weiss replied.

And wondered if he really would.

IT WAS THEIR SECOND nightfall on the mesa and Bolan was already counting the hours until they departed—or tried to, at least—under cover of darkness. There was stew on the fire, something with mystery meat that Bolan didn't want to think about. In his experience, wild game was often easier to stomach when he didn't have full details of the menu.

Half an hour short of mealtime, Bones came looking for him. "I believe I've been neglecting you," he said by way of introduction.

"Not at all."

"You've been out scouting. I consider that a hopeful sign."

"It's not exactly like that song," Bolan said, "but I'm getting there."

Bones frowned. "Which song is that?"

"'I Can See Clearly Now.'"

"Uh-huh. But better, day by day?"

"I'd like to have a look, if you've got time before the jungle chili cook-off."

"Suits me," Bolan replied, and followed Weiss back to the operating tent-cum-hooch where all his gear was stored. En route, he caught a glimpse of Marta watching them before she turned back to her conversation with the Jivaros.

Inside the tent, Bolan followed directions and sat on the edge of Weiss's makeshift operating table. It had come to the mesa in pieces, and Weiss would soon be leaving it behind, along with all the rest of his equipment. Bolan wondered what that loss would do to Bones, then told himself that life meant more than tents and tables, stethoscopes and scalpels.

"Straight ahead now, for me."

Bolan stared past Weiss, while the doctor examined his eyes with an ophthalmoscope. The light was sharp, just short of painful, and it left him seeing spots, but they cleared quickly.

"I believe you're on the mend," Bones said.

"Seems like."

"How long will you be staying, then?"

The question took him by surprise.

"You think I'm wearing out my welcome, Bones?"

"I think our host can tolerate one gringo at a time, barely, on a good day. Two's pushing it. He's a suspicious man, verging on paranoid, and who can blame him?"

"That sounds like you think I ought to leave."

"Proving that I don't need to check your ears."

"Will you be staying?" Bolan asked.

"We've talked about it," Bones replied.

"And?"

"I've explained to him that I'm not much of a joiner."

"How'd he take it?"

"No objections at the moment."

"But when push comes to shove..."

"I'm thinking about it."

Bolan saw an opening and went for it. "One way to finesse the bail-out," he suggested, "would be for both of us to take off together."

"You're scheming again, Sarge. I smell it."

"I won't deny it," Bolan said, "but we can talk about that later, when we've put some ground between ourselves and the *Lost World*."

"I don't want to fight my way out," Bones informed him.

"Can't say I like the odds much, myself. Maybe Salvato won't object if we both have a word with him."

"I'll think about it. In the meantime, what say we go have some monkey stew, or whatever it is, and then try sleeping through a whole night, for a change?"

Bolan felt the opportunity slipping through his fingers, but a death grip at this point would only make it crumble into dust.

"Sounds good," he said. "Except the monkey part."

"Maybe it's lizard. I was guessing."

"Great. A choice."

"You've eaten worse. I know you have."

"No argument. But I was hoping those days were behind me."

"Silly boy."

They left the tent together and found Marta Enriquez waiting near the exit. Eyes darting from one man to the other, she appeared to hope that something had been settled in her absence. Bolan shook his head, a movement barely visible, and saw the disappointment on her face. She expected bad news, and Bolan had delivered.

"The meal is almost ready," she informed them, as if that had been her purpose for lingering outside the tent.

Bones thanked her, slipped an arm around her waist and started toward the fire. Trailing the couple, Bolan wondered whether Marta had the nerve to go through with their plan.

He would know soon enough.

And if she failed them, it would be too late.

CHAPTER SIXTEEN

"Is there nothing I can say to change your mind, Nathan?"

Enriquez was on the verge of tears. Sitting alone with Weiss, inside the old tent where he worked and slept, she'd begged him to consider packing out with Cooper to some safer place. And he had once again refused.

"You mean a great deal to me, Marta."

"Yes, but not enough that you desire to live."

"It's not about a death wish, Marta. If you don't know that by now—"

"I know," she interrupted him, "that everywhere you travel in Brazil, somebody wants to kill you. The police, the army, mercenaries—there's no end to it. Remaining here isn't a gesture of devotion. It is suicide."

His shoulders slumped a little as he said, "There's nothing for me in the States. If that's your goal, you're better off trying without me. I'd just slow you down."

She turned on him, angry. "You think I care about America? You think that's what I want? To see Times Square or Hollywood and Vine?"

"I don't know *what* you're after, Marta. All I ever hear from you, these days, is 'Get out! Run away!'"

"If running saves your life, then, yes, I'd rather have you safe than hiding in the jungle like a fugitive, hunted by killers."

"Safe where?" he asked.

"Safe anywhere. A hospital or clinic maybe. Try another country. Use another name."

"Become another man?"

"To live, why not?"

Weiss smiled at that. "We have an aphorism—an old saying—in the States," he said. "I've no idea who coined it. Anyway, it says 'I wouldn't want to join any club that would have me as a member.'"

"I don't understand, Nathan."

"I don't fit anywhere, Marta. I haven't fit for years. I'll never fit again, with all the red tape, HMO bureaucracy bullshit. I can't help people if I have to keep one eye closed and the other on the bottom line. Hospitals don't want me. I don't want them."

"So, why not start your own. A clinic, somewhere. Let Ricardo help you. Spending other people's money makes him feel as if he has a purpose."

"And would you be my assistant?" Weiss smiled fondly as he spoke.

"I would, of course, if you ask me."

"You're dreaming, Marta."

She felt the tears spill over, streaming down her cheeks. "Sometimes a dream comes true."

"That hasn't been my personal experience," Weiss said. "Listen, when we leave here in a few days—"

"Leave here?" It startled her. "You won't stay with Salvato?"

Weiss shook his head. "We've talked about it. Patients couldn't find me here, or if they did, the climb would put them off. Another day or two, we'll relocate."

"And start the chase all over," Enriquez said.

"I hope not."

"Hope's not good enough," she told him earnestly. "You have to make a choice, Nathan."

"It's already been made. We'll go down in a day or two, find someplace good to camp. Hope for the best."

"I won't be there," she told him. "I can't stay and watch you die." She slipped a hand into her pocket, palming the syringe in darkness.

"You should go with Cooper, Marta. Leave tomorrow morning, if he's good to go. Leave all of this behind and make a new start."

Biting back a sob, uncapping the syringe, she said, "I'd hope it wouldn't come to this."

"It always does, my love." She heard true sadness in his voice as Nathan said, "I'll miss you."

"Kiss me, then."

He turned to face her on the cot. Marta reached up to cup his face with one hand, covering his lips with hers. Her other hand raised the syringe and brought it into place. At the last instant, stroking fingers tangled in the doctor's hair and clutched him tightly. Marta's lips smothered his small cry of surprise as the needle slid home.

The sedative was powerful, fast-acting. Weiss started to go limp before he could reach back and pluck the hypodermic from his neck. His hand flailed impotently, brushed his cheek, then fell against her shoulder. Weiss slumped against her, lips sliding away from hers as he released a long, bone-weary sigh.

"Sleep well, my love," she told him as she eased him backward, draped across the cot.

Recapping the syringe, she slipped it back into her pocket. She might still have need of it, before her job was done. A glance at her wristwatch told her it was nearly time.

Now all she had to do was wait.

And pray for strength.

I'M NOT a goddamned mountain goat, Downey thought, but he clung with desperation to the rope that creased his palms, dreading the fall that certainly would leave him crippled if it didn't kill him outright.

They'd agreed, after some terse debate that used up their remaining daylight, that it would be folly to approach the mesa's summit on the one and only clear-cut trail. Whoever waited at the top, unless they were complete mental defectives, there would be guards posted, and it didn't take a military strategist to know one man could sweep them from the hillside with an automatic weapon.

Sergeant Aléman had found the alternate approach and sent a scout ahead with rope to make it doable. His soldiers seemed to take it as a routine exercise, while Downey—with cautious support from Jones—reminded Aléman that one slip on the climb could doom them all.

At which point, Aléman had smiled and said, "Don't slip."

The climb would've been challenging enough for Downey in broad daylight, but in darkness it was doubly difficult. His boots slipped on the dirt and shale, pelting the men below him with a steady drizzle of debris, while those above Downey unleashed the same on him. His eyes stung and his nose itched, but he didn't dare release the rope to wipe his face. There was no lifeline looped around his waist.

Release meant plunging to the rocks below.

Release meant death.

It seemed to take forever, inching upward with the rope searing his palms, boots scrabbling for purchase on the rough walls of the cut. Below him, he could hear Jones cursing as he climbed, a steady litany that could've been a prayer, until sharp ears picked out the words.

Downey had done some cursing of his own, during the first phase of the climb, before he realized that it was best to save his breath. They had a hundred feet or so to cover, and he guessed that he was halfway to the top, though peering up or down was not an option for him at the moment. It was hard enough, climbing the rock face like an insect, without doing anything to amplify his vertigo.

And when they reached the top, what then?

The plan was vague: seek out whoever lit the fire whose smoke they'd glimpsed by daylight, creep up on them quietly, and deal with them. Assuming it was Nathan Weiss and company, of course.

But if it wasn't...

Downey thought the odds were in their favor, but he could be wrong. God knew it wouldn't be the first time. Still, he reckoned anyone they found atop the mesa had to be some kind of enemy. Bandits, rebels, a tribe of hostile Indians. The cure for all of them came from the barrel of a gun.

There'd been no way to tell if he'd hit anyone last night, in the chaotic jungle ambush, but he meant to change all that the second time around. This time, they'd get it right.

Downey was startled when strong hands reached down to hoist him from the cut and dragged him well back from the lip of the plateau. He scraped his elbows, stomach, knees in transit, but the pain was insignificant.

He'd made it! He was still alive!

And that meant someone else was bound to die.

"YOU'RE LEAVING SOON, I think," Salvato said.

Bolan met the guerrilla leader's eyes, seeking some kind of hidden meaning there, but found no secrets. "As soon as possible," he said. "We have a deal."

"Indeed. But I've been wondering, since we spoke last, what will prevent you from betraying us?"

"Why should I?" Bolan asked. He felt thin ice beneath his feet.

"You are American," Salvato said. "Americans despise all revolutionaries but their long-dead ancestors. Also, your friend has chosen not to run away with you."

"That's right," Bolan replied. "He chose. If you were holding him against his will, that would be something else. As far as revolution goes, I don't care one way or another. I came down to make a pitch. It's been made and rejected."

"No hard feelings, then?"

"What are we, children? Nathan made his choice. He'll have to live with it."

"In my experience, Yankees are not so—what's the word? Mellow?"

"A long hike through the woods and nearly going blind will do that," Bolan said.

"You've had a revelation, then?" Salvato seemed amused.

"Let's say I've reevaluated what's important."

"And you leave your good friend, after coming all this way to find him?"

"Free will," Bolan replied. "That's how it goes sometimes."

"You seem sincere," Salvato said. "Why don't I trust you?"

"It's the Yankee thing. You're getting me confused with some old man in Washington."

"Perhaps. But you'll agree that things might be much simpler for me if you never made it back to the United States."

"That's one way you could look at it," the Executioner answered. "Of course, that way of thinking has some built-in problems."

"What would those be?" Salvato asked.

"First, I won't lay down without a fight. You can't be sure how many men you'll lose, or if you might be one of them. And when the smoke clears, you've got Nathan to consider."

"Dr. Weiss?"

"He's no great fan of treachery. Kill me without good reason, by his standards, and smart money says you've lost yourself a medic."

"Who's to say that he would even know?" Salvato asked, smiling.

"You're underestimating both of us. I had you pegged as more intelligent than that."

"You weren't mistaken, Senhor Cooper. I will leave you to the jungle, if you wish."

"A fighting chance. That's all I ask."

"And you shall have it. One last question, please, before we sleep."

"What's that?"

"Would you have tried to take *O Médico* by force, if not for me and my soldiers?"

Bolan pretended to consider it, then shrugged. "I guess we'll never know."

"Sleep well, Yankee. You have a long journey ahead of you."

Alone at last, Bolan squinted to read his watch. It was a quarter past eleven, give or take, and Marta should have done the deed by now. The tent she shared with Bones was dark and silent. Bolan couldn't see the others—Abraham, Adam and Eve—but he assumed they would be present and accounted for when they were needed.

If they weren't, the plan would fall apart before they took their first step out of camp. They needed extra hands to get Weiss down the hillside trail, while Bolan covered them, and then to bear him on his way.

He settled back to wait for midnight, feigning sleep. Although his eyes were closed, his mind remained alert. The scenes played out behind his eyelids reeked of blood and gunsmoke, echoing with shots and screams. There were no happy endings, only different ugly ways to die.

Bolan didn't deceive himself. He wasn't absolutely combat-ready yet, but it would have to do. The good news was that as the last man down the mountain, he would have a relatively easy job, guarding the rear. If a pursuit began, there'd be no guessing as to who among Salvato's men were friendly or hostile.

In that case, Bolan's task would be to kill them all.

BLAS FELT the others watching him as he began to climb. His hesitancy when it came to scaling the plateau had been observed by several of the men, all younger, and Blas now felt that he had to prove himself. Accordingly, he led the way, with Chama at his heels, the others straggling out behind them on the narrow mountain trail.

If there were enemies atop the mesa, Blas knew there'd be sentries covering the steep approach. He didn't want a firefight with them, nothing that would rouse the camp—if there was anyone to rouse. To that end, Blas had taken a suppressor from his pack, where it lay long unused, and threaded it onto the muzzle of his Imbel pistol. It wasn't a classic movie "silencer" that could reduce gunshots to breathless whispers, but it should muffle the shots enough that sleeping men some distance from the scene would not awake.

Blas hoped so, anyway.

If they were ambushed on the trail, he calculated it would be disastrous. Those who weren't cut down by bullets would most likely plummet from the cliff while trying to retreat. Given his fear of heights, Blas hoped the enemy who fired on him had decent aim. Make it a killing shot, instead of one that merely wounded him and spun him screaming into the abyss.

Enough!

Blas recognized the negativity inside himself as a handicap, and potentially a fatal one. Distracted by the morbid thoughts, he felt a stone slip underneath his boot and clutched a root protruding from the mountainside, to keep himself from tumbling backward down the trail.

Moving on as if nothing had happened, Blas heard Chama

breathing heavily behind him, frightened. It made Blas feel better, to know his fear wasn't unique, and he pressed on to prove himself a leader. Prove himself a man.

How long until they reached the summit?

From down below, he'd estimated that the cliff measured one hundred feet, approximately. Once he started climbing, though, Blas lost his sense of time and distance, concentrating on the goat path just in front of him, frightened to lift his head and gauge the distance that remained. If he slipped and fell...

It's not like looking down, Blas told himself.

Slowing his steps until he barely moved, Blas raised his eyes. He was surprised to find that he had covered more than half the distance from ground level to the mesa's brim. No more than forty feet remained, the last bit passing in between two boulders where it would be natural for guards to lie in wait.

Taking another risk, Blas drew his muzzle-heavy pistol from its holster, thumbing off the safety. If he slipped now, he would only have one hand with which to catch himself, double the risk unless he dropped the gun and left himself defenseless.

No one's falling.

Step by aching step, Blas climbed the trail. He felt the others watching him, eyes boring into him like augers. Every muscle-straining stride brought him another two or three feet closer to his destination and the threat of weapons blazing in his face at point-blank range.

Maybe the guards would be asleep.

Maybe there were no guards.

Blas almost sobbed out loud when it began to rain. The trail would turn to mud in moments, might become impassable, his men slip-sliding into darkness even as he reached the summit, leaving him alone.

Enraged and frightened all at once, Blas ran the last few yards, knees pumping, lips drawn back into a snarl. Fat raindrops stung his face and scalp, but he was strong enough to keep his eyes open as he approached the rugged boulders.

Any second now...

Blas charged into the stony gap and found one man rising to meet him, grappling with a weapon caught beneath his rainproof poncho. He fired once into the startled sentry's face, once more into his chest as the man crumpled backward, going down.

There was another, rising on his left, no poncho but a long coat flaring to reveal an automatic rifle. Blas fired once, twice, three times, muzzle-flashes etching shadows on the rocky slabs before his second target fell.

He stood and swept the night for others, but there were no more. Not here. Two guards told him there was a camp nearby, but it wasn't immediately visible. No firelight beckoned from the darkness, and Blas was surprised to find the mesa's top nearly as thickly wooded as the forest down below.

How would he find *O Médico?*

The others massed behind him, pressing close. Blas turned to them, voice rasping as he ordered, "Find the trail. There *has* to be a trail!"

PRIMO SALVATO COULDN'T sleep. That was unusual, almost unprecedented. He was known among his men for an ability to sleep in almost any circumstances, whether on the eve of battle, under pouring rain or huddled in the branches of a tree.

What kept him from his rest this night?

Salvato wasn't psychic, nor did he know anyone who was. He put no stock in premonitions, yet a sense of dark foreboding had oppressed him since he'd spread his bedroll on the ground that night.

Something was wrong.

But what?

He'd felt the tension when he spoke to Cooper, and had nearly checked on Weiss, but he'd seen Enriquez join the doctor in his tent a short time earlier. Salvato didn't want to see them on the cot together, doing whatever they did in privacy. It would remind him that he found the woman attractive, that she stirred him in a way no woman had for years—and that she wasn't his.

Perhaps, if Weiss was gone…

Salvato pushed that thought away, unfinished. Weiss was more important to his men and to the movement than whatever feelings he concocted for a woman whom he barely knew. The doctor could protect Salvato's men against disease and mend their wounds, while the woman was a mere diversion, someone who could warm his lonely bed.

Get up and check on them, a small voice in Salvato's head insisted. Do it now.

He stalled another moment, then threw back his blanket as the first drops of another rain shower came pelting down. Rising, Salvato wondered what it had to be like to live in Mexico, or anyplace where desert baked beneath relentless sunlight every day. Someplace where flesh and clothing didn't rot from dampness and where weapons didn't sprout rust overnight.

Salvato took his rifle with him, stepping gingerly around his soldiers sleeping under ponchos, some of them in one- and two-man tents. He wondered if they dreamed, what thoughts of home and family relieved the constant danger of their waking hours.

The rain helped him focus, its tempo increasing until Salvato's wiry hair was plastered to his scalp. He held the Imbel autorifle close against his side to shield it, but the rain was everywhere. The piece would need another oiling soon, to keep the rust at bay.

What would he find inside the doctor's tent? There had been time enough for Weiss and Enriquez to be done with any sweaty grappling, and Salvato hoped that he would find them both asleep. It was enough for him to stand in darkness and to hear them breathing, satisfied that his nocturnal fears were groundless.

And when he was finished with *O Médico,* perhaps he'd check on Cooper.

That one troubled him, the way he shrugged off threats and intimations of disaster. Even with his eyesight compromised, Cooper displayed more courage than most of Salvato's guerrillas. A part of him wished that the man would join them, help invest the others with his fighting spirit, but Salvato couldn't overcome his personal suspicion where the Yankee was concerned.

Better to kill him and be done with it, he thought, but if he chose that option, then it had to be done without the doctor's knowledge. They were friends, or had been once, and Weiss might take it badly if he learned of Cooper's death.

Then let him disappear.

It was an easy thing to say, but something told Salvato it wouldn't be simple to accomplish. Cooper wouldn't easily be taken by surprise. He would defend himself, and that meant mortal danger for Salvato's men.

Perhaps for Salvato himself.

He would rethink the problem while he checked on Weiss, and maybe hope that Cooper meant what he had said about leaving without his friend. That would solve everything, and if the jungle claimed him after he was well away from camp, so much the better.

Standing in the rainy dark outside the doctor's tent, Salvato hesitated, one hand outstretched toward the canvas flap. He listened, leaning closer, hearing no sounds from within.

Asleep. That's good.

After another moment's delay, Salvato pushed back the tent flap, moving as slowly and quietly as possible. He stepped inside, maneuvering until he had a clear view of the doctor's cot.

There was something…

A sudden flash of understanding struck Salvato and he hurried forward, ripping at the neatly folded blankets.

Weiss and Marta.

Both of them were gone.

BOLAN WAS WAITING in the shadows, armed and packed, when the others crossed a shaft of errant moonlight. Abraham and Adam carried Bones between them, Marta Enriquez in the lead, while Eve brought up the rear. He hadn't questioned their decision to exclude Ricardo from the plan, assuming that they knew the young man well enough to judge how he'd react, while Bolan hadn't shared ten words with him since joining Weiss's company.

He stepped out of the darkness, hearing Marta catch her breath, though she'd been ready for him, knowing where he'd be. Around them, all was quiet in the sleeping camp. No sounds of movement, no one talking in his sleep.

By moonlight, Marta's face was well defined, the clearest image Bolan's eyes had registered in days. I'm almost there, he thought, and hoped that **his re**covery would be adequate if it came down to fighting in the dark.

Adam and Abraham had rifles slung across their shoulders, fierce determination written on their faces. Bolan guessed that they would go the limit for the man who'd given them a second chance at life.

He only hoped this wouldn't be the end, for all of them.

"We have three hours and forty minutes till the next shift change," he whispered. Bolan didn't have to check his watch. The numbers ticking backward in his mind were loud and clear.

"We're ready," Enriquez told him. "Lead the way."

He led them on a circuit of the camp's perimeter, staying inside the tree line, just in case one of Salvato's men woke up and chanced to look around. It added time to their retreat, but cutting through the middle of the camp would be a foolish risk, the chance of being accidentally discovered multiplied by six. One sound, one rebel stirring in the darkness to relieve himself, and they would be cut off from any hope of a clandestine exit from the mesa.

What about the sentries?

It was raining steadily now and Bolan counted on it to conceal the sound of their approaching footsteps. If the guards were dutiful and wide awake, he'd find a way to deal with them. The Ka-Bar was one silent weapon, and his bare hands were another.

If he had to fight the guards, there was no point in leaving them alive. Death silenced them forever, buying Bolan's team three hours and change, whereas a man rendered unconscious, even bound and gagged, might wake and free himself to warn the camp before they even had a chance to reach the forest floor.

Death it would be, then, if he had to fight.

For them, or for himself.

Their trek to reach the mesa's rim seemed longer in the dark, when they were taking care to make no sound. Bolan had covered the same distance with Marta in a fraction of the time, just one night earlier, when they had searched in vain for other exit routes from the plateau. This night, each footstep had to be precisely placed, each movement calculated not only for progress, but for safety's sake.

When they were halfway to their destination, Bolan hesitated, froze in midstride, one hand raised as a signal to the others. There'd been a popping sound somewhere ahead—or was it only his imagination?

No.

He heard the sound again, repeated swiftly. Even lacking intimate familiarity with every life form native to Brazil, Bolan was confident the sound had been manmade.

In fact, it sounded like...

Instinctively he closed his eyes, leaned forward, listening. The sound, so like a silenced firearm's rapid-fire report, wasn't repeated. In its place, he thought he heard whispered voices and the sound of scuffling feet.

Another heartbeat told him that the sounds didn't originate from his imagination. Footsteps advancing toward the camp told Bolan there were more than two men on the move, and so they couldn't be Salvato's watchmen.

"We've got company," he told the others in a hiss. "Fall back."

At least until the new arrivals passed, their great escape was temporarily on hold. But when the way was clear again—

From camp, a voice was raised, shouting in Portuguese.

"Salvato!" Enriquez said. "He knows we're gone."

Any pursuit the rebel leader may have planned was stalled, however, when a sudden blaze of automatic weapons fire lit up the camp.

CHAPTER SEVENTEEN

The gunfire startled Downey, literally made him jump as if he'd stepped on a live wire. Clutching his CAR-15 in a death grip, he nearly fired an accidental round himself.

"Who's shooting, goddamn it?" he whispered to Sergeant Alemán. "What the hell's going on?"

Stone-faced, the sergeant said, "To answer that question, we must advance."

"No shit? What are we waiting for?"

Jones glared at Downey for a moment, but he made no comment as the sergeant signaled their advance. The other Brazilians took it in stride, though none seemed overanxious to engage a force of unknown size, blazing away at midnight with a battery of automatic weapons.

Angry shouting reached his ears now, telling Downey that they hadn't walked in on the middle of some late-night target practice session. This was combat, pure and simple, but he didn't have the first clue as to who was fighting whom.

Just give me Weiss, he thought, addressing his entreaty to

no gods in particular. Maybe a little piece of Cooper on the side.

The carbine suddenly felt heavy in his hands, as if its weight increased with every step he took in the direction of the battleground. An image from their last skirmish appeared in Downey's mind and he turned to face Jones.

"You go in front of me," he snapped.

"What do you mean?"

"Just do it!" Downey jabbed the carbine's muzzle at his underling for emphasis.

"Okay! Jesus!"

"Pray on your own time," Downey said. "Let's go!"

He followed Jones and Alemán's commandos toward a point on the plateau where gunshots echoed and a swarm of muzzle-flashes lit the night like giant fireflies. Nearing the scene, Downey assessed the situation and decided that there had to be forty guns or more spraying the night with autofire.

Where was Weiss, in the midst of all that?

Where was Cooper?

Downey didn't know, and there was only one way to find out. They couldn't linger on the sidelines, waiting for the faceless belligerents to kill one another off. It might not happen, and the victors might still have sufficient energy and ammunition left to wipe out Downey's team.

The same risk came with plunging into the melee, but if they struck from the advantage of surprise and played their cards right, maybe they could find the doctor, pick him off, and then get the hell out of Dodge with their skins still intact.

Maybe.

Advancing through the trees, they formed a kind of ragged skirmish line. No firing yet, until they had a chance to sort out what was happening and what the two opposing sides were fighting for. For just a second, Downey wondered whether some of these same shooters were the ones he'd faced in the previous night's ambush, but he couldn't figure why they would be here.

Unless the mesa was their destination all along.

Had Weiss been moving toward this destination from the first day of their search? And if so, who else would've tracked him here to kill him?

Downey winced and ducked as a stray bullet whispered overhead. The busy shooters hadn't seen him yet, he was convinced of that, but some of them were firing indiscriminately, spraying trees and shadows, any targets they could see.

Almost there.

Downey's legs ached from jogging in a crouch; his shoulders, tight and hunched, burned as if the muscles were on fire. He knew his hands would start to cramp soon, if he didn't ease his stranglehold on the carbine, but Downey focused on the muzzle-flashes and on Jones walking in front of him.

There'd be no treachery this time, if he could help it. Jones would stay in front of him, no matter what, and if that got the big oaf killed, Downey would shed no tears. One back-stabber was plenty, and he didn't plan to give another one the chance Sutter had blown.

Another bullet whined past, and another. Sergeant Alemán and his commandos were all crouching now, advancing at a near-crawl, just when Downey wanted them to hurry. He suppressed an urge to break formation, reminding himself that the Brazilians were trained jungle fighters, untainted by concern for personal rewards that might destroy him if he wasn't careful.

Slow and steady, now.

But part of Downey's mind answered, To hell with that!

When Alémán signaled a halt, they were still forty yards from the main scene of action. Downey squinted through the darkness lit sporadically by gunfire, trying to mark targets, pick out landmarks. There were tents, he saw, and figures moving in the shadows, but he couldn't make out uniforms or weapons, much less faces. How could he find Weiss amid such chaos?

Alémán was moving down the line, whispering orders. "Choose your targets," he instructed. "When I give the signal, fire short bursts and make them count."

Downey wriggled behind a tree and braced his carbine, held it steady as he waited. Targets flitted in and out of view, making conscious selection an impossibility. He needed to be closer, but they had to clear a path first, shave the odds.

From somewhere to his right the sergeant shouted, "Fire!" The line erupted, adding still more smoky thunder to the night.

Alone within the maelstrom, Downey smiled and swept the field with automatic fire.

PRIMO SALVATO LAY beside the dead fire pit, searching for targets, firing when a shadow he could not identify showed signs of stealthy life. He thought he'd dropped two men so far, and prayed they weren't his own.

But who were they?

He'd just begun to rouse the camp, alert his men to O

Médico's disappearance, when a band of unknown gunmen suddenly appeared and opened fire. They came from the northeast, the same direction as the trail that granted access to the mesa, where his guards were posted.

Squinting over rifle sights, Salvato hoped the guards were dead. If not, it meant they had betrayed them and he'd have to kill them personally. It was preferable for them to be loyal and die like men, rather than to distract him when nocturnal enemies required Salvato's full attention.

There! Another one!

He aimed, fired and experienced a moment of elation as the target crumpled. Dead? Wounded? Salvato didn't know, but he hoped for the best.

And as he fought, he wondered where *O Médico* had gone, taking the others with him. The escape was clearly planned in advance. Before he sounded the alarm, Salvato had gone looking for Matt Cooper, the two Jivaros and the Tehuelche known as Abraham. All gone. The only one of Weiss's party still in camp was the effete one, called Ricardo, and he seemed sincerely startled by the news that he'd been left alone.

Salvato would've questioned the Tehuelche tribesmen who remained behind, but there had been no time. The shooting started as he called his men from tents and bedrolls, an alert to danger, and there'd been no letup since.

Who were these nightcrawlers who'd crept into his camp with murderous intent?

They might be army, but Salvato thought he would've rated helicopters and a somewhat larger strike force. Mercenaries were another possibility, but he could only guess who'd hired them, how they'd tracked him to the mesa.

If, in fact, they had.

Salvato thought of Weiss again, and he suddenly knew that the gunmen were there for *O Médico*. Salvato's men were incidental targets, pure victims of circumstance, but they would still die if they couldn't fight their way out of the trap.

Salvato wished he had more men, better weapons, explosives—whatever it might take to swing the balance in his favor—but he knew that they'd have to make do with what was available. His men had to make up in courage and spirit what they lacked in numbers and resources.

And he had to lead by example.

The battlefield was dark, chaotic, growing more disorganized and fluid with each passing moment. If he meant to save his soldiers and himself, Salvato knew that he had to act immediately, forcefully, to seize control and drive the raiders back. When they were fighting at the cliff's edge, his opponents could decide if they preferred to leap or die at Salvato's guns.

But first he had to rally his disoriented troops for a concerted defense of the camp. It wouldn't do, simply hiding and firing at random shadows while the raiders advanced. If they were overrun, fragmented, then the situation would be hopeless.

Salvato fought a sudden atavistic urge to flee and leave his men to sort the bloody business out themselves. Blind panic gripped him for a moment, but he quickly overcame it. When he first took up the rebel cause, he'd pledged himself to fight until he died or tasted victory. This night wouldn't bring final triumph, but it could provide another chance for him to prove himself.

Rising, Salvato called to his men, "To me! Fall in! Attack!" He punctuated the commands with short bursts from his autorifle, standing now, as he advanced to meet the enemy.

THE LAST THING Bolan wanted was to find himself embroiled in a firefight between Salvato's men and others he couldn't identify. The goal had been escape, not confrontation, and his team wasn't equipped or ready for a battle to the death.

As if they had a choice.

The fight had come to them, and while he still hoped to avoid the worst of it, escape hadn't been vastly complicated by the raiders who had come from nowhere to assault Salvato's camp.

Scratch that. They'd clearly come from somewhere, gaining access to the mesa by the same route Bolan and the others had employed one short day earlier. He thought again about the firefight overhead the previous night, and Bolan knew that it defied coincidence for gunmen to appear this way, completely unrelated to the former skirmish.

And if they'd ascended on the one good trail, it stood to reason that the strike force might've left its own guards to protect its flank, while making sure none of the enemy escaped. More danger, then, for Bolan's crew, assuming they could get past the invaders to attempt the steep descent.

Enriquez, crouching beside him in the darkness, asked, "What can we do?"

"Stick to the plan," he answered, speaking barely loud enough for her to hear his words over the battle din, "unless you want to try the other way we found."

She glanced at Bones, reclining on the sod where Abraham and Adam had deposited his silent form. "We can't take Nathan down that way."

"Agreed. So, it's the trail or nothing."

"We should hurry," the woman urged.

"They're busy," Bolan answered with a short nod toward Salvato's camp. "There may be new guards on the exit, though. We'll have to watch our step."

"I understand."

He hoped so, for a plan was hatching in his mind that would require firm understanding. "Take the others on ahead," he told Enriquez, "but stop short of the rim. Watch out for shooters on the way."

Her eyes widened with fright and she clutched his arm. "Where are you going?"

"Back to stir the pot a little," Bolan said. "I want to keep them occupied while we slip out the back way."

"But they're fighting now!"

"There's fighting," he informed her, "and there's fighting. I just want to turn the heat up. Bring it to a boil."

"Your eyes—"

"Are fine," he told her. Thinking, *Good enough for this, at least.*

For what he had in mind, discrimination was superfluous. It didn't matter which targets he chose, since none were allies in his flight with Weiss from the plateau. As long as he could agitate both sides in roughly equal measure, without getting tagged himself, his goal would be achieved.

The Executioner wasn't looking for a clean sweep this time. For all he cared, Salvato and his enemies could fight around the clock. In fact, it would be better for his purpose if they did. To heat the battle up without annihilating either side required as much finesse as taking out specific targets in the dark.

Enriquez was stalling, trying to change Bolan's mind. "I don't think—"

"Good. *Don't* think," he said. "Just *move,* and watch out for whatever men the new crowd left behind to block the way."

"But—"

"Just do it! If you plan on getting Nathan out of here alive, stop wasting time!"

She blinked at him, surprised and angry. Anger was all right, he thought, if it prevented Marta from delaying action with a roster of excuses. When she turned to Abraham and Adam, speaking in their native dialect, Bolan felt secure enough to turn away and leave them, backtracking toward camp and the uproar of battle.

Was there a blurry aspect to the muzzle-flashes guiding him along? The warrior didn't notice, didn't care. His eyes had healed sufficiently for him to find the action and to join it. At the moment, that was all he cared about. The only thing that mattered.

Buying time, for Marta and the others to advance with Bones. And when he joined them, when they fought through any opposition left behind to guard the trail, he hoped the soldiers fighting for Salvato's camp would be preoccupied with life and death, unable to break free and seek another fight elsewhere.

If anything went wrong, then Marta and the rest were on their own. In that case, Bolan wouldn't know what happened to them, and their fate would be in someone else's hands.

A few more strides brought Bolan to the killing ground. He scanned it for an opening, found one, and waded in.

A CLUMSY ACCIDENT SAVED Adriano Blas from sudden death. Leading the charge against the camp where he expected to surprise *O Médico,* he stumbled, lurching forward, and a bullet grazed his scalp.

The pain was shattering. Blood streamed across his face and filled one eye, half blinding Blas. A ragged sob escaped his lips, but even in that moment, Blas knew what a lucky man he was.

If he had stayed upright, not falling, then the slug that split his scalp would've exploded through his face and dropped Blas in his tracks, stone-dead. Through waves of searing pain that made his ears ring, Blas decided that the hand of Providence had tripped him, sparing him to punish Weiss and everyone who scorned the Fist of Freedom.

Rising to all fours, blood dripping from his scalp and face, Blas shouted hoarse encouragement to his guerrillas. Some of them ran past him, gaping at the spectacle he made, but Blas ignored their horrified expressions and exhorted them to crush the enemy.

He found his rifle, wiping crimson fingers on his pants to dry them before he retrieved the weapon. Blas raked a sleeve across his bloody eye socket and found that he could see again, albeit rather poorly. Dizziness surprised him as he rose, but it passed swiftly, yielding to a headache that surpassed any in his experience.

No matter.

Pain was simply one more obstacle to be defeated, nothing that he couldn't handle in pursuit of victory. Blas staggered forward, nearly all his men in front of him now, as he advanced into the battle ground.

There'd been a camp here, once, but it had turned into a killing ground. Most of the tents were flattened or hanging lopsided where bullets had ripped them. Men ran here and there, firing at shadows, sometimes running into other men and grappling hand-to-hand. Clubbed rifles, slashing blades and flailing fists marked points where combat was reduced to its most primitive.

Blas loved it all.

The veil of blood that covered half his face gave him a savage aspect, like some mad berserker run amok. Blas knew he had to seem barely human, and his feeling matched the mask he wore. Civilization sloughed away and left him one of Nature's snarling predators—but one who acted with deliberation and a conscious plan.

He had to locate Weiss. Once that was done, he could devote himself to punishing the men who had concealed *O Médico* and tried to murder Blas himself.

Such insolence would cost them dearly.

Fifteen feet in front of Blas, an enemy appeared, armed with a submachine gun. At his first glimpse of the bloody specter shambling toward him, he let out a high-pitched cry and raised his weapon.

Too late.

Blas triggered a burst into the stranger's chest and dropped him thrashing where he stood. Another target scuttled out of the darkness, firing from the hip, and Blas could hear the bullets whispering around him—left, right, overhead.

Another sign from Providence!

Returning fire, Blas stitched his adversary with a ragged line of holes from hip to shoulder, spinning him around, already dead or dying by the time his face struck Mother Earth.

This was more like it, spilling someone else's blood. Blas reveled in it, might have kept on firing at the two men he'd already shot, but others needed his attention. There was still resistance in the camp, still men with guns who challenged his authority and fought to keep him from *O Médico*.

It was the last mistake they'd ever make, on this, their last night living. Blas would teach his enemies the error of their ways, but they wouldn't survive to profit from the lesson.

Grinning fiercely through his mask of blood, clutching the Imbel autorifle to his chest, Blas marched into the bright heart of the killing ground as if he were Death's messenger, and thus immune to harm.

MARTA WAS TERRIFIED and trying not to show it. Clinging to the rifle she had found days earlier, in the Tehuelche village, kept her hands from trembling, but no weapon could forestall the tremors that she felt inside. Adam and Abraham were likewise armed, but neither had been trained in use of firearms and their burden left them nearly helpless. Eve carried a wicked-looking knife, but Marta doubted whether any of their enemies would let her close enough to use it.

She understood Cooper's plan, but it still felt like abandonment when he'd turned back and left them with instructions to proceed as planned. In Marta's mind, the plan had ceased to matter when invaders suddenly appeared and rushed the camp. Whether they'd left guards on the exit trail or not, the raid changed everything.

Marta was torn between an urge to stay and fight, and an impulse to flee blindly into the darkness, running aimlessly until she reached another cliff and found that there was nowhere left to go.

What, then?

Perhaps a leap of faith.

She thought about Salvato's men, who might've been pursuing them that very moment if the raiders hadn't struck precisely when they did. There'd be more wounded now, and no one there to treat them since she'd drugged Nathan and carried him away.

To what? An unexpected death at strangers' hands?

Marta led her companions slowly toward the mesa's rim, where boulders marked their access to the steep descending trail. Aside from fear, a sense of guilt oppressed her, telling Marta that she'd be responsible for anything that happened now to Nathan, in his helpless state, and also to their three companions.

Drugging Weiss and stealing him away had been her plan from the beginning. Cooper and the others had agreed to it, for Nathan's sake, but Marta bore the ultimate responsibility if anything went wrong.

And now it had.

Her pace had slowed to a crawl when Abraham hissed at her, startling Marta from her morbid reverie with a request for greater speed. She nodded, muttered an apology, and moved more quickly through the darkness toward their destination.

Each step brought her closer to the thing she feared: a challenge from the shadows, gunfire, Nathan dying in her arms before a bullet finally snuffed out her damning consciousness of failure.

Marta double-checked the safety on her rifle, as Cooper had shown her, making sure that the weapon was ready to fire. She had no expertise—had never previously fired a shot, in fact—but she would fight for Nathan and her friends.

Not fight, she thought, with Cooper's parting words in mind. Observe.

He had instructed her to stop short of the cliff's edge, waiting for him to return—but what if she had seen the last of him? Implicit in his order was the possibility that Cooper might be killed or wounded while he carried out his desperate plan.

In which case, full responsibility for Nathan and the others would rest squarely on her shoulders, whether she was capable of saving them or not.

She would be ready if that happened, albeit within the limits of her skill and courage. Frightened as she was, Marta would fight and kill for Nathan and her friends. She would give up her life, if need be, for their sake.

With that resolve in mind, she found a measure of her fear replaced by sadness that their lives had come to this. Her dream had been to spend a lifetime helping Nathan heal those who would otherwise have no one, spreading hope in a milieu where it was often difficult to find.

That dream was shattered now, but there was still a chance they could survive as fugitives, perhaps escape to lead a modest life somewhere beyond the reach of enemies. Marta had no idea where such a sanctuary might exist, but she would gladly spend her last days searching for it, if she could have Nathan at her side.

First, though, she had to salvage something from her bungled plan. She had to rescue Nathan and the others if she could, escape the mountaintop that had become a killing ground and find them all a temporary place to hide.

Ahead she heard male voices murmuring, their conversation punctuated by metallic sounds of weapons being primed and checked. Raising a hand to stop the others, Marta whispered warnings to them, then crept slowly forward by herself, to meet the enemy.

STIRRING THE POT required an expert's touch and timing. First, Bolan had to observe the murky battleground and roughly plot the distribution of opposing sides, no minor challenge in the dead of night, with fluid battle lines.

The good news was that Bolan didn't favor either side to win the firefight, meaning he was free to fire on anyone and everyone in camp—but carefully. His goal wasn't to kill them off, or to give either side an edge by whittling down the other's numbers.

Quite the opposite, in fact.

He had an angry hornet's nest in front of him, but Bolan wanted an inferno that would keep the various combatants fully occupied while he escaped with Bones, Marta and the others. Every shot the clashing bands of hostiles fired would further numb their ears and spike their rage, so that a few stray shots along the mesa's brim should go unnoticed.

So he hoped, at least.

And failing that, some of the attackers sought to peel off from the main event and help their sentries on the cliff, they'd have to deal with opposition at the campsite first. Whichever way the action went, Bolan would benefit from an intensive killing frenzy in the camp.

Beginning now.

Bolan had found his place—the first one, anyway—and marked his targets by their muzzle-flashes. Peering through the Steyr's optic sight, eyes smarting from the cordite haze but clear enough for this work, Bolan found a point just short of where his targets lay in darkness, firing at an east-west angle through the camp.

Who were they?

Bolan neither knew nor cared.

He fired a short burst toward his faceless targets, 5.56 mm bullets kicking up a storm of turf and shredded ferns a foot or so in front of their position. Ricochets might sting them, but he wasn't firing for lethal effect.

The muzzle-flashes faltered, then redoubled their intensity, while Bolan shifted to a new location, slinking through the shadows. Bullets flew around him, leaving the Executioner to duck and weave on instinct, dodging unseen messengers of death. It only took one hit to stop him cold and maybe doom the others, but he had to take that chance.

Another field of fire, another clutch of targets. These were firing north-south through the killing ground, dueling with shooters on the other side. Bolan lined up his shot, aiming above the snipers' heads this time. He squinted through the Steyr's sight at darkness, stroked the trigger lightly and held steady as a half dozen rounds flew downrange.

Move again, hugging shadows and wearing the night as a cloak. Bolan sought his next vantage point, picked out a deadfall on the camp's southeastern perimeter, and was halfway there when a dark form rose in front of him, slashing at his face with a rifle butt.

He turned and hunched, took a glancing blow on his left shoulder as he drove the Steyr's muzzle deep into his adversary's gut. The trigger squeeze was reflex, three rounds ripping through the young guerrilla's body at waist level, spewing gouts of crimson from behind.

The dying man collapsed backward, his weapon spilling loose from spastic hands. Bolan hurdled the corpse and reached his goal, tumbling behind a bulwark formed when two large trees went down together, branched intertwined, roots snaking through the air like clutching tentacles.

He waited for a moment, to find out if anyone had glimpsed the kill and tracked him, but the only rounds incoming felt like strays, too high and wide to mark a serious attempt on Bolan's life. He wriggled for position, found it and began to scan the camp again in search of targets.

There.

He spied a trio of guerrillas, scurrying from one position to another while the firefight raged around them. Bolan raised the Steyr to his shoulder, led the point man by a yard and fired a short burst. He couldn't see or hear the bullets' impact, but the foremost runner stumbled with a cry of pain and went down sprawling, clutching his right leg.

The other two raced to their leader, firing from the hip in all directions while they stooped to pick him up, then loped back toward their starting point. Fear and frustration kept them firing even after they were under cover, when they should've been binding their comrade's wounds.

Perfect.

A few more well-placed rounds and Bolan could fall back to rendezvous with Marta and the others. Hoping they were still alive and playing safe, he rose again and sought another target in the night.

CHAPTER EIGHTEEN

Primo Salvato felt that he was losing ground. He couldn't prove it by surveying the chaotic battleground, all shadow-shapes in hectic motion, but he had a sense of forces shifting into an alliance that would crush him and his soldiers if he didn't take decisive action soon.

The problem was, he had no clue where he should start.

His first attempt to rally a defense had nearly cost his life. Shouting and firing from the hip, he'd found himself alone in no-man's land while bullets whined around him from all sides. His swift retreat had been humiliating, but at least it saved his skin.

Surprise had thrown Salvato off his game, although he was embarrassed to admit it. First, there'd been the shock of finding Dr. Weiss and his companions missing from their beds. Then, as Salvato roused the camp to organize a search, his unknown enemies had swept in from the east with blazing guns, trying to kill Salvato and his men. The one-two punch had staggered him, and only now was he recovering enough to mount an organized defense.

Salvato hoped that it wasn't already too late.

This time, instead of shouting orders to his men—which would be overheard by enemies and pin a target on his chest— Salvato started creeping through the camp, seeking survivors who would follow him to rout their foes.

The first comrade he found was dead, drilled through the left eye by an expert marksman or a stray round fired in panic. Moving on, Salvato found his first survivor several yards beyond the corpse—and nearly took a bullet of his own, when young Luis Echeverria thrust an Imbel submachine gun in his face.

Salvato managed to identify himself and calm his fellow rebel, moving close and whispering his plan for an assault that would reclaim the camp and driver their enemies over the cliff, a hundred yards away. Echeverria agreed, bobbing his head, and crawled after Salvato as his leader wormed into the darkness, seeking others fit to fight.

Salvato thought the search would drive him mad. Instead of charging headlong toward his enemies, he crept through mud and whispered to the comrades he discovered on his circuit of the camp. He was rewarded twice by finding wounded enemies along the way, wielding his knife with savage fervor to dispatch them, but the finds only confused Salvato further.

One of those whose throat he slit appeared to be a military regular, complete with shoulder patches on his tiger-stripe fatigues that marked him as a member of Brazil's hated security police. The other wore a kind of patchwork uniform no soldier on the government payroll would ever don, even as a disguise.

The mix baffled Salvato. There were several guerrilla "armies" in the Mato Grosso region that competed for supplies and recognition in the media, and while that competition sometimes led to violence, none of the rebel bands Salvato knew of would collaborate with state authorities to crush a rival.

Would they?

But if that bizarre scenario was true, who hated him enough to strike a devil's bargain with the enemy? And who knew where to find him while he was in hiding with *O Médico?*

Another possibility occurred to him. The second corpse might be a mercenary guide, employed to track Salvato's soldiers through the jungle. That scenario, at least, confirmed the supposition that they had been trailed from Weiss's campsite, through the forest.

What about the prior night's jungle fireworks show?

Salvato realized he was no closer to solving that puzzle now than he had been twenty-four hours ago, and it made no difference in his present situation. Unknown gunmen were trying to kill him right now, and Salvato had no time to think about where or whom they were fighting the previous night.

He only wished they'd all been killed before they'd found his hiding place.

Slowly and cautiously, Salvato gathered eight men who retained their weapons, ammunition and the will to fight. Together on the camp's southern perimeter, his soldiers listened while Salvato hatched a plan.

Instead of charging toward the center of the camp, where automatic fire converged from every side and they would surely die in seconds flat, he meant to lead his strike team counterclockwise, sweeping the perimeter, killing whatever enemies they found, collecting more comrades along the way.

If they found themselves outnumbered at some point, they would retreat, regroup and strike off in the opposite direction, picking off stragglers until they came full circle and their adversaries were destroyed.

It sounded good in theory, anyway.

And if they failed, at least Salvato would've tried.

Prepared for anything, or so he thought, Primo Salvato led his men into the darkness marked by muzzle-flashes, homing on the scent of death.

WHILE SALVATO PONDERED the riddle of mismatched enemies, Bolan experienced a revelation of his own.

And this one nearly claimed his life.

He had continued on his way around the camp, firing short bursts at various combatants here and there, shooting to kill only when he was personally threatened. That was rare, given his stealth and skill, but luck is also part of any battle—and the Executioner's nearly ran out as he was getting ready to evacuate the killing ground.

Just one or two more well-placed bursts, to keep the pot boiling, and he was out of here. Another sixty seconds, maximum, before—

The hulking shadow came from Bolan's left, choosing a kind of awkward football tackle when a point-blank gunshot would've canceled Bolan's ticket in a fraction of a second. There was no time to be grateful, though, as Bolan's adversary hit him with a burly shoulder and the muzzle of his weapon whipped at Bolan's legs.

It was a good move, smoothly executed, but it didn't pack a killing punch. Bolan went down, then struck back with an elbow shot to his assailant's head and rolled away to gain some distance.

Doggedly, the big man followed him, rising from hands and knees to make another rush. Again, he could've fired his weapon but he didn't, making Bolan wonder if the piece was jammed or if its magazine was empty. Either way, he had a split second to raise the Steyr AUG and block a buttstroke that could easily have cracked his skull.

Bolan retreated, parrying the way he had in boot camp cudgel duels. The sharp moves were familiar, but he had no helmet, his opponent's weapon wasn't padded, and the storm of gunfire crackling all around them might abort the contest. Bolan, for his part, would've been glad to shoot the big man who was crowding him, but the attacker seemed to read his mind, refusing to let Bolan slip beyond arm's reach.

They fought that way for several seconds in the darkness, rifles clacking solidly together as both men sought an advantage, neither willing to surrender it and thereby throw his life away. Bolan gave his assailant points for stamina and knew he wouldn't win the fight by simply blocking moves. He had to capture the offensive, turn the fight around and take it to his enemy.

If only…

Bolan saw his opening and took the chance. Instead of blocking the next swing aimed at his face, he ducked beneath it, dropping to a crouch, and slashed the Steyr's butt into his adversary's groin. A squeal of pain escaped the figure looming over him, but Bolan's enemy still had presence of mind enough to jab at Bolan's head while he was doubling over, going for the kill.

Bolan rolled to his left, avoided the bone-crushing blow

by inches, and responded by whipping his weapon into the back of his enemy's buckling knees. The big man dropped, using his rifle as a crutch to keep himself from falling on his face, but that move left his back exposed just long enough for Bolan to complete his triple play.

The Steyr rose and fell, impacting solidly where skull and vertebrae were joined. The first shot drove his adversary down, face pressed into the mud. Another made sure he'd be staying there until somebody came to carry him away.

The smart thing would've been to run, but Bolan's curiosity had been aroused. The dead man was a full head taller and a hundred pounds heavier than the average Brazilian soldier, that discrepancy compounded by the fact that he was carrying a CAR-15. Bolan removed the weapon from arm's reach, on the off chance a miracle occurred, and then he rolled the corpse over onto its back.

At first, the darkness and a layer of clinging mud confused him, but his eyes were clear enough to recognize the dead man when he'd brushed some of the filth away. He'd beaten this one once before, nonfatally, when they had tangled in Belém.

One of Blaine Downey's spooks.

And where there was one Company employee, Bolan knew there might be others.

Overcoming his surprise in record time, he rose and fled the camp. Marta and Bones were waiting for him, needed him, and in that moment Bolan realized that they were in the middle of a very different, very deadly game.

BLAINE DOWNEY DIDN'T KNOW where Jones had gone, and that fact made him almost as unhappy as the constant swarm of bullets flying overhead. He pictured Jones sneaking around behind him, looking for a chance to score where his friend Sutter dropped the ball, drawing a bead on Downey's head.

The raid had gone to hell in nothing flat, and Downey's first priority was living long enough to get off the mountain. After that, if need be, he would pick a compass point at random and start walking, anything to put this godforsaken place behind him forever.

But first, he wanted Nathan Weiss.

Downey had only seen the bastard once, in person, but he'd been tracking Weiss for the best part of a year, determined not to let Weiss evade the penalty for his subversive activities. Every day the doctor walked at large on God's free Earth was an insult to everything Downey believed in.

And that would end this night, if Downey had his way.

If not...

Was he prepared to die here, for a taste of sweet revenge? Downey considered the alternative, escaping with his job unfinished, fabricating yet another in a long line of excuses for the Langley brass, and staying silent while they raked his ass over the coals.

No good.

He had enough cash squirreled away to lead a modest life in some backwater like Bolivia or Paraguay for half a dozen years, but then what would he do? Hire out to some crime syndicate as a security consultant, trying to exert some pull with old friends in the States?

A fresh burst of fire from his left got Downey moving, crawling lizard-like past flattened tents and scattered bodies. There was one tent clearly larger than the others, bullet-riddled sides hanging like tattered curtains now, but clearly Weiss's lair. He'd need the room for surgery and storage of supplies. If he was still alive and still around, it made as good a place as any to begin the final search.

All Downey had to do was get there without being shot.

He made it after several anxious moments, wriggling underneath the tent flap to explore within. Though hidden from the gunners ranged around him now, he didn't stand. Bullets still slapped and rustled through the canvas overhead, passing like vitriolic thoughts in search of someone to offend.

Downey was carrying a flashlight but he didn't use it, didn't need it to explore the tent. He knew almost immediately that he was alone inside it. No one would've lingered in the shadows here, exposed to gunfire from outside yet blind to any warnings of approaching danger.

Downey spent just long enough inside the tent to verify his first impression, checking to make sure that Weiss hadn't been shot and laid out in a corner somewhere, hidden by the shadows. Satisfied that there was nothing more to see or feel inside the bullet-riddled tent, Downey retreated to the exit, waiting there until he saw an opportunity to crawl outside.

What next?

If Weiss wasn't inside his tent, he could be anywhere. Most medics weren't combatants, Downey knew, which made them cowards in his mind and made him speculate that Weiss had fled the camp at the first sound of gunfire. If that was true, he could be anywhere on the plateau or scrambling down some hidden path to make his getaway.

The bastard could be slipping through his fingers once again, and Downey wouldn't even know until it was too late.

That thought almost brought Downey to his feet, but he retained enough control to quell that impulse in the nick of time. This didn't have to be a suicide assignment, even now. He could forget Matt Cooper and the woman, focus solely on the target who had haunted him these past twelve months.

If he could only find the doctor…

And blow his brains out.

Mouthing curses in the darkness, Downey crawled away to seek his victim in the dark recesses of the killing ground.

PRIMO SALVATO SQUEEZED the trigger of his Imbel MD2 and watched his 5.56 mm bullets drop a total stranger in his tracks. The target seemed to be a soldier, but Salvato couldn't vouch for that unless he saw dog tags, and he had no intention of collecting any souvenirs.

His men followed Salvato as he crept forward, passing the corpse, seeking his next target. They'd picked off four, so far, but he was chafing at the sluggish pace of their advance. Salvato wanted action now, to drive the interlopers from his hideaway, but any mad charge through the storm of fire that raged around him would be tantamount to suicide.

Stay slow and steady, then.

Someone among his enemies had other thoughts on how to win the fight, it seemed. From the northeastern quarter of the camp, a sudden howling rose, accompanied by gunfire from a dozen weapons, more or less. Plainly, a rush was coming that could sweep the camp before Salvato carried out his plan.

Salvato kept his head down, snapping orders at his men until they formed a ragged skirmish line. They all had cover, of a sort, behind tree roots or stones, one man reclining in a coffin-size depression in the earth. If they were careful, made their shots count every time, Salvato thought they had a chance to break the charge and turn the tide of battle in their favor.

Maybe. With a stroke of luck.

"Wait for my signal," he commanded. "No one fires without my order."

Up and down the line they nodded, shadow-heads bobbing in darkness. If they failed Salvato, these could be his final moments, but if they stood fast and followed orders to the letter, there was still a chance they might prevail.

Salvato watched the muzzle-flashes blinking at him, heard the bullets whining overhead, and waited for the enemy to start his headlong dash across the camp. They would be in the open, vulnerable, but Salvato knew enough of combat to remember that his men were frightened and fatigued. It wouldn't be enough to simply point their guns and hold the triggers down. An Imbel assault rifle's 30-round box magazine lasted only two and a half seconds on sustained autofire, and while ignorant civilians imagined that every burst scored a kill, most shots fired in battle were wasted.

Cool heads and clear eyes were what Salvato needed now to defeat his enemies. Each wasted shot increased the likelihood of being overrun and slaughtered by the strangers in his camp.

With one last shout, the charge began. Salvato waited, breathing through clenched teeth, his index finger slowly tightening around the trigger of his weapon.

Just a little closer...

Salvato squeezed the trigger, sent two rounds hurtling downrange, and then the rifle's slide locked open on an empty chamber.

Cursing bitterly while those around him fired, Salvato wrenched the spent magazine free and discarded it, pulling another from his belt pouch. In his haste, he fumbled, dropped the magazine, had to retrieve it, feverishly blowing dirt from the bright cartridges.

He glanced up toward the charging line of enemies and froze.

Running a stride or two behind the foremost gunmen in the line, Salvato recognized a shambling figure smeared with blood and muck. Despite the big man's gory mask, Salvato would've known him anywhere, the face emblazoned on his memory from prior confrontations.

Adriano Blas!

Somehow, for some reason, the Fist of Freedom had attacked Salvato's camp. He didn't understand it, though he'd never seen precisely eye-to-eye with Blas on strategy, but now a sudden flare of rage consumed him.

Blas had done this to him. Blas had ruined everything.

Salvato tried to load his rifle, fumbled again and realized that he was holding the magazine backward. As he reversed it, softly cursing, a spray of bullets swept the ground in front of him and hurled mud into his face.

Lurching backward, Salvato dropped his weapon and its magazine, clawing his eyes. Gunfire continued all around him as his vision cleared, and by the time he started groping for his weapon once again, Salvato knew he was too late.

The raiders were almost upon him. Those who had weath-

ered the firestorm were shouting and firing, forty feet or less
from overrunning his position. Desperate, Salvato jerked his
pistol from its holster and pointed, jerking the trigger in rapid-fire, feeling the solid kick against his palm.

One of the bold attackers stumbled, sprawling, but it
wasn't Blas. The others scattered, veering off to left and right,
still firing as they tried to flank Salvato's position. He
glimpsed Blas retreating and sprang from his place of concealment without giving thought to personal safety.

He could not allow Blas to escape after this.

Energized by his rage, Salvato raced after Blas, empty pistol in hand, gaining ground by the second. Near the camp's
northern perimeter, Salvato judged that he was close enough
and risked a snarling leap.

He landed on his rival's back, one arm around the big
man's neck, and brought the pistol down on Blas's head. Together, grappling like two frenzied animals, they toppled to
the muddy ground.

THE ESCALATING rifle fire behind him told Bolan that he had
done his job. Now, he was on his way to join Marta Enriquez
and the others, hoping that he'd find them still alive. A few
more yards to go...

And suddenly he knew he was too late.

This time, the firing came from Bolan's front, the general
location of the trail that was their planned escape route from
the mesa. Even as he recognized the sound and its direction,
Bolan sought an optimistic explanation for it and struck out.

He ran.

Trusting his eyes and other senses, Bolan sprinted through

the darkness, following the sounds of combat from the mesa's rim. It sounded like a minimum of six or seven weapons firing simultaneously, which meant Bolan's friends were probably in trouble.

Almost there.

He picked out muzzle-flashes in the darkness now, two clusters of them separated by some thirty feet of open ground. Taking a chance, he guessed that Marta's team would be the furthest from the rim. He veered in that direction, coming in behind them, and had nearly reached his destination when the Jivaro called Eve stepped silently in front of him, a sharp blade pressed to Bolan's throat.

"You know me, right?" he asked her, wondering if she spoke any English.

"Why so late?" she asked him as the blade withdrew.

"I got hung up in traffic," Bolan answered, brushing past her, moving toward the firing line.

"Thank God you've come!" Enriquez said, greeting him between short bursts from her assault rifle. "We can't get past them to the trail."

He glanced at Bones, still dreaming in the midst of his narcotic sleep, and wondered if the hellish racket would arouse him sooner than expected. Then again, if he could sleep through this...

"How many are there?" Bolan asked Marta.

"Just four, I think."

Just four. With decent cover, four could be an army. Four could hold a critical position until Hell froze over and the damned went ice skating.

"I'll try to get around their blind side," Bolan said, half

smiling at the unintended irony. His own vision was nearly back to normal, and it struck him that he might've got his eyesight back just in the nick of time to watch Bones and the others die.

"Be careful," Enriquez urged, while switching ammunition magazines. Beside her, Abraham and Adam both had rifles, taking turns with 2- and 3-round bursts to keep their enemies from getting cocky.

"I'm always careful," Bolan said.

He was already looking for an angle, with the lie still on his lips, when something changed about the racket from Salvato's camp. Bolan froze in his tracks, assessing it, and in another heartbeat recognized the difference.

Some of the angry voices weren't as distant anymore. They had drawn closer and were gaining by the second.

"Someone's coming," he told Enriquez.

"What?"

"From camp."

She glanced around, worried. "You're sure?"

"Another minute, you can ask them."

Enriquez clearly understood that it could only be bad news. Salvato's men or the intruders, either one might shoot first and ask questions later—if they ever got around to questions.

"We should go," he cautioned.

"Where? The guards—"

"Not that way."

"What, then?"

He answered with a question of his own. "Feel like a swim?"

CHAPTER NINETEEN

Adriano Blas was high-stepping toward the tree line, nearly safe, when someone tackled him and whipped some kind of bludgeon hard across the right side of his skull. He stumbled, reeling, cursing as he fell, deadweight on top of him.

Though stunned, frightened and hurting, Blas was far from helpless, even now. His adversary was about to strike again, perhaps cave in his skull, when Blas rolled to his left, bucking, and drove an elbow back into the tackler's ribs.

A pained grunt from his enemy rewarded Blas, but it wasn't enough to free him. Once again, the bludgeon struck him, this time at the juncture of his neck and shoulder, sending flares of pain along his arm. The next time he lashed out at his unseen opponent, Blas found that the arm responded sluggishly, almost a phantom limb.

Another blow, but Blas expected it, hunching his burly shoulders, rolling with the impact. It still hurt, but there was no critical damage.

His adversary wasn't large, but he was strong and wiry.

Blas could tell that from the bastard's grip, the weight across his back, the force behind his numbing blows. If Blas didn't dislodge him soon, one of those strikes would find his skull and it would be the end of him.

Blas arched his back, pushing with hands and knees, his left arm nearly buckling. Like a wild horse in a rodeo, he lurched and twisted to unseat his rider, pitched this way and that. Failing to free himself in that manner, Blas did the next best thing and threw himself sideways, rolling, so that he wound up on his back, with his attacker pinned beneath him.

That was good and bad, as Blas quickly discovered. While the bastard couldn't club him now, an arm encircled Blas's neck, the biceps flexing tight against his windpipe. At the same time, Blas heard a metallic clicking somewhere to his right and strained in that direction, feeling panic as he saw a semiautomatic pistol pointed at his face.

The weapon clicked again, and then once more.

Empty!

The strangling arm around his throat muted the rebel leader's cry of triumph, premature in any case, but it couldn't forestall the hot rush of adrenaline through Blas's body. He had come *that close* to death, and yet survived.

The battle wasn't over yet.

The arm around his throat grew tighter, pulling his head backward, and Blas gave the bastard what he seemed to want. Risking a death grip that would finish him, Blas drove his skull into the mute attacker's face, followed immediately by a second stunning blow.

Blas felt two things at once: a spurt of wet warmth in his hair, and sudden relaxation of the arm around his neck. Reacting to the second with a born survivor's speed, he rolled free of the strangling grip and scuttled well back from his adversary, putting ground between them. By the time he staggered to his feet, the other man was on his knees.

Blas squinted through the darkness and his pain, seeing the face, needing another moment for the recognition to sink in. Surprise replaced some of the aches he felt, then, staring at the man who knelt in front of him.

"Is it you, Salvato?"

"Who else would it be?" the smaller man replied, breathless. "You came to kill me, after all."

A sudden rush of understanding told Blas everything he had to know. "You stole *O Médico!*"

"Stole him? I saved his life, you stupid shit."

Blas snarled and sprang to the attack. He aimed a high kick at Salvato's head, too late to pull it as he saw the kneeling man release his empty pistol and produce a knife as if by magic. Raising his left arm to block the kick, Salvato swung his knife. Blas felt the blade bite deep into his thigh.

Howling, he fell upon Salvato, left hand clutching at Salvato's wrist, grinding the fragile bones to make him drop the knife. With his free hand, Blas gripped Salvato's throat, squeezing with every ounce of strength that still remained to him.

But it was fading fast.

Blas felt it going, spurting in time with his pulse from the severed femoral artery, drenching his pants and Salvato's with life in its most primal form. He had minutes to live, without help, and Blas knew there'd be no help this night.

He'd missed *O Médico,* and it was about to cost him his life.

Still, he gripped Salvato's throat with crushing force, squeezing and bearing down with all his weight, his total consciousness focused on thumb and fingers biting into flesh. Slowly he felt Salvato stiffen underneath him, watched the eyes roll back until dead white was all he saw.

And still, Blas held his grip, refusing to be duped by some third-rate performance. He would clutch the bastard's throat until his men arrived to carry him away. They'd have to pry his fingers from Salvato's neck or bury them together, locked like lovers in a last embrace.

"You see?" he whispered to Salvato as the darkness closed around him, smothering his dreams. "I win! You see?"

"A SWIM? What do you mean?"

The panic Bolan heard in Marta's voice told him she understood him perfectly. "We're running out of options," he reminded her. "It's that, or stand and fight."

She thought about it for another fraction of a second, while the sounds of their converging enemies drew closer. "What about Nathan?" she asked.

"We'll handle him."

"I hate this," Enriquez said.

"Tell me about it. I don't have my swimming trunks."

Forcing a smile, she nodded. "Yes, all right."

It was another moment's work to brief the others, while more bullets whined around them in the darkness. Abraham and Adam kept their stoic masks in place, but Eve recoiled a step, shaking her head. Adam reached out to grip her arm, squeezing, and gave an order Bolan couldn't understand. This time, Eve nodded, but her fear was palpable.

"They'll do it," Enriquez told him.

"Good. We need to move right now."

A closer, louder burst of fire punctuated Bolan's comment. Swiveling to face the nearest enemy, he answered with a short burst from the AUG to keep their heads down.

"Go!" he ordered. "Hurry!"

Enriquez led the way, with Abraham and Adam bearing Weiss between them, Eve trailing her husband, and the Executioner assuming the rear-guard position. They had only fifty yards or so to travel, but the enemy was fast approaching.

It was a long-shot gamble, but he saw no other hope of getting off the mesa, much less extracting Bones. The only half decent trail was closed to them, and they possessed no climbing gear, even if there'd been time to reach the narrow cut he'd found with Marta, on the mesa's western face.

It was the waterfall or nothing, and with enough luck, Bolan thought they might survive it. Whether they'd be fit to outrun enemies after the drop was anybody's guess, but they would have to take it one step at a time.

For several moments Bolan hoped that they had lost their enemies in darkness. It would take time for the new arrivals from the camp to huddle with the sentries, try to find out what was happening, and set off in pursuit. His hopes were dashed, though, when he heard voices approaching and saw two pale flashlight beams lance through he darkness.

"Hurry up!" he called to Marta, worried that she wouldn't hear him. Nonetheless, she seemed to pick up speed, the Indians between them likewise running faster now.

Bolan hung back just far enough to intercept any point men

their enemies might send ahead. Gunfire would mark them and provoke fire in return, but he wouldn't let the pursuers overtake Marta and Bones, if he could help it. One way or another, he would get them to the drop.

Whatever happened after that was up to Fate.

His mind flashed back to Downey, wondering how Langley's man in Brazil had found Salvato's jungle hideout, whether there were airborne reinforcements on the way to seal the place and cut off any possible retreat. It seemed unlikely, inasmuch as air support was commonly employed with the first wave of troops to strike a target, rather than as some afterthought.

Were more troops waiting at the foot of the plateau, to intercept escapees? They would have to take that chance, but Bolan reckoned there would be no organized surveillance on the waterfall, if Downey's men had even noticed it.

They had one chance, and it was fraught with danger.

But sometimes, one chance was all it took.

BLAINE DOWNEY HAD forgotten all about the waterfall. He'd glimpsed it briefly, circling the plateau's base with Sergeant Alemán's strike team, but it was nothing that concerned him, and the firefight on the mesa had driven all extraneous thoughts from his mind.

Downey had found one of the Indians who shared the doctor's camp, gut shot and bleeding out behind one of the tents. He'd tried to grill the wounded man, but language stood between them, and the tribesman had been bold enough to spit in Downey's face. That final insult tripped a switch in Downey's brain, and by the time he finished hammering the native's face it was nearly unrecognizable as human.

The exercise had helped Downey, to some extent, but he was still no closer to his target. Neither could he find Matt Cooper or the woman who ran Weiss's errands.

Wait, the small voice in his head warned Downey. If all three of them are gone...

What could it mean, except that they'd escaped from camp before he got there with the soldiers? When the shooting started, Cooper and Weiss had to have split, taking the bitch along for company.

Where would they go?

The mesa was blown, in terms of offering sanctuary. The only hope of finding safety lay below them, in the jungle. If Weiss made it that far, he could pick a compass point at leisure and run for his life, leaving Downey with egg on his face one more time.

"No, you don't!"

Unaware that he'd spoken out loud, Downey spent a moment scanning the camp, recovering his sense of direction. They'd come in from the northwest, and the one clear trail they'd marked lay east of the camp, perhaps a hundred yards beyond the slaughter ground.

If Weiss was running, logic said he'd go that way. Even if hunters blocked his progress, it was still the route that Downey needed to pursue.

Alone?

He looked around for Jones and couldn't find the moron anywhere. The darkness had a way of sucking people in, making them disappear. It worried Downey, losing track of Jones, but if the prick was stalking him, he'd take his chances. Weiss was more important at the moment.

Downey couldn't let him slip away this time.

He found a point of reference and began to scrabble eastward, following the camp's perimeter, using whatever cover he could find along the way. There was no safety in the darkness, bullets hissing aimlessly through space around him, slapping into trees and men with absolute impartiality.

He crawled past wounded men and corpses, pausing for a moment when he found two locked together in a cold embrace. One clutched the other's throat and wrist, the other held a blood knife that had to have found its mark before they fell together, grappling out the final moments of their lives in blood and filth.

Downey peered at their lifeless faces, recognized neither and crept around them, coming back inexorably to his chosen path. A few more yards would see him clear of camp, such as it was, and he could then try to improve his time on foot, instead of wriggling lizard-like among the slain.

Downey was clear and scrambling to his feet when someone rose in front of him, an automatic weapon leveled at his chest, and barked something at him in Portuguese. He didn't understand a word of it, straining his eyes to see if it was one of Alemán's commandos, but he couldn't tell.

Should he reply in English, or would that insure his death? What could he do to save himself?

In one move, Downey dropped to his knees while raising his carbine and squeezing the trigger. The piece was set for 3-round bursts, and Downey triggered four bursts in his panic, almost cheering as he saw his bullets scoring solid hits.

The nameless adversary fell, but as he crumpled to the earth, instinct tightened his trigger finger, ripping off an aimless burst into the night.

He almost missed.

Of half a dozen rounds unleashed, a single slug struck Downey in the upper left-hand quadrant of his torso, tumbling through his lung and shattering the shoulder blade to exit from his back. The impact pitched him over backward, and he felt the carbine tumble from his fingers.

Helpless, Downey lay beneath the stars and watched them wheeling overhead. He couldn't move, could hardly breathe.

"Goddamn it," Downey wheezed, "it isn't fair."

And cursing bitter Fate, he slowly closed his eyes.

THE NIGHT HAD TURNED to madness. From her own plan, dangerous enough that she had little hope of actually living through it, Marta found herself committed to a scheme that smacked of certain death.

But she was running toward that fate, regardless.

For she had no other choice.

As far as she could tell, the unknown raiders meant to slaughter everyone in camp without exception. They had come in shooting, without warning, and made no attempt at taking prisoners. If there was any hope in facing them, she guessed, Matt Cooper wouldn't have suggested that they flee.

And flight it was, a headlong race with death in one form, toward destruction in another. Picturing the river and its waterfall, Marta envisioned plummeting toward jagged rocks below, flesh torn, bones shattered, water flooding lungs that fought for any trace of oxygen.

And what of Nathan?

In his present state, he couldn't even try to save himself. He'd be a tumbling rag doll in the water, absolutely helpless.

If he plunged beneath the surface—as he had to, assuming there was depth enough below to break their fall, he couldn't swim or even count on floating properly.

In that moment, she knew what had to be done and silently resolved to see it through, regardless of the danger to herself. Whatever happened, Marta would do everything within her power to keep Nathan safe and help him to elude his enemies. Until her dying breath, she would protect him from the world and from himself.

How much longer?

Marta wasn't sure, but she remembered covering this ground one short day earlier, albeit at much slower speed. She knew the river had to be close, but with the noise of battle from the camp, it was more difficult to pick out nature's sounds.

Marta was concentrating so intently on the river that she nearly stumbled into it. One moment, forest undergrowth was all around her, clutching at her hair and clothes; the next, she glimpsed the water just in front of her, before her boots slipped in the mud and she went down onto one knee.

The others joined her seconds later, Cooper bringing up the rear. From Marta's right, not far away, she heard the falls now. If they'd been a few yards closer to the rim, she could've felt the spray upon her face.

"We're out of time," Bolan advised her, breathing heavily. "The choice is either make a stand right here, or take the plunge."

No choice at all.

"I'll go first," Enriquez said. "With Nathan."

"Can you handle him?" Bolan asked.

"Someone has to.

"Right. Okay. Here's what you do."

She set the automatic rifle's safety as he told her, slung the weapon so it lay across her back, the strap in front between her breasts. Adam and Abraham held Nathan upright, facing Marta, until she could wrap her arms around his waist and interlock her fingers at the back.

"He'll try to drown you without meaning to," Bolan said. "Bodies float. You may wind up beneath him, but you'll need to breathe. Try going in feet first, if possible."

"Tie us together," Marta urged him.

"Bad idea," the tall American replied. "You couldn't shake him then, no matter what. If anything goes wrong, he'll drag you down."

"Dammit!"

"You want me to, I'll take him," Bolan said.

She was surprised to feel a sudden rush of something that resembled jealousy. "He's mine," she answered. "Help us in the water, please."

As they were lifted, all hands taking part, she wrapped her legs around Nathan's and crossed her ankles. The last time they'd lain in that position, he had been inside her. Now she wondered if they'd ever be that way again. Would Nathan even speak to her, after she had betrayed him? Would he—

"Ready!"

At the sound of Cooper's warning, Marta filled her lungs with air and shut her eyes. The water's chill surprised her, but she didn't have much time to think about it. In another heartbeat, they were both submerged, then bobbing in the current, breaking surface, rolling, down again.

She heard Nathan spluttering, close to her ear, and rolled in the water to put him above her, praying that he still had strength enough to drag a breath. Marta could feel them speeding now, and knew it wouldn't be much longer until they—

The launch, even expected, was a terrifying moment. She had never seen a roller coaster, much less ridden one, but Marta understood the primal fear of falling. Instantly her heart was in her throat, the wind and water roaring in her ears.

Feet first! she thought, and hung on to her lover for dear life.

IT WAS a strange dream, Nathan Weiss decided. First the baptism, which had no frame of reference in his personal experience, but he could see the robed choir wading out to join him, singing "Hallelujah" or whatever.

And he found it very odd, how long the preacher held him under water, as if testing both his faith and physical endurance. Stranger still, the preacher had Mack Bolan's face, but that was simple lunacy. Bolan was dead, and even in his lifetime Weiss had never known him as a Bible-thumper.

Falling!

Uninitiated as he was into the panoply of Christian ritual, Weiss knew it wasn't normal for the guest of honor at a baptism to be shot from a cannon. Nonetheless, he heard the roar distinctly, felt the liftoff as the blast propelled him into space.

Weiss tried to fan his arms, thinking the dream might let him sprout a pair of wings, but they were pinned against his sides. Frustration veered toward panic as he realized his arms *and* legs had somehow been immobilized. How could he fly, for God's sake, if he couldn't even move?

Weiss almost lost his fear of falling when an angel's voice addressed him, curiously speaking only into his left ear. Instead of being high and mighty, it was a familiar voice, one that he almost recognized from—where? Why was the angel shouting, when he felt her lips against his face?

The message made no sense at all to Weiss: "I love you! Hold on tight! I love you! Hold—"

The shock of impact and submersion forced Weiss back to consciousness, breaking the soporific potion's grip on mind and body. Stunned by his explosive entry to the pool he'd never seen, chilled to the bone and drowning, Weiss thrashed frantically to free himself from the embrace that pinned his arms and legs. He felt himself sinking and knew that he would die unless he broke that hold.

And suddenly it vanished.

Instinct brought him to the surface, gasping, spewing water with an earthy flavor from his mouth and nostrils. His sinus cavities burned fiercely and the pain helped clear his head.

Somehow, although he'd reached the surface, Weiss was still deluged with water from above. It took another moment for his mind to grasp the concept of a waterfall, and then he stroked away from it, eyes probing darkness for the nearest bit of terra firma.

Don't forget the angel.

Weiss hesitated, paddled in a circle, eyes sweeping the surface of the pool. Was that a body floating ten yards to his left?

Still sluggish, but regaining strength with every stroke, he swam in that direction, found a figure with a rifle strapped across its back floating facedown, and used the water's buoyancy to help invert the floater. Through a haze of drifting spray, he recognized the face.

"Marta?"

She didn't answer, but her eyelids fluttered and she coughed a spout of water from her throat. Weiss knew he had to get Marta ashore—wherever shore was—to prevent her drowning on the water that she'd already inhaled. Each second counted now, if he was going to prevent brain damage, even death.

Weiss chose a compass point and stroked in that direction, one arm towing Marta while the other paddled. Somewhere overhead, a warbling cry competed with the thunder of the falls, seeming to blossom in his ears. Before Weiss had a chance to track it, something struck the surface of the pool and raised a bright plume several meters high.

Jesus, they're bombing us! Weiss thought.

And paddled faster toward the shore he couldn't see.

BOLAN WAITED until the last moment, until the others had vanished downstream and the sounds of pursuit were almost upon him, before he slung his AUG and dived into the water. Instantly the current seized him and propelled him toward the falls.

Bolan didn't resist. He raised his head twice, taking breath, and on the second time saw dark shapes clustered on the river's bank where he'd been standing seconds earlier. One of the hunters pointed and his comrades raised their weapons.

Bolan dived, incoming gunfire barely audible beneath the water's surface. Bullets plunked around him, spent their force on impact as the current swept him out of range. His lungs were aching in another moment, but he knew it couldn't be much farther to the falls. The churning water told him he was almost there.

And still, the drop surprised him. One moment, he could stretch out an arm and graze the river bottom with his fingertips. The next, his head broke water without rising and a dark gulf yawned beneath him, bright spume plummeting a hundred feet or more, as if he had been dropped into the largest water slide on Earth.

Except there was no slide, nothing to stop him plunging headfirst toward the pool and earth below. Remembering his words to Marta, Bolan struggled through a crude half somersault to drop feet-first.

At this height, this velocity, it wouldn't matter how he landed on a rock or solid ground. He would be mangled beyond recognition, either way, and dead before he knew it. In the water, though, landing feet first could spare him being knocked unconscious, even crippled from a broken neck.

The drop took only seconds, but it seemed to last a lifetime. Unlike Bolan's several hundred jumps from airplanes, there was no ripcord to pull, no parachute to brake his fall. Instead of coasting gently down, his body gained velocity with every foot he fell, until the water's glassy surface rushed to meet his pointed toes and Bolan plunged into the deep, cold dark.

He'd filled his lungs before impact, and still they nearly emptied as he sank, bubbles from his explosive entry making him feel as if he'd landed in a huge glass of champagne. There'd be no giddy feeling if he drank it down in celebration, though. Just gagging, strangling death.

His feet scraped bottom and he kicked off toward the surface, stroking powerfully. Bolan knew it was possible to get disoriented under water, even miss the surface altogether, but his concentration didn't fail him. Just as colored spots began to swarm in front of his eyes, a sure sign that his brain was being starved of oxygen, he broke the surface with a gasp and hung there, treading water in the dark.

"Matthew?"

He turned toward Marta's voice, relieved that he could see her on the shore, surrounded by the others. Counting heads, he realized that Bones was on his feet and standing at the woman's side.

Trouble, he thought, but there was no way to avoid it. They'd already come this far, and if Bones didn't like it, he could climb back to the mesa's top and parley with the men who'd come kill him. Maybe they would meet him halfway down and save him some exertion.

Bolan reached the shore a moment later, many hands extending to assist him as he scrambled from the water. Facing Weiss, he waited for the tirade, but it never came.

"Cliff diving's always been a fantasy of mine," Bones said. "Of course, I thought I'd be awake."

"You could go up and try again," Bolan suggested.

"Not right now. Marta explained about the uninvited company."

No pun intended, Bolan thought. And said, "You got that right. I recognized one of them from Belém. He's CIA."

"They don't give up," Weiss said.

"We've got a lead right now," Bolan reminded him, "but we could lose it anytime."

"Where are we going?" Bones inquired. "I've just about worn out my welcome in Brazil."

"They say Bolivia is nice, this time of year," Bolan replied.

Bones brushed the sopping hair back from his face and smiled. "You think they need a doctor, Sarge?" he asked.

CHAPTER TWENTY

The Bolivian frontier

They traveled light and made the best time possible, ever alert to any indications of pursuit. The first day, when a military helicopter overflew their route of march, Bolan expected an attack that never came. By day three on the trail, against his own best judgment, he was starting to relax.

"They've given up," Bones said that night, over a meal of fruit and monkey meat. "You did it, Mr. Cooper."

Bolan hadn't shared the doctor's optimism. "It's too early for congratulations," he replied. "Until we cross the border, it's still anybody's game. And if we make it to Bolivia, you'll find a whole new list of problems waiting for you."

"The eternal optimist." Weiss smiled, then sobered as he said, "You took a major chance on me, that I'd cooperate when I came to my senses."

It was Bolan's turn to smile. "You want to tell me when that happens?"

"No, I mean it. You were gambling with your lives, all of you."

"Staying with Salvato wasn't any kind of option," Bolan said. "He had a shoestring operation on its last legs when we met him. It was only a matter of time until someone picked him off."

"I could've fought you on the trail, refused to leave the country," Weiss pressed.

"You could've," Bolan granted, "but it made no sense. You're fresh out of supplies, no tent. What could you do?"

Bones looked around him as he said, "I might start over with my loyal staff."

Bolan saw Marta glance away. The Indians returned his gaze, unflinching. "You still can," he said. "It's a big world out there, but the door to Brazil has been shut in your face. You'd be wise to accept that fact and move on."

Bones cocked his head, showing the face he wore when he played devil's advocate. "And if I don't? Then what?"

"Then we say adios, or the equivalent in Portuguese. I've done my part, Bones. If you really want to die that badly, I can guarantee you no one else will try to interfere."

Weiss stared at Bolan for a moment, letting that sink in, then smiled and said, "Maybe I'll give Bolivia a try."

"You know," said Bolan, trying once more for the jackpot, "you could still come home."

"I don't remember where that is."

"Find someplace new," the Executioner suggested.

"Sarge, that's what I'm doing."

Right.

"I wish we could've brought Ricardo with us," Weiss remarked a moment later.

Marta fielded that one. "He'd become too friendly with Salvato. I was worried that he might betray us."

"Still, his links were useful."

"In Brazil," Bolan said, "not Bolivia."

"You're right. Out with the old, in with the new." Another frown. "Except, I don't feel new."

"Give it some time, Bones."

"Right. I hope you're right."

Day four turned out to be their worst since fleeing the plateau. Torrential rain pursued them like an enemy, flooding their meager trail and slowing progress to an infuriating minimum. They fought for yards of ground, instead of miles, each step an ordeal in the deluge and the quagmire it created. Rain like this was a phenomenon unknown outside the tropics, alien and unimagined by the residents of "civilized" locales. That night, huddled together in a cold and hungry camp, Bolan remembered that the jungle wasn't friend or enemy to man.

The jungle didn't care if any of them lived or died.

Day five, against all odds, dawned bright and clear. The rain forest still dripped and steamed from its most recent soaking, but the birds and animals were back in force, resuming their boisterous routine. The trail wasn't exactly dry, but it was better, and they made fair time. A little after midday, Bolan's GPS device flashed the coordinates that he'd been waiting for.

"Okay," he said without fanfare, "this is officially Bolivia."

"Looks like Brazil to me," Bones said.

"Bear that in mind," Bolan replied. "We ought to put a few

more miles behind us, just in case there's someone on our trail who isn't packing one of these."

"You mean, the Company?" Weiss asked.

"I'm thinking anyone at all. There's no point tempting Fate."

"I guess I've done enough of that to last a while," Weiss said.

They marched into the afternoon, Bolan on point, with Abraham and Adam taking turns on rear guard. The natives were outside their normal range, but they still knew the forest's quirks and cues. If someone was pursuing them on foot, Bolan trusted the Indians to spot a tail before he could.

That night, in camp, Bolan unpacked an item he'd been saving for the finish line. It weighed ten pounds and took five minutes to assemble, from its small transmitter to a fanlike dish antenna that opened to the rough diameter of a dinner plate. The battery, which tested positive, contained enough juice to dispatch a single high-speed message skyward, toward a small communications satellite, and on from there to Stony Man.

The box and dish were Bolan's ticket home.

"What will you tell them?" Weiss inquired.

"I send coordinates and hope we both show up on time," Bolan replied.

"That's all?"

"What else is there?"

"I'm guessing you could ask them for a snatch team, if you wanted to."

"They wouldn't send one," Bolan told him frankly.

"Oh?" Bones seemed surprised.

"In case you hadn't noticed, this has been a solo operation. I'll be stretching it to get a lift."

"Swimming against the tide?"

"They understand friendship, up to a point. But, then again, there's policy."

"I understand," Weiss said.

"I hope you do. This was a one-time-only offer, Bones. Whatever happens in Bolivia, Colombia or Katmandu, they won't be sending anybody else. Ever."

"I hear you. It was my mistake. I've tried to make it clear I wasn't asking for a ticket out."

"You still have time to change your mind."

Weiss thought about it for a moment, then leaned back and shook his head. "No, thanks," he said. "I've figured out the reason why you can't go home again."

"Why's that?"

"Because home isn't there. It doesn't last."

"Be sure, Bones."

"It was wrong for me to ask for help I couldn't use. I'm sorry for your trouble."

Bolan passed a hand in front of his eyes. His old friend's face was crystal-clear. "No trouble," he replied. "Just same old, same old."

"Yeah. I know the feeling." Rising from his place beside their small campfire, Weiss said, "You'd better book that flight. Party of one. I'm turning in."

"I'll see you in the morning."

"Bright and early, Sarge. We have a long way still to go."

Bolan keyed in pickup coordinates and sent the message. Even as he pressed the button, he experienced a sense of let-down, as if he was failing Weiss. It was irrational, he realized, but there it was.

"It's not your fault," Enriquez said, coming up beside him in the night.

"How long have you been reading minds?" Bolan asked.

"I read faces, sometimes hearts. It was my error, Matt. We can't make Nathan safe against his will."

"Too bad you didn't have another hypo," he remarked.

"I did," she answered, "but I tossed it yesterday. He has to make his own choices."

"And you?"

"I choose to stay with Nathan. We will see what happens next."

"You think he'll really try Bolivia, or turn around and head back to Brazil?" asked Bolan.

Enriquez smiled. "Nothing he does surprises me."

"I guess you're getting used to it by now."

"It's never boring." Watching Bolan break down the transmitter, Enriquez asked, "When is your rendezvous?"

"Twelve hours," Bolan said. "It takes some time to put these things in play."

"Will they come here?"

He shook his head. "I picked another spot, not far away."

"When are you leaving?"

"Sunrise, give or take," he said.

"I hope you make it safely."

"Same to you." Bolan tracked Weiss with his eyes. "You could do worse."

Enriquez bent and pressed her lips to Bolan's cheek. "Sleep well."

"Good night."

He buried the transmitter fifty feet outside their camp, trusting the jungle to corrode and devour its components before any chance discovery by someone who could recognize it. Returning to the fire, he found Adam and Abraham observing him as he lay down and focused on the long, dark corridor of sleep.

The next day's hike would be an easy three klicks to the pickup point, with more than ample time to reach it if he left at dawn. There would be no prolonged farewells, and he anticipated no diversions on the way, but he'd allowed himself eight hours for a march that should take three, at most.

Hedging his bets.

When he was confident that there was nothing left to plan or double-check, the warrior blanked his mind and closed his weary eyes.

EPILOGUE

At 6:00 a.m., Jack Grimaldi was flying as much on caffeine as he was on aircraft fuel. The Bell LongRanger helicopter had been ready and waiting when he arrived in Santa Cruz, an hour-long flight from La Paz by Learjet, on the eastern slope of the Andes. Beyond Santa Cruz lay the wild, and another two hours by air to keep his date with Bolan.

Grimaldi had been waiting in La Paz for three long days, living on room service and hanging near the telephone. He wouldn't catch the squeal direct from Bolan. That would go to Stony Man, but Hal Brognola wanted him in place and ready when the signal came. The previous night, it had. Twelve hours to the pickup at a point perhaps a day's march in from the Brazilian border.

That was all Grimaldi had, so far. He didn't know if Bolan would be fighting his way out, if he would be alone or traveling with company. Grimaldi hadn't been included on the mission briefing, and he didn't need to know the details.

He was flying in for Bolan. Anything beyond that was su-

perfluous—unless, of course, it had to do with being blasted
from the sky.

His flight was cleared with the Bolivian air force, a partner with the U.S. in the so-called war on drugs. Grimaldi
hadn't seen much warfare in La Paz or Santa Cruz, but there'd
been ample signs of affluence to make him think the war was
being lost at home.

Forget it.

Cocaine wasn't part of the equation this time. He was
strictly on a mercy mission, lifting Bolan out of whatever assignment had delivered him into his present state. Grimaldi
concentrated on his instruments and made himself a promise
that he wouldn't ask for any details, even if the big guy came
aboard like King Tut, wrapped in bandages.

Be cool, he thought. It's just another milk run, like deliv-
ering the mail.

Reflexively, he checked the chopper's fuel gauge. There
was juice for the round trip, and then some, but a little reas-
surance never hurt. It was a long walk back to Santa Cruz
from the coordinates that Stony Man had given him, a trek
Grimaldi wanted to avoid at any cost.

Bolan had been through that and worse, he guessed, in the
past week. Leaving Brazil on foot, blazing his own trail in the
process, meant the soldier hadn't been on any holiday retreat
himself.

The helicopter's GPS device was locked on to the same coordinates Bolan had beamed to Stony Man the previous night.
Grimaldi doubted that Bolan had been on the site when he
broadcast that signal—too risky—but he would've bet his
life on Bolan being there this day.

A large-scale topographical map of southeastern Bolivia lay on the vacant copilot's seat beside him, folded to display the area including Bolan's LZ coordinates. Grimaldi had boxed the spot with a black marker, and stealing glances at the map now, he confirmed the presence of a hilltop rising eighty feet above the forest floor. If Bolan scaled that modest peak and there were no trees on the hill itself, the pickup should be relatively easy.

According to the GPS, he was almost on top of Bolan's hill. Another quarter mile to go, which told him it was time to change course, circling wide of the mark to approach from the north. He didn't want to be predictable and make it easy for the heavies, just in case they were expecting him.

Grimaldi kept the Mayday channel open on his radio, not broadcasting, but waiting for a message if Bolan was able to transmit. He didn't know what kind of gear his old friend was packing, whether he had any radio at all, but if he did—

"Is that the Stony Man Express?"

The voice was tinny in his headphones, but Grimaldi would've known it anywhere. "You've got the Jackpot, Sarge. What's your situation?"

"Standing by solo, at the coordinates. I'm clean."

"I'm glad to hear it," Grimaldi said, grinning now. "I'll be on top of you in five."

THE HILLTOP WASN'T flat, but its crest was clear and large enough for Grimaldi to land the thirty-nine-foot chopper. Bolan flagged him, then retreated out of contact range, shielding his eyes against the storm of rotor wash as the Bell Long-Ranger set down. Grimaldi kept the engines running, rotors spinning, as Bolan ran forward, crouching, and scrambled into the cockpit.

A moment later they were airborne, banking to the north, then circling westward toward a looming, saw-toothed line of mountains. Bolan shook the hand Grimaldi offered him and told the pilot, "I'm surprised to see you."

"You know me," Grimaldi said. "No social life. I hang around the house, hoping for invitations to a party."

"This one's over," Bolan said, "but I could use a designated driver."

Grimaldi smiled. "Going a little heavy on the jungle juice, I take it?"

"You have no idea."

"Well, anyway, it's over."

Not for Bones, Bolan thought. But he said, "It's over. Right."

"Are you okay?" the pilot asked. "No hits?"

"A little tired, that's all."

"You want to go in back and catch a nap, it's ninety minutes back to Santa Cruz."

"I'll just stay here and rest my eyes," Bolan replied.

"Suits me," Grimaldi said. "We aim to please."

Closing his eyes, Bolan allowed the helicopter's droning noise and deep vibration to invade his mind and banish conscious thought. He didn't want to think of Nathan Weiss, Marta Enriquez and the others he had left behind to make their own way in the jungle. They were survivors, in a sense, but they were also innocents, seeking a place Bolan feared might not exist.

Weiss sought a place where he could help patients regardless of their race or ideology, ignored by the authorities even when those he treated were outlaws or rebels. Marta, Bolan thought, was simply looking for a place where she could spend her life with Weiss, both of them happy, unmolested by the outside world. The Indians who traveled with them likely wanted nothing more than to survive.

They were like children who had run away from an abusive home, learning that there was no safe haven in the world.

Or was there?

Bolan hadn't found one yet, but he kept hoping, too. It might be foolish optimism, but without it, how could he go on? How could he fight and risk his life for something better, if he honestly believed that something was forever out of reach?

His eyes opened to find the rain had stopped. Sunlight was breaking through the clouds.

"Not sleepy, after all?" Grimaldi asked.

"I can't afford to sleep right now," Bolan replied. "There's still too much to see."

A long-lost sword.

A willing heroine.

A quest to protect humanity's
sacred secrets from falling
into the wrong hands.

Her destiny will be revealed.

July 2006.

GOLD
EAGLE ®

VANISHING POINT

**A U.S. aircraft carrier carrying a top secret weapon
is hijacked in the Pacific....**

The USS *Stennis* has been hijacked and on board is the
X-51—the most advanced unmanned aircraft ever
built. As the carrier becomes a war zone and the crew
succumbs to a poison attack, a covert three-man unit
called Able Team is the last line of defense against
a global shock wave.

STONY MAN®

#82

*Available
April 2006 at your
favorite retail outlet.*

GOLD
EAGLE®

GSM82

TAKE 'EM FREE
2 action-packed novels plus a mystery bonus
NO RISK
NO OBLIGATION TO BUY